MIRRORSCOPE

MIRRORSCOPE

Jess Artem

iUniverse, Inc.
New York Lincoln Shanghai

MIRRORSCOPE

iUniverse, Inc.

For information address:
iUniverse, Inc.
2021 Pine Lake Road, Suite 100
Lincoln, NE 68512
www.iuniverse.com

ISBN: 0-595-32217-4

Printed in the United States of America

Contents

PROLOGUE

Galileo Galilei, you are arraigned before this most Holy and Sacred Tribunal for reasons that have been detailed in your trial and to which you have admitted and most solemnly confessed under oath. Namely that, contrary to the teaching of the Holy Scriptures, you claim that the Sun is stationary and does not move from east to west and that the Earth moves and is not the center of God's creation.

Galileo Galilei, it is one thing to subscribe to false and heretical doctrines and opinions in private, but you have attempted and persisted against all authority and Divine guidance to publish your heretical views to faithful Christians here, in Rome, and throughout the Christian commonwealth. This transgression incurs all the penalties, pains, and censures this Holy Office and its sacred Canons may justly impose upon such unholy delinquencies and heresies. Yet, thanks to our merciful lord—and the opinion of those counseled to bear witness to your expertise in the study of mechanics and optics and the practical application and worth of such inventions—we are willing to absolve you from the harshest penalty that may be imposed upon your pernicious and heretical crime if you, in honest and sincere faith, hereby renounce upon oath your false doctrine.

Furthermore, so that your false claims and opinions shall not deceive or corrupt others, in contradiction of the teaching of the Sacred and Holy Scriptures, we order both that your book *Dialogue of Galileo Galilei* be banned by public edict and that you be confined and detained under the jurisdiction and pleasure of this Holy Office for a period not less than three years. As a salutary penance we impose upon you the additional order that you recite the seven penitential psalms once a week for the duration of your incarceration.

Galileo Galilei, you are hereby ordered to kneel before the Most Eminent and Reverend Lord Cardinals, Inquisitors-General of this Tribunal, and abjure your false and heretical pronouncements and accept the jurisdiction and sentence of this Holy Office.

*   *   *

Galileo knelt as ordered and recited his abjuration before the assembled Lord Cardinals of the Tribunal.

I, Galileo Galilei, kneeling before this most Sacred and Holy Office, pray forgiveness for my sins and declare that the doctrine that the Sun occupies the center of creation and does not move, and that the Earth moves and is not the center of creation, is false and contrary to Holy Writ. Furthermore, so that such false and heretical opinion shall not be repeated, I swear on oath and touching with my hand the Most Holy Gospels, such false doctrine shall not be held, defended, or taught in any manner, oral or in writing, and that it is my duty to declare and denounce to the Inquisitor-General anyone who claims or supports the said false doctrine. Finally, if I contravene any part of this solemn oath, I submit myself to all the pains and penalties ordered, imposed, or decreed by this Holy Office.

I, Galileo Galilie aged seventy years, most solemnly abjure and renounce the said false doctrine. Signed by my own hand this day, in Rome, June 22, 1633.

1

The Road to the Monastery

Dr. Scott Ferris reached for the on/off knob of his Mercury's Motorola and, with a flick of the wrist, brought reality back to a bright autumn day in October 1956—and the job of driving his companion, Lee Drexler, to Mt. Palomar Observatory in Southern California.

Scott and his partner on this drive were two of the very first graduates to emerge from the California Institute of Technology's new astronomy faculty, and Lee was now on his way to join the team operating the giant 200-inch telescope. Both he and Scott had graduated from Caltech in 1954, though Lee had first gone down to South Africa for a while to help his mentor, Professor Roy Roxborne, study the bright, highly energized nuclei of the Seyfert galaxies—observations best conducted from observatories in the Southern Hemisphere.

Scott had elected to go straight to Mt. Palomar, accepting an offer to help refine galaxy redshift-distance measurements that Edwin Hubble had come to believe indicated the distant spiraling galaxies were all rushing away from one another. Dr. Hubble had made this remarkable discovery in the 1920s, initially with the 100-inch telescope on nearby Mt. Wilson, and then later refined the recession rate with the 200-inch telescope when it was commissioned in 1948—the same instrument Lee was soon to train upon the immensity of the universe.

Although Dr. Hubble had been instrumental in pushing for the construction of a telescope more powerful than Mt. Wilson's—and had done much of the fundraising and initial testing for the new one—now, after a quarter of a century of ground-breaking research, he was ready to call it a day, at least as far as observations were concerned. With advancing years, the comfort of carpeted and oak-paneled administration offices, on Mt Palomar Drive, down in Pasadena seemed a more appealing option than the cramped, often freezing, conditions of the observing cage. He would still direct the observations, of course, but would now let younger astronomers, such as Lee Drexler and Scott Ferris, spend the tedious long hours observing at the mountain-top observatory.

Hubble's discovery of galactic recession was quickly gaining in popularity amongst the majority of the world's astronomers and already some prominent cosmologists were speculating that it might be the result of some primordial explosion, or 'big bang', as it had been dubbed by Professor Ted Howell at Cambridge in the UK, which gave birth to the universe. In short, the universe was now considered to be expanding in all directions.

Scott Ferris was attracted by this notion too and was already enthused with the prospect of helping to trace the origin of the universe back to its first moment in time. Gaining evidence to verify our cosmic origins and being asked to help in this important endeavor by the most acclaimed astronomer of the twentieth century was an opportunity beyond his wildest dreams. True, he harbored a few initial misgivings that the quest might undermine the teaching of his fundamentalist Christian upbringing and, more particularly, the Old Testament version of the creation event, but he hadn't dwelt long on the apparent dichotomy. Heck, he was an astronomer, not a preacher, and wasn't about to question Dr. Hubble's historic observations now that he had been given the opportunity to further the great man's work. Anyway, looking for our cosmic origins was tantamount to looking for God, in Scott's view, and if God happened to appear in the eye-piece of Scott's telescope, why, perhaps science and religion could somehow be reunited after three centuries of bitter secularism! Of course, this research might not reveal the *face* of the creator, but at least it might illuminate to some degree the methods he, or she, had used to fashion it. Scott felt comfortable enough with that to embrace the task with the confidence that he wasn't in breach of the Holy Scriptures.

Though Scott Ferris and his colleague were now embarking upon the same grand research program to study the origin and evolution of the universe, their paths to the professional and geographical summit to which they where now headed had been very different. Scott's background was solidly agrarian; he had grown up amidst the hardship of his family's subsistence-farming community in the U.S. Midwest and even today, after several years being groomed in philosophy and physics, first at the University of Chicago and then at

Caltech, he still retained the rustic, happy-go-lucky hillbilly appearance of the farm boy. Short and stocky, he had a cheery freckled face that beamed with unpretentious good humor. With a thatch of unkempt straw-colored hair, Scott Ferris looked to all the world as though he would be happier riding a John Deere than the observing cage of the world's most sophisticated and powerful telescope.

If Scott Ferris's appearance belied his rural heritage, his partner's on this journey to Mt. Palomar couldn't have been more different. Lee's lanky, athletic build, military-style moustache, and finely-chiseled urbane features exuded an image of privilege and well-groomed sophistication—a young Clark Gable, perhaps, or a youthful Gregory Peck.

Lee Drexler came from a community of East Coast artists, and his childhood had been spent amongst the artist community of New York's Greenwich Village. His father, George Drexler, was a noted member of an expressionist art movement in the 1920s, and his parents' home was constantly a center for the bohemian, the eccentric, and the artistic radical. Lee's mother was an accomplished concert pianist when she met Lee's father, but following the birth of his younger sister, Lisa, she reduced her public performances to spend more time with her two children. Ethel Drexler found that the ideal solution was to give private piano lessons from their large townhouse on Bowery Street. Lee still recalled with pride the intense intellectual gatherings and the fierce artistic and philosophical debates that seemed to gravitate around him. Revolution seemed the order of the day, almost every day, when Lee was young.

When the time came for Lee to consider his own career prospects, he had contemplated continuing with his family's artistic vocation, but in the end he decided on a career in science. Lee reasoned that if one was going to explore the mystery of creation, the mystery of existence, then science was a more rigorous and objective pursuit in which to do it, being less open to the vagaries of subjective interpretation, vanity, or fashion. Lee's father proved surprisingly sympathetic, even offering encouragement by pointing out that the ideas of several of the most acclaimed scientists in the modern era, such as Albert Einstein and Niels Bohr, and many in antiquity, such as Tycho Brahe, Kepler, and Newton, had been influenced by the beauty and symmetry evident in nature. In this regard, then, he had no particular qualms about his son's chosen path. On the contrary, the prospect of a tenured position and regular income guaranteed by a university or research institution more than compensated for the vicissitudes of the artist's life.

Actually, Scott and Lee had become friends while Lee was studying astrophysics at Harvard. Scott Ferris had visited the observatory there one summer and they had hit it off right away, cementing their friendship when Lee moved to Caltech.

Today, they had eased out of Pasadena soon after 3 P.M., picked up Interstate 15 at Corona, and then driven south in the direction of San Diego. At Escondido they made a left and joined what was once the old mule trail that had been used to bring the building materials up to Mt. Palomar's summit. It was paved now, of course, but still a slow, twisting, hairpin-laden journey.

The intensity of the strong sunlight piercing the clear blue sky above them belied the increasing crispness of the autumnal air as Scott's ageing Mercury convertible slowly climbed through the rock-strewn, fir tree-dotted landscape that marked their ascent up the 6,000 ft summit of Mt. Palomar. They had decided on the 'open' option of Scott's convertible on their departure from Los Angeles, but now, some two-thirds of the way to their destination, and some 4,000 ft above sea level, they periodically tugged at the zippers of their leather flying jackets to shield themselves against the dropping temperature.

'You doing OK, Lee? We can stop and put the hood up.'

'I think I'll make it, Scott. Besides, we'd better get used to the fresh air; we're gonna get a lot of it in the next year or so.'

'Gee, Lee,' Scott pondered wistfully after negotiating a full-lock hairpin that nearly brought the lurching vehicle to a complete standstill, 'when you listen to the problems poor old Galileo had to contend with way back then, I'm sure glad we are living in the twentieth century, an age where we have the freedom to publish scientific discoveries without fear of censorship or persecution.'

'Yeah, they even burned poor old Bruno at the stake for backing Galileo a few years after that. The Catholic Church sure was mad at those guys for contradicting the Papal doctrine that the Earth lay immutable at the center of the universe.'

Lee still found that particular part of the story the hardest to take. Tying people to a stake and burning them alive didn't seem like a very Christian thing to do. In Lee's mind, it smacked of desperation, an act of someone who feared the prospect of change—and perhaps a loss of authority.

'We've come a long way since then, Lee. We now accept the telescope as an instrument with which to develop a more rational explanation of the universe rather than having to rely on astrology, superstition, or religious doctrine. The church now look after their own flock and don't try to influence the scientific picture we guys are putting together.'

Lee let his gaze fall on the red plastic finger of the speedometer and watched as it slowly indicated increasing velocity.

'I sure hope scientific debate can be conducted in a rational and unbiased manner, Scott, but that Velikovsky affair recently had a lot of people jumping up and down shouting foul.'

Scott Ferris reached again for the column-mounted gear stalk and shifted to a lower gear as they encountered another hairpin bend.

'Velikovsky? You mean that rumpus about the guy who claimed to have come up with some proof that the moon had been ejected from Jupiter or some such crazy notion?'

'I think it was Venus that was ejected from Jupiter, Scott. He was some Russian émigré who fled to the States to avoid Stalin's persecution of intellectuals and academics. The public loved it. He wrote this best-selling book, *War of the Worlds*. No, the title was *Worlds in Collision*. It reached number one on the *New York Times'* bestseller list and they made his publisher drop it. It was almost like a book-burning party from Galileo's time.'

'Who did, Lee?'

'Oh, some of the more conservative members of the astronomical establishment, together with the help of some prominent academics in the universities. Apparently, Velikovsky's publisher had a strong textbook division, and the universities agreed amongst themselves, under pressure from some influential astronomers, to stop ordering the textbooks unless they dropped Velikovsky's book from their lists. It must have been a difficult decision, with *Worlds in Collision* selling like hotcakes.'

Lee himself had never quite understood what the fuss was all about. After all, if the idea was so crazy, so improbable, why make a big fuss about it? Could it be Velikovsky had hit some raw nerve and exposed an idea—*a possibility*—the astronomical community preferred not to contemplate because they thought it impossible? What's so crazy about the idea that astronomical bodies might be formed by ejection, he had often wondered to himself. Just because we haven't actually seen it happen doesn't mean it's a flat-out impossibility.

'Well, at least they only burn books today, Lee!'

'Yeah, I guess he did give his critics some reason to ridicule his ideas, though,' Lee added, by way of bringing his friend up to date on the pros and cons of the controversy as he understood it. 'By claiming that the birth of

Venus took place in recent historical time and is recorded in biblical texts—that sure can't have helped his case.'

Scott Ferris tugged back the sleeve of his leather flying jacket just enough to check the time. The three-hour drive from Pasadena had gone smoothly and now they were less than twenty minutes from the summit of Mt. Palomar. The increasingly barren landscape now held few trees and was littered only with dried, bleached grass, coarse scrub, and protruding rocks, evidence of the long snow-covered months that normally began in the second half of November, blanketing the summit of Mt. Palomar until the spring.

'Twenty minutes to go, Lee! Looks like we'll be there before dusk. Hell, it doesn't always go like this. Rain, snow, broken radiator, you name it—even ran out of gas one time. Can you believe that? Had to hitch a lift from a maintenance crew that happened to come along!'

'Good work, kid. You know, it's not so long ago they used to have to ride the mule train all the way to the top.' Lee gave his companion the thumbs-up, paused a moment to take in the scenery, then returned to the problem of book burning.

'Another problem for Velikovsky was that Venus has the most circular orbit of all the planets. If it had happened the way Velikovsky claimed, it's unlikely it would have ended up in its present state so quickly—gravity is too slow a force to allow that. Mind you, in principle it would seem fair at least to consider the proposal rather than simply throw it out by picking on shaky circumstantial historical proofs. It would be a travesty if science started to assume the role the church once held in deciding what is possible and what isn't.'

The dome housing the giant telescope now loomed on the skyline above them. Glistening white and majestic in the stillness of the late afternoon sun, the structure had a surreal appearance that was emphasized by the extreme isolation and altitude of its location. It looked to Lee as if someone had sprinkled fairy dust on the barren mountain landscape and some giant mushroom had sprung up overnight.

Scott flipped open the car's glove box and fumbled with a bunch of keys. After satisfying himself that he had located the right one to unlock the observatory's perimeter gate, he dangled it before his colleague.

'Actually, now that you mention it, I do remember something about the Velikovsky affair. Wasn't your old boss at Harvard mixed up in that? I seem to remember his name cropping up.'

'Yeah, Burmann. He was director of Harvard College, where I did my graduate studies. He was the astronomer who organized most of the opposition to Velikovsky's book. He just went ape over the fact that someone from another discipline would question the prevailing astronomical wisdom. Like most attempts at censorship though, it had its backlash and made even more people take notice of what it was they were attempting to play down. Ironically, it made the book even more popular. As it turned out, it was taken up by another publisher and again topped the bestseller lists.'

Scott Ferris looked in the rearview mirror, more out of habit than in the expectancy of seeing a vehicle anywhere in the vicinity of this desolate location, then gave his passenger a sideways glance.

'Well, as long as you don't go looking for planets popping out of the gas giants, Lee, I guess they'll stay off *your* tail. What exactly are you going to be studying up at the Monastery, now that you've finished helping out on Roxborne's research?'

'"Monastery?"'

'Oh, that's what we call the living quarters up at the 200-inch. Once you join the team up here, it's not much different than taking on the monastic life. You're locked away from society for weeks on end and they won't even let you crack a bottle of wine over dinner—no wives or girlfriends either! It's a pretty ascetic existence, but you get used to it—depends how long you are up here for.' Scott let out an ironic laugh. 'You'd soon go crazy if it weren't for the observing.'

'Maybe I should have brought a habit. I could shuffle about in the dark and really play the part! Actually, I want to compile a photographic atlas of the more unusual, disrupted galaxies. By the way, Scott, thanks for your support in the committee with regards to my observing proposal. Without your recommendation, I wouldn't be sitting here right now. Varscher and Linkowsky didn't look too kindly on my original proposal to study the Seyfert galaxies. I thought at least I'd get the backing of Varscher since I helped out on his nova distance program. Apparently he didn't seem to trust my reliability for some reason.'

The car lurched to a stop in front of the observatory's perimeter gate and Lee opened the door.

'I thought you did great work recalibrating the distance of novae in M31, Lee, but when you started having those independent ideas about those young blue stars in the local group of galaxies having abnormal redshifts, even I wondered for a moment if you were really 100% committed to the galactic distance calibration Hubble has established.'

Scott Ferris had read Lee's paper claiming these hot young stars had redshifts that appeared to be systemically higher on average than the measured overall redshift of their host galaxies, but he treated the claim with a degree of skepticism. The research had not been verified by other astronomers and it would, if true, complicate the galaxy/redshift distance formula that Hubble had established, a formula most now accepted as evidence for the expansion of the universe. Scott personally thought it better if this report was quickly buried, not least because any perceived undermining, or questioning, of the big bang cosmology would hardly further his friend's career.

'Well, I wouldn't take it too personally,' he added by way of assuring his colleague that the present picture was now most likely correct. 'They are probably more concerned with pressing on quickly to confirm the big picture. By comparing nova and star clusters in our galaxy and M31, we can get a more accurate measure of distance and rate of expansion. Your work on that wasn't the most glamorous, perhaps, but it was an important piece in the puzzle nonetheless. But, it's true,' Scott added by way of consolation, 'they could have shown a little more gratitude.'

Lee watched as the car rattled over the metal cattle grid and stopped just inside the perimeter fence. He pushed the iron gate shut, slid back onto the Mercury's bench seat, and pulled the door shut.

'You're still working on the way stars evolve, right?' Lee asked.

'Yeah, with Humphrey Perlmartta. We are trying to refine the mass/luminosity scale—get the true brightness and gauge with more certainty their true distance, and thus the distance of their host galaxies. We know from Hubble's observations that the greater a galaxy's light is shifted towards the red end of the electromagnetic spectrum, the faster it is receding from us. What we want to refine is the exact rate of recession.'

It's an amazing discovery, Scott. The biggest change in our picture of the cosmos since Copernicus overturned the Earth-centered belief of his day. We sure are privileged to be among the very first to observe with the 200-inch mirror. I'm still intrigued by those Seyferts spirals that have nuclei that shine more like stars. There must be a heck of a lot of energy being generated in that small region.'

'Well, don't stray too far off the allocated observing schedule, buddy. Hayman keeps a close eye on preserving the continuity of the research program that's revealing the expansion of the universe, and there'll soon be a queue of people applying for time on the 200-inch. Besides, you can always follow up these objects when you get a bit of spare time from your atlas compilation work. Hey, can you believe these number plates! "M31," that's Karl David-son's; he's in the photo-developing lab. "ORION 3," that's Howard Douglas; he's in spectroscopy. You know what I'm gonna get? A Ford Galaxy. Hell, I spend so much time looking at 'em, I might as well drive one!'

Lee was surprised at how few vehicles occupied the observatory's parking area. There were no more than five. For an enterprise of such grand ambition, one might imagine many more people would be involved at the research site. The scarcity of human activity only emphasized the air of monastic solitude and stillness. The fourteen-storey high domed sentinel, gleaming white and silent—except for the faint hum of a motor buried deep somewhere behind its closed and intimidating Gothic façade—appeared eerily temple-like. A shrine to the Scientific Age. It certainly impressed upon Lee the distinct feeling that he was about to embark upon a journey that would condemn him to long hours of solitude. It would, he thought, be something akin to those who fol-low the monastic path. True, his vision, his meditation—his search for cosmic truth and revelation—would be directed outwards rather than in, but the com-mitment, the long hours of lonely contemplation, raised the comparison in his mind.

'Gee, I feel on top of the world already! What are we up here, 6,000 ft?' Lee asked. They parked the car in a space reserved for Dr. Ferris and walked to a narrow ridge some distance from the main building. As they gazed down upon the San Diego basin, a trail of brownish haze indicated the position of both San Diego and L.A. in the distance.

'Yeah, something like that—5,600 to be exact. If the lights of San Diego and L.A. grow much brighter, though, there's going to be a light-pollution problem in the future. That wasn't a concern when they drew up plans to site the 200-inch up here in the 1930s.'

'Hey, let me show you your cabin, then I'll introduce you to the boss. We can meet up later in the staff canteen.' Lee dumped his gear at a small but comfortable cabin and then followed Scott over to the main building to meet the director.

Professor Huber Hayman was a man seldom tempted to trifle with the inconsequential. It wasn't that he was anti-social—though some thought him rather aloof—or that he hadn't the time, or inclination, to attend to the bureaucratic and administrative duties that leadership brought with it. No, if he gave the impression that he had little time for such mundane duties it was simply that, as director of Mt. Palomar Observatory, he was more concerned with events that took place billions of light years from Earth and expected anyone who joined his team to feel the same—though one might be forgiven for wondering where such enthusiasm for the stars came from.

He was now in his early sixties: silver haired, of sallow complexion and slender frame. His wardrobe, which seemed to consist entirely of baggy suits of striped charcoal, presented more the image of a man who'd spent his life attending to clerical work—an accountant or a bank manager, perhaps, rather than someone entrusted with overseeing research into the farthest reaches of time and space.

But appearances often belie vocational conviction, and so it was with Lee's new boss. Professor Huber Hayman was a man on a mission, and that mission was protected by a strict and absolute adherence to the path mapped by Edwin Hubble and his discovery that all the galaxies in the universe had been speeding apart since the primordial big bang. It was Huber Hayman's mission to gather photographic evidence with the giant light-gathering mirror under his direction and prove to the world that science now held the keys that would unlock the mystery of creation. If those toiling under his charge up at the 'Monastery' might have been considered 'monks,' he was the High Priest, the Head Abbott, leading the enterprise forward toward its most Holy Grail.

'Welcome to Mt. Palomar, Dr. Drexler! You join us at a most exciting and eventful period in our research program.'

Lee took the director's limp hand and was ushered into an office on the ground floor of the main building. The director made no obvious move to indicate they would spend much time in the office, and continued without directing Lee to sit down.

'I, and the faculty members of the observing committee, welcome you to Mt. Palomar Observatory and trust that the facilities here will provide you with the opportunity to further our galaxy research program into the expansion of the universe. Thanks to Hubble and his disciples, and with the help of this powerful new tool, we are pushing the limits of the observable universe back almost to the beginning of time. With your help, Dr. Drexler, and the rest of my team of dedicated astronomers here, I'm confident that before long we shall have some fundamental answers to determine not only how the universe evolved but what likely course it will follow in the distant future.'

'From studies of nearby galaxies currently underway, we have been able to make a good determination of the distance out to the local group. Once we know the redshift/distance of these, we can study more distant groups and thus gain a more precise determination of the universe's rate of expansion. I believe you've had some experience with our sister 100-inch telescope over at

Mt. Wilson, so you will be familiar with the basic operating procedures we use here. The 200-inch has a far more sophisticated tracking mechanism and many other novel labor-saving devices that make the job of observing considerably easier. Perhaps one day we shall have fully-automated telescopes that may be directed from a comfortable office by remote control, but I'm afraid we are not there yet. I'm sure you will find the 200-inch a great improvement over the telescopes in our other facilities, though.'

Lee sensed a brief window of opportunity to respond as Hayman paused briefly in his astronomical sales patter to flick a switch on his desktop communications console and put a call on hold.

'It's a real privilege to join the team, Professor Hayman. Scott Ferris has brought me up to date on the progress you are making here—I can't wait to begin my research.'

Hayman seemed not to register what Lee had said, because he was now bent over his communications console issuing a command to his secretary in another room. 'Miss Archer, would you call Dr. Robbins and ask if he would mind rescheduling our meeting to tomorrow morning. I have Dr. Drexler with me who's just come up from Caltech, and he needs to be given a quick run-through our facilities upstairs. I can see him tomorrow at ten o'clock if that's convenient?'

The director put down the phone and turned back to Lee. 'Sorry about that. I had a meeting, but it will probably hold.' He looked at his watch and ushered Lee toward the door. 'Let's go and take a look upstairs. The sooner you get to know your way around, the better. I'll have to be back soon, but we can make a start.'

Lee followed as the director led the way round the bare concrete-walled corridor, past administration offices, machine workshops, libraries, and photographic labs. They pushed through a swing door, climbed a steel stairway that sent their clattering footsteps echoing through the concrete well of corridors, and reached a mezzanine, then it was up another steel stairway before pushing at a door that opened onto a raised walkway that encircled the inside of the domed building.

Lee had already visited several large 'scopes in his brief astronomical career, of course, but what towered before him now seemed like the Eiffel Tower by comparison to anything he had witnessed before. Painted battleship grey, the mechanical contraption was of titanic proportions. As his gaze traveled from the huge welded sheet-metal horseshoe, which was the size of a tennis court and acted as a pivot for the towering 100-ft frame and its 15-ton glass mirror, he was struck by the ship-like presence this marvel of engineering gave off. In fact, it was unsurprising that it did exhibit ship-like qualities: many of the telescope's largest parts had been assembled in naval shipyards, as these were the only places big enough to weld and rivet the huge pieces of sheet metal and steel girder.

'This is pure twentieth-century Gothic,' he thought to himself. 'If medieval man had designed and managed to construct a monster of such mechanical dimensions, it would surely have looked like this.'

With no apparent concession to either human comfort or sense of the aesthetic, it was simply a giant mechanical trap for gathering the image of celestial objects, the faint light of which started its journey long before our solar system was born. It was, he thought, a kind of metaphorical 'cosmic spider's web,' woven by man, and he would soon be spending long nights waiting patiently at its center, ready to pounce when the sticky emulsion of his photographic plates had trapped sufficient photons for him to gorge on another galaxy—perhaps even a cluster of galaxies, if he was lucky.

Before he had time to pursue such comparisons to the world of arachnids, he became aware of Professor Hayman descending a flight of metal stairs that led down to the concrete floor of the huge domed building and beckoning him to follow.

Standing next to the director, from this lower perspective, the giant construction looked even more imposing.

'When you think that all this started with Galileo's little hand-held spy glass, Lee! It's truly amazing what we've ended up with today.'

'Yeah, and the universe is a bit bigger than it was in his day too, that's for sure.' Lee was momentarily awestruck at the thought he would soon be at the helm of this, the largest telescope ever built—and using it to probe depths of space never before witnessed by human eyes.

'There have been a lot of developments in the telescope field since Galileo's time, that's for sure. This little baby is the culmination of some 300 years of continuous improvement—state of the art, and about as big as it is possible to get. Can't build a bigger glass mirror; it would break under its own weight.'

Lee knew some of the problems associated with casting the huge glass mirror, but he played ignorant and encouraged Hayman to continue. 'Took several attempts before a chunk of special Pyrex glass was successfully cast, didn't it?' he proffered.

'Yes, we had difficulty keeping the cooling-down even all over. The first two attempts had to be abandoned. Finally a solution was found, but even then, the whole process of cooling, grinding, and polishing took ten years. The original chunk of glass weighed twenty tons, but after all the grinding and polishing, it ended up at the present fifteen.'

'Didn't the war interrupt construction, Professor Hayman?'

'Yes, it did, Lee. But even when construction was completed we needed a further two years of grinding and polishing the mirror before it was finally commissioned.'

'The entire structure took twenty-one years to build from the conception of the original plans, and we finally started observational work proper in forty-nine. It's proved a great benefit in furthering the redshift/distance law and strengthening our belief in the expanding universe. Let me show you how we get up to the prime focus cage.'

Professor Hayman turned and gestured to a metal basket, reminiscent of the gondola of a hot air balloon, suspended in the middle of the gray skeletal frame some eighty feet above their heads.

'That's where you're going to be spending most nights, Lee. You'll need to know how to operate the lift.'

They climbed a stairway to a metal landing where the lift waited and climbed in. Hayman snapped the waist-high guardrail securely shut and punched a green button on the console that started their ascent towards the domed roof. Only the low hum of the lift's motor and the occasional echo of someone intermittently hammering on a piece of metal in the concrete bowels of the building below them broke the eerie silence.

Upon reaching their destination, and docking with the prime focus cage, Lee scrambled into the metal gondola and settled himself on a leather-covered metal seat that looked like it had been borrowed from a piece of agricultural machinery.

'Hey! This is like riding on those fairground Ferris wheels. Hope it's got a safety harness!' Lee Drexler called across to his instructor, who was still on the lift. 'You'd think we astronomers would block the view of the mirror down there, sitting here right slap bang in the middle of the tube! How high off the ground is this thing?'

'Oh, some eighty feet—and we don't supply a parachute, so be careful you don't go sleep-walking or something.'

Lee looked gingerly over the edge of the metal cage and made a mental note to heed the advice, as the director quickly continued. 'Yes, one would think the observer would block out some light. But actually the mirror's so large, from its perspective you appear little bigger than a fly on a dustbin lid, so it really makes little practical difference. It's a remarkable coincidence, Lee. Our dome here is 135 feet tall and 137 feet in diameter—the same as the Pantheon in Rome! Well, Lee, I have to get back to the office. I'll get one of our night assistants to give you a more thorough look over the 'scope and its control system when we get back down.'

The director hit the descend button after Lee had scrambled back onto the platform, and the cage slowly retraced its trajectory towards earth.

'Tomorrow you will want to take a tour of the other facilities we have here, Lee. I'll arrange for one of our ground staff to show you around our sister 'scope, the Schmidt 48-inch, which is used for wide-field photography. We are well on the way to completing a photographic survey of the whole sky for reference purposes with the 48-inch. Do you know how long that program would have taken with the 200-inch?' Professor Hayman rounded on him with the excited air of a quiz master, impatient to divulge the correct answer.

Lee hesitated.

'Five thousand years!' Professor Hayman jumped upon Lee's hesitancy, clearly pleased to impart this piece of interesting statistical information. 'FIVE THOUSAND YEARS!' he repeated proudly. 'The different size reflectors, then, are invaluable for tackling different jobs. Not that you actually observe anything directly as you would with a normal telescope,' he demurred with a touch of regret. 'These are basically just very large cameras with the image recorded on photographic plates during hours of careful tracking. Long gone are the days of observers like Percival Lowell and the Earl of Rosse, who looked directly through the eyepiece and attempted to record what they saw by making sketches,' Drexler offered as they touched down and disembarked from the lift.

'Yes, indeed. Thanks to the initiative of Hubble and his colleagues and the foresight of George Ellery Hale in managing to persuade the Rockefeller Foundation to donate the six million dollars needed to finance the construction, we have here the two most powerful instruments in the world—use them wisely, Lee!'

Lee followed the director back up the metal steps and paused at the landing.

'The Carnegie Institution of Washington built the earlier big 'scopes over on Mt. Wilson, so why exactly did the Rockefeller Foundation vest ownership of this observatory to Caltech, Professor Hayman? They didn't even have an astronomy faculty at the time.'

Lee knew some of this story but was never completely sure of the political twists and turns that accompanied the building of the 200-inch.

'Well, remember, Carnegie owned and operated the Mt. Wilson observatories. The newly formed California Institute of Technology hadn't any major observing facilities, so this was to be a joint venture; Carnegie supplied the very first astronomers and we now operate under a joint agreement. The directorship of Palomar alternates between Carnegie and Caltech.'

'Well, Scott Ferris and I sure are privileged to be among the first to have graduated from Caltech's astronomy department...but it's a little ironic that we're starting to observe at a time in history when the visual 'scopes have probably reached the limit of resolving power.'

'Oh, I think you'll have plenty to look at before this baby is out of date, Lee!'

Lee knew that this was indeed true and didn't doubt for a moment that the new telescope would keep him busy for a long time to come. But there were other windows being opened onto the universe now that extended astronomical observations beyond the purely visible part of the electromagnetic spectrum.

'It looks like the new radio telescopes that have been developed at Jodrell Bank in the UK and Parks in Australia could become important tools to help us see beyond the visual spectrum,' Lee continued.

'Well that's true, Lee, but these new instruments complement rather than supplement the visual observations. In fact, we are working closely with the radio astronomers at present—especially one of our people, Frank Sedgwick, who has gone down to Parks. He has found some very high energy sources at various positions in the sky, and one of our tasks is to try and get a visual fix to see what's there. We have got a fairly good fix on one of Sedgwick's chaps, and it looks like it's a galaxy, though a very strange one.'

Lee had heard a rumor to this effect, but it was all very hush hush with only a small number of specialist people working on the secret project.

'We think it may actually be two galaxies in collision,' Hayman continued, sounding as though he were imparting a piece of information in strict confidence. 'At least, that is what it looks like from the rather indistinct images we have gotten so far—though it's still a little early to tell. We've got a pretty good fix on some others too, and the curious thing is that they all appear to have patches of radio emission coming from two lobes strung symmetrically across the central galaxy. Tim Silver, who collaborates with Professor Howell at Cambridge, thinks this might be a result of energetic material somehow being ejected from the central galaxy—but Howell's team would be looking for something like that...'

Hayman shot Lee a confidential wink.

'Any process that might look like a method for creating new matter to shore up their Continuous Creation theory!' He laughed. 'Theorists! Stick with the observations, Lee. That's the only thing that counts in this game!'

Lee knew that Professor Howell at Cambridge, in the United Kingdom, had garnered a reputation as a bit of a maverick with his alternative to the big bang and was a constant source of irritation to some in the astronomical establishment, but he thought it prudent, here, to keep quiet about the fact that he rather admired Howell's rebellious nature and his alternative cosmological theory.

'Well, this is an area I hope to be studying. I'm particularly interested in just these kinds of galaxies, the ones that appear to be disrupted in some way. My first observing run is still scheduled for Wednesday night, right?'

'Your run is cleared for Wednesday, yes.'

They made their way back to ground level, and the director escorted Lee to the main entrance.

'Well, you'll want to get straightened out. The dining room is over there, past the library; you can't miss it. You can get a pretty decent meal there when Rose Miller and her staff are on duty, otherwise you'll either have to cater for yourself, or share what the others are preparing. You'll also get to meet some of the other staff. Welcome to the team, Dr. Drexler. I hope your observations here will prove most fruitful.'

'Thank you, Professor Hayman, so do I.'

As Lee turned to gaze up at the domed building, now bathed in the hue of a rose-colored sunset, his thoughts reverberated with the news of the secret project and the knowledge that he would soon be using the very instrument needed to confirm it.

2

A Most Unusual Discovery

The headlights of Mike Martin's pickup momentarily illuminated the tall, shadowy figure making its way across the frozen landscape in the direction of the ghostly domed building of the 200-inch telescope. Though he and his passenger, spectroscopist Dr. Paul Janow's glimpse of the figure was little longer than the flash of a flickering strobe as they bumped over the frozen track and came to an unsteady stop in the observatory's parking lot, they were left with the unnerving impression that they had just witnessed the apparition of a WW11 Bomber pilot. Dressed in a one-piece blue flying suit (the kind that's plugged into the electrical circuit for heating), brown 'bomber' jacket, and heavy leather boots, the scurrying figure clasped tightly an attaché case. All that was apparently missing from the apparition was the period leather head gear, goggles pulled tightly over his head, and a B52 revving impatiently on the tarmac, ready for take-off.

'Who the heck's that? I thought the war was over!' Paul Janow rubbed his eyes and strained his head toward the pickup's windscreen in an effort to better recapture the scene he had just witnessed.

Dr. Mike Martin cut the pickup's V8, rolled down the side window, and listened for a moment. The stillness was broken only by a faint hum coming from the direction in which the pilot headed.

'Oh, that's Lee Drexler. He's off on another bombing run.'

'Hey Lee!' Mike Martin cupped his hands to better channel the direction and distance of his quip. 'Who are you targeting tonight, the Ruskies?'

Dr. Martin's jibe languished on either deaf ears or insufficient range, for the B52 pilot disappeared through the main entrance of the 200-inch building without hesitation or comment.

*   *   *

'Hi, Robert, are we all set? We're tracking the Virgo cluster tonight. There's a string of six disrupted galaxies I need to look at. Should be around an eight-hour exposure in all. Can you open the lid please when I get settled into the cage?'

Robert Hale was Lee's night assistant for this run, as he had been for most of Lee's other sorties into the extragalactic realm over the past five years, and he knew the procedure that was required to get his pilot airborne. With a thumbs up, he waited as Lee climbed into the cage that would deliver him to the cockpit of his intergalactic time machine, then turned and headed for the control desk that would enable him to point Lee toward his intended target.

'Robert, can you hear me?' Lee hit the button on the intercom. He laid aside a sheaf of finding charts then carefully slid a large glass photographic plate into the positioning holder, above the slit that would focus the faint reflected beam of starlight sent to him from the giant mirror below.

The tinny affirmation, crackling up from ground control, sounded to Dr. Drexler as though it were being sent from another planet.

'OK, Robert, when you're ready, let's go. Right ascension 14 hours, 16 minutes; declination plus 21 degrees, 27 minutes. Thank you. That should give us WE-47, Vega 5.'

Dr. Drexler leaned back on the leather-covered 'tractor' seat and waited as the giant girdered tube of the 200-inch telescope slowly began to transport him up and out to its designated elevation, between heaven, earth, and the slowly-widening slit in the huge domed roof.

'You should be on target now,' crackled ground control after some five minutes of almost imperceptible transport within the giant dome. Indeed, so utterly smooth was Lee's progress as the telescope turned, it seemed as if he were at rest and the huge domed building rotated about him. How ironic, he thought, such a simple illusion had once caused men to believe that the sun rotated about a stationary Earth!

Another thing Lee found rather ironic was that in order to get an exact fix on the guide star that would lock them onto the object to be studied, one had first to fix its position by looking at it through a small microscope. It amused him to think that this microscopic view was then amplified a million-fold by telescopes such as the one he was about to focus. How strange, he thought, to be able to glide so effortlessly from the microscopic dimension to the macro in one simple move. One time, after smoking a little marijuana one of his more 'adventurous' Caltech friends had given him to help while away the long hours of physical inaction, he wondered if, indeed, there was any real difference between the two instruments of magnification. We assume one looks out, to the boundless cosmos of planets, stars, and galaxies; and the other in, to the microscopic domain of atoms, molecules, and cells. That's the way it's always been. But could the perceived distinction be an illusion? An illusion born of a conceptual misunderstanding similar in magnitude to the Earth/Sun rotation paradox faced by Copernicus? Lee hesitated, unsure of the answer. One thing was certain: if there were no difference it would certainly alter our concept of space and time and our place in the universe, that was for sure! But he hadn't dwelt long on the philosophical implications of this conundrum before the effects of the drug wore off. He was an astronomer, not a philosopher, and he would let others grapple with such mind-boggling concepts if they wanted to.

Lee fixed a star between the guide microscope's crosshairs and called down to ground control to begin the tracking. He turned off the small pen light on the control panel, leaving only the dim red glow of his back-up light, then leaned back and let his gaze drift upward to the scattering of glittering stars framed in the slit of the vast blackened dome. He had only now to wait. Wait out the next hour or so in his cramped cage until the film of emulsion covering his photographic plate had trapped enough photons to reveal events that had taken place eons ago, halfway across the universe.

Usually, he had to check tracking only occasionally to make sure the guide star hadn't shifted position—so while one could take a brief doze, sleeping right through the run was out of the question. Then, of course, there were other objects to target and plates to replace in the exposure slit. Tonight, Lee intended to track six exposures in all. Some long, some short. Some using different color filters to cut through obscuring gas and dust and bring out fine detail, emphasizing different chemical elements, etc.

This particular January night, the temperature was well below freezing and, while this steadied the atmosphere and helped to obtain fine quality photographs, it made the task of carrying out his mission considerably more difficult and was the reason Lee had his flying gear on. This was a tip that Scott Ferris had passed on to him: 'Go get a flying suit, Lee,' he had once told him at Caltech, 'one that you can plug into the electric circuit of the prime focus cage.

That's the only way you're gonna survive up on Mt. Palomar in winter.' And so it was that Lee now bent down and plugged two small cables to the connectors of his suit and dialed the temperature gauge to mark 3.

There were few other creature comforts to while away the lonely nights. One could read a little or jot down some necessary calculations on a notepad, but even that was difficult in the freezing, ill-lit, cramped conditions. Most nights Lee would take a sandwich up with him, but liquid refreshment was avoided to pre-empt the call of nature. One of the few comforts was being able to listen to music. This was piped up to the cage from ground control and listened to through a small loudspeaker built into the cage—or one could use headphones. He kept a small selection of tape recordings in Robert's control room. Mostly these were classical recordings, not only because the symphonic works lasted for an hour or more, but also because the grandeur of the music, Beethoven and Mozart in particular, lifted his spirits and inspired meditations upon the immensity of creation to which he bore witness. This night he had the urge to meditate upon the same music Galileo might have listened to as he gazed upon the heavens three centuries earlier with the first small handheld telescope.

'Robert, could you give me some seventeenth century Italian choral music, please? Yes, that's right…yes…Palestrina. Set the wake-up call for 6:30. If all goes according to plan, I shouldn't need you 'til then.'

Lee replaced the handset, adjusted the volume control next to the loudspeaker, then settled back and drifted into an earlier century.

*   *   *

A loud buzzer suddenly going off next to his ear brought Dr. Drexler abruptly back to the present and the realization that the night's observing run was now over. Lee stirred himself, fumbled for the intercom, and affirmed to ground control he was now semi-conscious, ready to pack up the night's catch and come down.

'Good morning, Lee. Soon have you down, buddy. Hang on.'

Observing was never an easy task in the freezing cramped conditions, and Robert Hale knew that Lee, because of his height, suffered a greater disadvantage than most. Tall or not, while he had the utmost respect for those who could endure such physical discomforts, he had little wish to emulate them himself.

'I fired up the stove in the canteen. You got a jug of Brazil's best brewing down here, Lee.'

'Thanks, Robert. You're a blessing. I hope tonight's run was worth the wait. Lee gathered together the glass photographic plates and placed them carefully in a plastic box. He then unplugged the electric heating cables from his suit and stepped into the lift.

'OK, take her away.' The lift separated from the prime focus cage and Lee started the slow descent back to earth.

Before heading for his dormitory to catch some well-deserved sleep, Lee passed the plates to his assistant with the instructions to take them over to the developing lab and have them ready for inspection later that day.

It was getting on for 4 P.M. by the time Lee had woken, showered, and made his way over to the photo lab to check on the night's run. His optimism that the photos would turn out well was buoyed by the last night's low temperature and steady atmospheric conditions. As he studied the first photograph, he was not disappointed.

'Looks good, Dan.'

'We'll have the last one ready in about half an hour, Lee.' Dan Hartmann, the lab's chief developer, was busy pouring developing fluid into a large rectangular glass dish when there was a knock at the door and Scott Ferris looked in.

'Hey, Lee. You're up early. How's the photo album coming along? Found any extraterrestrials yet?'

Lee knew the author of the Midwestern twang and responded without taking his eye from the small tube-like magnifying glass he was using to examine fine stellar detail on the photo.

'Ha, ha! No, but I do have some strange looking galaxies, Scott! Come and take a look at these weirdoes I got last night. Some appear to be ejecting huge amounts of matter from the nuclear region. One looks like it's splitting in two to form a separate companion.'

Scott Ferris joined Lee at the light box and examined one of the photographs intently for a minute.

'What the hell's going on there, Scott?'

'Looks like some explosion is ripping the galaxies apart, Lee—that's the first impression. But why would they blow up like that?'

Dr. Drexler pulled up a chair and passed the magnifying tube to his colleague. 'Could they be splitting into two or more separate companions, maybe? And what do you make of these jets that appear to be coming out of the nucleus? It looks like they wind back around to form spiral arms in some cases.'

Lee picked up another plate and placed it on the light box.

'I got a call from Victor Ambarzumian recently. He's looked at similar examples in the atlas compiled by Hubble, and he's convinced that new galaxies are formed by ejection from the nucleus of existing ones. He suggested that twenty years ago, but nobody listened. Seemed the general consensus was to go with the merger hypothesis.'

'Why did he call you, Lee?'

'Oh, he saw some of the photos I had published a while back in the *Observatory Journal* and wanted to know if I thought we could resurrect his idea.'

'And...do you?'

'Absolutely. I can't see any real alternative, Scott. It's what the images seem to be telling us. You've got to start believing your own eyes at some point in this game. In my view, Victor mounts a very compelling case for this hypothesis, based on the visual evidence.'

There was a knock at the door, followed by the entrance of a tall, barrel-chested, irascible-looking fellow in his early sixties wearing baggy Levis, high-heeled leather boots, and a red 'cowboy' shirt. The shirt was piped along the cuffs and breast pockets in gold braid and fastened, at its ill-fitting neck, by a black bootlace tie that had a large jewel-like stud imbedded in it. The intruder's immediate appearance was that of a prize-fighter or, perhaps, a wrangler from the county rodeo. Either way, his complexion was that of someone who had recently just escaped being throttled or thrown off. He dabbed at his broken, flushed face with a small handkerchief as he surveyed the occupants of the lab.

'Anyone at home?' The visitor's voice was surprisingly high pitched considering its barrel-chested origin, and its accent suggested an East European parentage. 'Ah! Dawktourr Scott and Dawktourr Lee! May I enter?'

'Only if you leave your spurs outside, Oscar. You know how they rough up the parquet,' Scott Ferris replied with mock disdain.

Oscar Olitsky had come to the U.S. after the war and gained his Ph.D. in astrophysics at Cornell University, before being taken under Professor Varscher's wing and groomed in galaxy evolution theory over at Mt. Wilson. He had been one of the first Carnegie astronomers to come to Mt. Palomar and had built a reputation for expressing extremely wild ideas and exhibiting bouts of unpredictable behavior.

'You're not in one of your "moods," I hope.' Lee put down his glass plate and backed off in a show of feigned apprehension.

Oscar Olitsky threw his head back and let out a bullish snort. 'Hah! It's early, and I haven't met any of those "scientists" that "claim" to carry out "research" in this hallowed institute. Besides, I have successfully carried out my ballistic experiment! It makes me very happy to tell you it WORKS, my friends!'

'*Ballistic* experiment?' Lee Drexler repeated in mock horror.

Olitsky was clearly excited and looked like he had something of immense importance to impart. He stood holding the door, seemingly transfixed by the positive news he was about to deliver

'I get too much zee turbulence in my lines of zight, guys,' he finally uttered breathlessly. So I get my assistant to bring me a shotgun and I blast a hole clean through my troubling airs. BOOM! Now I zee so clearly like astronomers have never before zeen!'

'Well good for you, Oscar.' Scott Ferris attempted to both placate and congratulate their unruly visitor at the same time. 'I'm pleased to hear your little experiment was such a success and it makes you happy. But may we respectfully remind you, this is an astronomical research institute, not a weapons-proving ground. By the way, can we help you?'

'I've come to pick up my precious photos of colliding galaxies. You two young punks are not stealing them, are you, and calling them your own?'

'No, Oscar. We are not stealing, copying, or plagiarizing your precious photos. We take our own, don't we, Scott?' Lee intoned wearily. 'And by the way, Oscar, they are not colliding, they're dividing.'

'Ha, you will see!' The East European in his cowboy outfit moved toward the window and paused, as though momentarily losing the thread of what he was saying, but then quickly rallied and continued, 'Dawktourr Lee, you are wasting your time compiling another atlas when I have already captured so many beauties to prove my theory that the galaxies are all bumping into each other like…like cars down there on your ridiculous freeways! Why waste your time looking for more examples, eh?'

'Yep, Oscar's in a good mood today—you can kinda tell, can't you! Don't go upsetting him, Lee, he's got a got a firearm stashed away up here!'

'Yeah, and I hope he's got a license to use it,' Dr. Drexler muttered under his breath, in an effort not to inflame the situation.

'Oh, don't worry! I send 'im back down the mountain with my assistant. I just use 'im to prove my theory. How come it's so easy to get a gun here in

California anyway, eh? Everybody walking around with a gun. Anybody would think your civil war was still on!'

Scott Ferris thought it prudent to steer the topic of their conversation away from the subject of highway pile-ups, firearms, and their lack of effective control in the USA. He shot the cowboy-astronomer a glance and offered Lee a light-hearted summary of Olitsky's main contribution to their craft.

'Oscar's not only an astronomer and a weapons expert, Lee. He's an artist, aren't you, Oscar? He doesn't just photograph the galaxies, he sketches them too. But sketches of colliding galaxies are—how shall we say—open to *artistic license*, Oscar. Lee here, on the other hand, is looking for visible, photographic proof. You want to be careful people don't accuse you of imagining those bridges of material between your colliding galaxies, like Percival Lowell imagined canals on Mars!'

Olitsky pulled a bunch of photographs and some papers from a filing cabinet and let out a strangled laugh. 'Don't worry about my eyes, guys. Why would I use zee ballistics unless my eyes could appreciate the subtlety of such a brilliantly conceived experiment?' He made a move toward the door, clutching his papers. 'Well, must to run.'

'Hey! Oscar, before you go, what do you make of this? I took it last night with a red filter.' Lee got up and dangled a photograph between his fingers. 'M87—it looks like there's a faint counter jet to the famous blue spike emanating from the nucleus. What do you think?'

Olitsky moved suspiciously to take the black-and-white photograph. He took a pair of spectacles from a braided breast pocket and scrutinized the picture intently.

'Lee, I'm glad you discovered this—and not one of those other bastardos!'

'I take it you agree with the proposition then, Oscar?'

'It sure looks like there's something there, but it's probably the result of tidal forces from an unseen companion galaxy.'

'You and your colliding galaxies, Oscar! When are you going to admit these are jets of matter that have been ejected from the nucleus?'

Olitsky straightened and slid the glasses back in his shirt pocket. 'When people provide the clear proof to convince me, Dawktourr Lee. Until then, I'm sticking with my collision hypothesis. But, I have to admit,' he offered generously, 'you are compiling an interesting catalog. How long have you got to go on that, anyway? You've been working on it now for five years, no?'

'Four, actually.' Lee made to snatch the photo from Olitsky and hide it behind his back. 'And there's a heck of a lot of galaxies out there, Oscar—you haven't found them all.'

Oscar Olitsky slapped Scott Ferris on the shoulder and made for the door, pausing only long enough to retrieve several papers that had slipped from the bundle he had scooped up, then turned on his cowboy-booted heel and gave them a conspiratorial wink as he went out. 'Keep searching, guys...keep searching.'

'Phew! That was a close shave, Lee. I thought you were going to stoke the volcano there for a minute. Poor old Olitsky's a volatile creature and doesn't take too kindly to people who can't see his colliding galaxies.'

'Yeah, I know. Fortunately, I also know that he rather admires my work, and the fact that we are both closely involved in the same area of research. I just happen to have a hunch that he is wrong on this. But he is a brilliant scientist and it's kind of unjust that he should be squeezed on his observing schedule and excluded from committees just because his ideas are outside the mainstream.'

'Yeah, it's a cut-throat business. Everybody wants to be the first to join up all the dots.'

'Actually, Lee, I was looking for you. Something interesting has come up.'

'Oh yeah, what's that?'

Scott Ferris moved to settle himself on the edge of the desk next to the light box.

'You remember the puzzling spectrum I got of the star-like object at the radio position of 3C 29 a couple of years back?'

Dr. Drexler looked up with interest. 'Why, yes, we talked about that. The spectrum was unlike anything we had ever seen before in a star; it never made sense to anyone. It was never resolved was it?'

'Right, exactly! Well, Bob Simmons has just called me to say that Harry Maynard at Parks in Australia got a precise fix on 3C 328 during the recent lunar occultation. Precise enough for our people to try and get visual identification at the radio location.'

'And?'

'Well, Simmons wasn't allowed to look for it himself because of some procedural red tape, so Marty Schwitters was asked to make the observation. Wait for this! He got a spectrum of an even brighter star-like object at one of its two small radio positions and, as with 3C 29, at first he couldn't understand it. Yesterday, in a sudden flash of recognition, he realized that it was simply the spectrum of Balmer lines in hydrogen, *but shifted to the red end of the electro-magnetic spectrum by 16%!*

'Are you kidding?' Dr. Drexler straightened and was now giving Scott Ferris his full attention.

'No, Lee, I'm not. Hayman has called a meeting for 3:30 Saturday afternoon down in Pasadena to discuss the discovery, and he wants everybody to attend so Schwitters can brief us.'

Dr. Drexler grabbed a pencil and scribbled some quick calculations on a piece of paper.

'Gee, at a rough estimate…based on Hubble's redshift law…I would say this object must be some 2 billion light years away, Scott.'

'That's not all. Bob and Jim Grenshaw rechecked the spectrum of *my* starlike object at the radio position of 3C 29 and found that *it* had an even greater redshift: 37%. That indicates 3C 29 is something like 4 billion light years distant.'

Dr. Drexler let out a low whistle and tapped the blunt end of his pencil on the desk.

'This is incredible! It puts these stars beyond the distance of the most remote galaxies. It doesn't seem possible. The only objects that appear anything like this are the Seyfert galaxies—they have a very bright, compact, variable nucleus.'

'Yes, Lee. But those are *galaxies*.'

'I've gotta be in on this. I should be finished up here Friday night.' Lee pinned the previous night's photographs in a line on the notice board then picked up the magnifying tube and tossed it thoughtfully from one hand to the other. 'What time did you say, 3:30?'

'Yeah. Bring along anything you think might be relevant. I'll see you there. I'm going on down today.'

*   *   *

Dr. Lee Drexler was a little early as he strode purposefully along the polished marble corridor of the Mt. Palomar Observatory headquarters. He pushed through the swing doors of the auditorium and spotted Scott Ferris already seated a couple of rows from the front of the rapidly filling hall. Lee squeezed along the aisle and sat down next to him.

'Hey Lee, good to see you made it on time. Looks like it's gonna be a pretty full party. Most of the people from Caltech seem to be here as well as several from other observatories.'

The excited buzz of people filling the hall suddenly died as Professor Hayman and an elegant companion, about half his age and sporting a bowtie, climbed onto the rostrum and sat down. After carefully spreading a paper before him, Professor Hayman tapped the microphone, cleared his throat, and waited until the noise in the hall had abated.

'Ladies and gentlemen. Thank you. Thank you. Thank you for coming. As you will have heard, something important and very unexpected has turned up. I wanted to brief you all and discuss the implications before the press gets wind of it. You know how they not only expect us to make earth-shattering discoveries up at Mt. Palomar, but to have instant explanations ready for them when we do! My office is going to be swamped with inquiries when this new development leaks. I'll need some kind of press release ready.'

Hayman leaned over, whispered something in his companion's ear, then turned back to address the assembled gathering.

'This is Dr. Marty Schwitters from Caltech. Would you like to give us an overview of what you have found, Dr. Schwitters?'

Dr. Schwitters took the handheld microphone, went over to the slide projector, and flashed the image of a radio galaxy on the screen. Overlaid on the galaxy were concentric lines indicating 21-cm radio contours.

'Thank you, Professor Hayman. Some of you may recall that Hadley Collins and colleagues' efforts to get a lunar occultation fix on 3C 29 with the radio telescope at Jodrell Bank a couple of years ago proved unsuccessful. Well, last week, Harry Maynard, using the 210-meter dish at Parks in Australia, had the opportunity to try again as the moon was occulting 3C 328. This occultation proved successful and an extremely accurate measurement of the position of 3C 328 was relayed to us by Frank Sedgwick at Parks.

'I managed to get a spectrum with the 200-inch of the star-like image at one of the two bright radio locations and while at first, as with 3C 29, I couldn't fathom the lines in the spectrum, two days ago, in a sudden flash of inspiration, I realized that it was simply that the familiar Balmer lines in hydrogen had been shifted towards the red end of the electromagnetic spectrum—by 16%.'

A gasp of astonishment issued from the hall, as Schwitters continued.

'A 16% increase in redshift on the Hubble scale represents a distance for our radio star of some 2 billion light years. Dr. Simmons and Scott Grenshaw immediately checked the spectrum of 3C 29 again and found its lines shifted to an even greater degree, to 37%, representing a distance of some 4 billion light years. I repeat,' he added seriously, '4 *billion* light years.

'Obviously, these objects, whatever they are, cannot be stars—at least not any kind of star that we are familiar with in our part of the universe. Stars in our galaxy are, at most, some 100,000 light years distant, and those in the nearest galaxy, Andromeda, are no more than 2 million light years away.'

'Because fluctuation in energy output of both 3C 328 and 3C 29 is seen to vary on time scales as short as a few days, we know they must be intrinsically small. Initial calculations indicate something not much bigger than the diameter of the solar system—a comparative *atom* when one considers the billions of stars that make up the typical galaxy. In view of this, these mysterious radio stars—or "radztars," as I prefer to call them because of their high redshift—must be the most powerful astronomical objects ever discovered. A good deal more powerful than a typical galaxy containing hundreds of millions of stars and with an energy output some 40% greater than Cygnus A, the most powerful galaxy known.'

'Well, that is a brief synopsis of what we know about these remarkable objects. It is clearly an important and quite unexpected discovery, and I know you would all be keen to learn of it as soon as possible. I'm afraid there are more questions than answers available at present, but I will be happy to try and answer any you may have. Like the rest of you, at the moment about all anyone can do is speculate as to the reason for the unusually high redshift of these star-like objects.'

Dr. Schwitters pointed to a hand raised toward the back of the hall. 'Yes, Dr. Pawling, you have a hand up!'

'What evidence do we have that 3C 328 is variable in energy output?'

Dr. Schwitters cleared his throat and gave his bowtie a slight but precise horizontal adjustment. As he did so, his vision seemed to evaporate momentarily behind the thick glass of his pebble-lensed spectacles.

'In the two years since the discovery of 3C 29 and 3C 328, optical observations have indicated quite rapid variation in light output on a short time scale. There is also evidence from the historical archives; researchers at Yale University have examined the Harvard College Observatory collection of astronomical plates going back more than seventy years, and they find the star now identified as 3C 328 has varied significantly in brightness during that time. Some bright flashes have varied in as short a time as one month.

'Yes, Oscar?'

Oscar Olitsky rose to his feet and toyed momentarily with his glasses, opening and shutting first one arm, then the other before putting forth his question.

'Dawktourr Schwitters. About ten years ago, Professor Ted Howell at Cambridge in the United Kingdom suggested in his paper *Cosmic Supermass* that objects with mass a million times that of the sun might exist in our galaxy. More recently, he and Professor Bainbridge, also from Cambridge, estimated our newfound radio stars must be one hundred thousand times more powerful than a supernova. My question is theeze: do you think our newfound radztars might be zee supermassive star going BOOM!—exploding in zee big time?'

Oscar's theatrical performance drew a murmur of laughter from the delegates, though Schwitters remained concentrated on the proposal put to him.

'Rather difficult to say at this stage, Oscar. They originally considered powering their massive supernova by nuclear energy, but that didn't seem efficient enough. I believe they are now looking at gravitation as the power source. Very massive collapsed objects do conserve huge amounts of energy—especially rotational, or spin, energy—and so this *might* be a possible reservoir if we can find a way to release quickly. The possibility of converting gravitational and rotational forces into radiation or explosive energy is predicted by Einstein. Additionally, a sufficiently strong gravitational field may cause photons to be redshifted as they approach the Schwarzchild radius of a massively collapsed object.'

Oscar Olitsky waved his glasses at Dr. Schwitters.

'Two of my colliding galaxies could create the required radiation!'

Lee gave his colleague a playful dig in the ribs with his elbow and stuck his thumb out in mock agreement.

'That's an interesting possibility, Oscar, and the sort of idea that needs to be more fully explored. But remember, we are talking about small objects here.'

Dr. Schwitters scanned the delegates. 'Any other…? Yes, Dr. Gardner.'

'Dr. Helen Gardner, Goddard Space physics Lab. Dr. Schwitters, do you think it possible the high redshift might be caused by something other than Doppler displacement due to the expansion of the universe? Could it be a relatively local object, perhaps situated in our galaxy?'

'Well, if it were, Helen, it would make our job a lot easier.'

Again, a ripple of laughter spread around the hall.

'For one thing, it need not be anywhere near as powerful. For another, its star-like appearance would be understandable, and, indeed, expected. However, from all the refinements that have been made to Hubble's redshift/distance formula over the past forty years or so, we know redshift is a reliable indicator of an object's position in space. So we must, I believe, proceed for now on the assumption that our present understanding of physics is correct and, difficult as the problem appears, it will in the end be solved without the need to tamper with established physical laws.'

Lee raised a hand, and waited for Dr. Schwitters' recognition.

'Dr. Drexler?'

'Dr. Schwitters. In the process of compiling my atlas of disrupted galaxies, it has become clear that the Seyferts have unusually bright, compact nuclei and they are observed to vary in brightness over short time scales. Might they appear to us as a radztar if seen from a great distance?'

'Well, we haven't detected any evidence of spiral arms that normally characterize the Seyferts observed relatively nearby, Dr. Drexler. But it is possible a very bright nucleus is outshining the lower intensity material in the arms. One can't rule this out at present. This is something you will probably want to work on.'

'Any other questions or thoughts? Yes, Scott?'

Scott Ferris took a slide box from his briefcase and rose to his feet. 'I recently took a photograph of M42 and was surprised to find that it appeared to be in the process of blowing itself apart. Er, I have a slide here…if you would like to project this…'

'Yes, certainly Scott, bring it up to the slide projector.'

Scott Ferris squeezed out into the aisle and mounted the rostrum. After checking his slide was properly displayed, he picked up a wooden pointer and turned back to the audience.

'This is a shot I captured after a three-hour exposure with the Mt. Palomar 200-inch. As we can see here, some huge explosion seems to be ripping the entire galaxy apart.'

'In view of this obvious explosion, might it be that radztars are remote galaxies that are radiating strongly due to some explosive event in the nucleus—perhaps with the hot, energetic surface facing in our direction?'

Dr. Schwitters and Professor Hayman turned to study the photograph with interest. Hayman then scribbled in his notepad as Schwitters offered his judgment on the image.

'It's possible, Scott; we can't rule it out at this stage. Some huge explosion certainly appears to have ripped the galaxy apart for some reason, and we would expect it to shine unusually brightly—at least for a brief period. But let me remind you once again, whatever these radztars are, the emitting region must be small—we know that because of the wavelength involved—so, if it comes from something the size of a galaxy, it must originate in the nuclear region.'

The director and Marty Schwitters fielded several more questions as the meeting progressed. Eventually, after some forty minutes of excited exchanges, Hayman looked around the hall and decided the meeting had reached its conclusion.

'Any other questions? No? Well, we will then wind up at this point for now. Thank you for your questions, thoughts, and comments. These are early days yet. The surprise redshift has only just been discovered, and the true nature of these star-like objects, whatever they are, will have to await further concerted observation in both the visual and radio spectrum.'

'Oh, Scott, I believe you were going to scan in the ultraviolet, is that right?'

'Yes. Dr. Drexler and I have already made some observations of Seyferts—which are also bright in the ultraviolet—and have had some good results using this method of identification. We are going to scan the radio galaxies to see if anything shows up strongly in the ultraviolet. We're hopeful, as the Seyferts are rather similar to these radio stars in many respects—apart from the very high redshifts.'

Hayman was about to get up when a hand went up in the front row.

'Oh, one last question? Yes, at the front there.'

'Thank you, Professor Hayman. Richard Ovandean, Kit Peak National Observatory. These cosmic radio sources, whether they are distant galaxies or some exotic kind of unknown star, do we know what's causing the intense radio emission?'

'Yes, I can answer that one, Richard. It is synchrotron emission caused by charged particles moving in a strong magnetic field. This is most likely the result of high temperatures and energetic events taking place in the nucleus of the galaxy, if indeed it is a galaxy. This process has been well studied in the high-energy-particle laboratories at both Fermilab and Los Alamos in New Mexico. Well, thank you everybody. I shall prepare a statement for the press, informing them that astronomers at Mt. Palomar in the USA appear to have discovered the most distant objects ever observed.'

The meeting broke up and the delegates quickly formed into small groups and conversed amongst themselves excitedly as they filtered slowly from the hall.

'Whadya make of that, Lee.' Scott Ferris lit a Marlboro as they reentered the cool marbled hallway and headed toward the exit. 'Looks like we've just increased the scale of the universe by a few billion light years!'

'Yeah, as I pointed out, the Seyferts are similar to radztars in many respects—with a small, bright nucleus and variable energy emission. But there's something that doesn't quite add up, Scott. It's their small star-like appearance that bothers me. They just shouldn't shine like stars at that incredible distance. Even with the longest exposure on the 200-inch, the farthest galaxies appear as dim, fuzzy objects.'

Lee pulled open one of the two swing doors, stepped back to let his companion through, then followed Scott out into the blinding light of a sun-drenched courtyard.

'Whatever they are, Scott, we'll need to work closely with our radio telescope colleagues to find out if there are many more of these objects out there. If we get more radio fixes, we'll need to use the 200-inch to try and get more visual detail.'

'Well, I'm up for a late vacation next week. This'll certainly give me something to mull over during the break. Call me if anything new breaks.'

'Will do, Lee.'

3

A Stormy Night at the Monastery

The darkening sky heralded the threat of a storm brewing somewhere in the back of the San Gabriel Mountains, to the east of Pasadena. But that was not the only thing that threatened to scupper Lee and Morton Goodfellow's tennis match against their two local friends, Tyler Moore and Marcus Greenfield. Dr. Lee Drexler's wife, Kay, was becoming concerned that he wouldn't make it back to Mt. Palomar before it broke.

'Hey, guys! Better wind that game up. There's a storm getting up and Lee's got to get back to Palomar before it breaks. I know you guys could play all day, but this is not the U.S. Open.

'OK, honey!' Lee paused midway through a serve and waved to his wife. 'We're at 5-3, third set. Won't take long—we've got 'em on the ropes here—another couple of minutes.'

Kay Drexler, no slouch herself when it came to a game of tennis, was pulling clothes off the line and stuffing them hurriedly into a wicker basket. Dressed in red canvas sneakers, tight-fitting khaki-colored cotton pants, and white tee shirt, her trim, athletic figure was testimony to a regime of regular physical exercise.

'Well, don't drop your serve, Lee, I've got to get Connie to her art class by three o'clock, and there's packing to do.'

A few drops of rain were already falling as Lee and Mort sealed the game and met their opponents at the net with a friendly handshake.

'Well played, guys! Thanks for the game.' Lee checked the sky and furrowed his brow apprehensively. 'Looks like we sealed it just in time. Just my luck! Due back to work, and I won't be able to see a darn thing!'

'What do you guys do up there when the weather's bad—play cards or something?' Marcus Greenfield was more into gigs than galaxies, being the lead saxophonist of a local jazz band. He had never himself been anywhere near a telescope.

They hurriedly gathered their equipment together and turned for the house as a clap of thunder rumbled ominously in the distant mountains.

'Oh, there're plenty of other things to do, Marc. Always some reports to write or papers to catch up on—a lot of research work. I've got to start planning the next batch of galaxies to study. Then I have to plot the coordinates against the Schmidt sky survey, stuff like that.'

'The *what* survey?' Marcus slipped his tennis racket into its sleeve and pulled the zip tight as they entered the house.

'Oh, it's a photographic survey carried out a few years ago by Edwin Hubble. It covers about three quarters of the sky from the Northern Hemisphere. I'm just picking out the brighter, more unusual looking galaxies and getting a better resolution with the 200-inch. You should see some of the weird-looking galaxies I've been capturing.'

Lee strode to the refrigerator and pulled open the door. 'You guys want a beer?'

'Better not, Lee. Kay'll declare us *persona non grata* if we stand around drinking beer when you've gotta get back to work!' He then added quickly, 'You mean they're not all like those lovely Catherine-wheel spirals?'

Lee cracked open a Coke threw back his head, and gulped straight from the can. 'Well, we used to think so. But with the big new 'scopes, we are seeing all kinds of different stuff now.'

'Lee! Don't forget these; it's going to be chilly up there now we're getting into the fall.' Kay tossed her husband a pair of heavy woolen socks, which he playfully immediately threw back to her under-arm.

'OK, honey. Can you find my scarf too—you know, the one I got from your Mom last birthday. I'll need that in the cage, even with the hot suit.'

Tyler grabbed his jacket and made for the door while the others followed, picking up their holdalls and rackets.

'It sure was sure a good move to level that waste ground and build the court, Lee. Thanks for the game; next time you're down from the mountain we're gonna get our revenge for that thrashing. Ciao, Kay!'

As Lee watched his friends run down the driveway and jump into their cars, several large drops of rain hammered the roof of the porch. He closed the door quickly and returned to the kitchen.

'Hey, Dad, you gonna be away long this time?' Lee's twelve-year-old daughter, Connie, had carefully lined up several different sized paint brushes on the kitchen table and was using the end of one to dig dried paint from a small jar.

'Oh, I'll be home soon, just as soon as I've taken a few more pictures for my photo album You be a good girl and look after your little sister now. When I get back I want to see some more of those fine pictures you've been doing too. If you keep up with those art studies, you'll have an exhibition one day in one of those posh art galleries downtown.'

'You mean like Granddad?'

'Sure, honey.' Lee gave his daughter a peck on the cheek. 'Just like Grand-dad.' He went to the drawer, withdrew a paper bag, and put the brushes in it. 'Art runs in the family. Why, I might have been an artist too, if I hadn't fallen in love with the stars.'

'I think Granddad's pictures are really weird, Dad.' Alicia, Connie's younger sister, had come in with some small glass jars of poster paint and was settling them unsteadily on the kitchen table. 'They don't look like the stuff we draw at school—don't even look like photos of things either,' she added as an afterthought.

Lee rushed to catch a jar that was rolling toward the table's edge and stood it upright, as his wife pointed to the hall clock. 'That's because he's…well…trying to express his own point of view, honey.'

'To train as an artist, you've first got to learn to draw things as they are, then you can change things later. Connie, have you got those small pointy brushes your art teacher told you to bring?'

Dr. Drexler grabbed a holdall with one hand and stuffed items of clothing into it with the other. 'Heck, I'll have to go. I should be back before nightfall in this weather.'

With a promise to call as soon as he was safely back, Lee kissed the girls, gave his wife a hug, and headed for the door. After struggling on the porch a moment to open a brightly colored umbrella, he splashed towards his car.

*   *   *

The windshield wipers were rhythmically slapping time to a Dixieland beat emanating from the car radio as Lee Drexler slowed to a stop in front of the observatory's perimeter gate. He had encountered intermittent rain on the drive up, but now it was sleeting quite heavily and he pulled at the collar of his anorak before jumping out to open the gate.

'Hell, I've got to speak to Hayman and get some remote control fixed up on this gate. We've got the most sophisticated piece of scientific equipment here and a stone-age method of getting to it.'

The Dixieland beat and its rhythm section continued their mesmerizing duet as the car rattled over the cattle grid and Lee located his parking space and finally cut the motor. Gathering his bags, he hurried through the driving sleet and dashed up the steps and into the foyer of the observatory offices.

'Holy smoke, you've picked a great time to come back up!'

Lee turned to see Scott Ferris leafing through a magazine in the reception foyer.

'Hey, Lee, welcome back.' Dr. Ferris got up and shook Lee's gloved hand. 'I was just waiting for a break in the sleet. I want to check something over in the library. 'How was the vacation?'

'Great! Can't wait to get back to work. This darn storm has wrecked my chances for now though. Do you have any idea how long this is due to last?'

'The metro guys reckon about three to four days—though if the wind changes direction we could see it clear a bit sooner. Did you get the data on the ultraviolet scans I sent along?'

'Sure, thanks. They were waiting when I got back from Berkeley. What's the latest count on the radio-quiet radztars we've found by this method now?'

Lee knew that the program to identify the radio-quiet radztars using ultraviolet filters was being carried out at several observatories now, and he had learned, while on vacation, that several more had been discovered using this method.

'Around a hundred now. It's certainly evident most seem to be radio dormant. Every week now the filter scans are turning up more. Some of the guys over at Kit Peak are checking the visual magnitudes and passing on candidates for us to do spectrographic analysis. I'll need your help to check one or two more when you've got a bit of free time.'

Dr. Drexler gave his coat a shake and hung it on a peg by the entrance.

'Sure, as soon as this cloud cover passes we can have a go. Get the plates ready. In the meantime, I want to plot the positions of the radio sources against some of the galaxies from my atlas.'

'You got something in mind there?'

'Well, you never know, Scott. I've got so many galaxies now that are all torn up inside—there must be something very energetic going on in the nucleus. It might turn up something. Anyway, I'm not going to be doing any observing until this storm passes, that's for sure.'

'Well, good luck, buddy.'

Scott Ferris went to the door and looked out.

'I gotta brave it, Lee. I said I'd meet up with Pete Harrison. He wants to discuss something to do with galaxy clustering in Hercules. Apparently he's found some peculiar chains of galaxies. I'll be in the library 'til about ten. Come by later if you're at a loose end.'

Scott Ferris greeted a couple of other astronomers who had congregated at the door. Suddenly, with an excited hoot 'n' holler, they launched themselves through the door and into the flaying blackness beyond.

Lee picked up a bundle of papers from his mail locker and, when he found a slight break in the driving sleet, grabbed his umbrella, dashed over to his dormitory, and started to unpack.

He hadn't made it over to the library that evening. By the time he'd unpacked, taken a shower, and had a bite to eat in the canteen, it was well past 9:30, so he decided to make a start on checking the positions of radio sources in the *Third Cambridge Catalog* against his disrupted galaxies.

The *Cambridge Catalog* was the latest to be drawn up of energetic radio sources. Lee peered at it now, shuffling black-and-white photographs and sky charts methodically on his desk. Three had been put aside as possible candidates for closer inspection, and he returned to them now, holding them up to his desk light.

'*Very* interesting. This looks like it matches up better than I thought.'

Muttering to himself, he checked the other two images carefully and then double-checked their radio position again in the *Cambridge Catalog*.

'Phew!' In amazement, he let out an involuntary gasp and dropped the photos onto his desk. 'There's a correlation here *between* the radio sources and some of the most disturbed galaxies in the atlas!'

Lee leaned back in his swivel chair and let his eyes rest momentarily on an electric clock that hung over the door. To his surprise it registered 3:20 A.M. The storm had increased quite considerably too since he began his search, and now he was suddenly conscious of the wind and sleet flaying angrily at his cabin's window. Rubbing his eyes, he got up, crossed to the window and tugged at a cord to close the blind.

Returning to his desk, Lee pondered for a while the startling implication of what he had just discovered.

'These are radztars! These are radztars! The radio sources are radztars and they are aligned across the disturbed galaxies—and the *most* disturbed galaxies at that!

'Jeez! The tiny radztars are not far off. They're being ejected from local disrupted galaxies! Or, at least, they are in some way associated with them.'

Lee gazed at a framed photograph of Edwin Hubble hanging on the wall.

'And you, Edwin, had us believing the universe was expanding, that the redshift was a measure of distance!'

The implications of what he had just discovered crowded his head.

'This means it can't be true! The radztars are associated with—at least—*some* of the nearby galaxies.'

Lee picked up the photos again and gazed at them.

'But…if redshift is not a measure of distance for radztars, then perhaps it's not for galaxies either!'

The last thing Lee was aware of that night was the time. To his surprise, the clock now indicated that it was 5:30 A.M. Kicking off his shoes, he turned off the lamp and slumped onto his bed.

The storm had abated and the sky was beginning to clear by the time Lee stirred. He got up, pulled back the blind, and peeped out onto the glistening snow-covered landscape. It was now mid-morning, and he knew he had to seek the good counsel of his friend and colleague, Scott Ferris. He had to get someone to double-check the previous night's discovery and confirm that it had not been some dreadful mistake.

Lee located Scott Ferris's office and knocked on the door. Failing to get a reply, he peeked inside. Seeing no one there, he turned to leave and bumped straight into Dr. Ferris, returning with a paper cup of steaming coffee.

'Hey, Lee! You're jumpy this morning—careful! What's up?' Scott Ferris brushed at the flecks of spilt coffee covering his right arm.

'Sorry, Scott. I was looking for you. Can I talk to you for a minute?'

'Sure, come on in. Why don't you grab a coffee from the machine?'

Dr. Ferris entered his office, cleared some papers off a low glass coffee table, and pulled up a couple of chairs.

Lee dropped two coins into the coffee machine, waited a moment, then gave it three hard bangs with his fist to help with the dispensation of a paper cup just as Oscar Olitsky happened to round the corner.

'Hey, that's Caltech property, Dawktourr Lee!' Oscar's chiseled face beamed radiant with mock concern at Lee's assault on the vending machine.

'I don't care *whose* property it is, Oscar!' Lee stooped and corrected the alignment of the paper cup, which had jammed in the machine's dispenser. 'I just want it to do what it is supposed to do! By the way, I might have a little surprise for you. Are you around later?'

'Surprise? I love surprises—you know me! What do you have in mind?'

'I think we've found a local radztar!—I'll tell you about it.' Lee pulled the paper cup from the machine and headed back to Dr Ferris's office.

'OK, right, I'll get that to you right away, Jesse. You want the latest photon-flux reading too, right? Right, I'll dig it out…yeah…sure…yeah, OK.'

Scott lowered the phone and gestured towards the glass-topped coffee table and its two bamboo-framed chairs.

'Looks like you need that coffee, Lee. You been up all night or something? I was over at the library 'til late. Did you stay late studying those radio positions?'

'That's exactly what I did, Scott. You're not going to believe this. It's fitting together like a jigsaw puzzle!'

Scott Ferris put his coffee on the glass table and settled himself.

'What exactly is fitting together like a jigsaw puzzle?'

'The radio sources! The radio sources from the *Cambridge Catalog*. Some appear to align with the disrupted galaxies in my atlas. I couldn't believe it. I had a hunch it might be worth a try. If this is correct, Scott, it could shake things up real big.'

Dr. Scott Ferris pulled at his knees to raise himself in the low chair and suddenly looked serious.

'Are you sure?'

'As sure as I can be at the moment.' Lee took the Cambridge radio source maps from a folder and spread them out on the table. 'Look, these three are all associated with my atlas of disturbed galaxies; and what's more, they are *more* strongly correlated with just that section of the atlas which comprises the most obvious examples of explosions.'

Scott Ferris studied the photos and radio positions carefully then leaned back again in his chair and scratched the back of head.

'Lee, the radio sources have been identified as *radztars*, for Christ's sake. Are you saying they are aligned with nearby galaxies?'

'I'm saying that's what the observations are indicating.'

Dr. Ferris leaned forward again. 'You realize what this means—if it is true?'

'You tell me, Scott.'

'If it's true…' Ferris continued, choosing his words with obvious deliberation, 'if the radztars are associated with these nearby galaxies…then…then the
redshift cannot be indicative of enormous distance.'

'And…' Lee urged his friend to continue.

'And if it is not indicative for radztars…perhaps it's not for galaxies either.'

Lee Drexler jumped to his feet, crossed to the window, and looked out.
'Don't I just know it! I couldn't sleep last night. I was up 'til 5:30 pondering
the implications. Scott, this could be revolutionary if it is confirmed. It would
indicate that the Hubble redshift law has been violated and that the cosmological model we have been forging over the past forty years is wrong in some
fundamental way.'

Scott Ferris leaned back on the circular floral-printed cushion and lit a cigarette.

'Lee, I don't like the smell of this. I've personally spent the past ten years
painstakingly refining Hubble's distance scale, and you suddenly come along
and say it's all a waste of time and we are going to have to go back and start all
over! There must be some mistake; everything has been proceeding smoothly
for the past forty years, and now you claim the redshift law has been violated.
This is some claim, buddy. It's gonna take some pile of evidence to prove this.
You'll be up against some pretty hard evidence going the other way, you
know.'

'I know Scott, but what can I do? I can't pretend the association doesn't
exist, for Christ's sake! I have already drafted an initial report of the finding,
since I couldn't sleep last night. I believe there's a Caltech meeting taking
place in March. That will give me time to make further checks before making
a formal announcement.'

Lee took a sip from the paper cup and set it back on the table.

'What we need to do next is look carefully at the relevant photos and see if
there is any visual confirmation of a connection between the galaxies and the
radztars. If they have been ejected from the galaxies, there may be material
evidence to back up the radio association.'

Scott Ferris stood up and stubbed his half-smoked cigarette in the ashtray.

'What *you* need to do, Lee. This is putting Hubble's reputation on the line,
and I'm not sure I want to be a part of it. A lot of folk have invested a lot of
time and effort confirming the great man's redshift law, and they aren't going
to be too pleased to be told their observations over the past forty years have
been wrongly interpreted. "Sorry, guys. You've got it all wrong. You'll have to
go back to the drawing board!"'

Lee paced the room.

'So? You're not suggesting that respect for historical reputations should take precedence over the observations, over a new discovery? That's a slippery slope, Scott, when genuine scientific inquiry winds up taking a backseat to prejudice and dogma. We might as well give up on objective research and become a bunch of apologists for the status quo. And, besides, it would be unethical.'

'Well it's your reputation that could be on the line, Lee.'

'Aw, come on. It wouldn't be the first time in the history of science we've needed to adjust our concepts, our ideas, in the face of an unexpected discovery. If the observations are valid, they'll stand up to rigorous critical analysis. If they don't—well, at least the scientific method will have been vindicated and the conventional position strengthened.'

Scott Ferris got up and looked at his watch. 'If I were you, Lee, I'd sleep on this. Think it over carefully. You need to thoroughly check your evidence before you go public. If you make some wild-assed claim that you can't confirm, it could hurt your professional standing.'

Lee picked up his papers and put them back in his case.

'You're right, I'll sleep on it and double-check before making any official announcement. Are you submitting a paper on the radio-quiet radztars at the March meeting, by the way?'

'Yeah, but now we are going to have to see if any of these are found around your atlas galaxies. I'm not sure I can help you with this, Lee. I'm very committed to the Hubble redshift relation. I've invested so much of my time in it, I'm not gonna chuck it all overnight. You might have to deal with this observation of yours by yourself for now. If you get some more proof, maybe—*maybe*—I'll have a look at it.'

Lee knew his friend was indeed strongly committed to Hubble's expanding universe, but he felt a touch of unease that he should so quickly adopt a defensive posture rather than embrace the new finding and seek to establish its validity. He sensed it might be hard to get Scott Ferris to help him prove his discovery, at least in the short term.

Lee moved to the door, paused before exiting and said: 'Well, let's see how this develops.'

4

March 1967: Presenting the Good News

Dr. Lee Drexler had sat patiently listening to the various presentations on the Caltech Colloquium agenda but had found most of little real interest, save one talk by a Danish astronomer who had presented evidence that some companion galaxies appeared to be distributed preferentially along the axis of rotation of the dominant parent. He made a note to catch up with Professor Oluf Erikson after the meeting wound up and learn a little more about this apparent axial distribution. But now it was his turn to take the rostrum and present the results of his research, that radztars appeared to be aligned with some of the disrupted galaxies he had cataloged. With nervous excitement born of the gravity of the message he was about to deliver, Lee gathered together his papers, sky charts, and photographs as the last speaker left the podium, and he was called by the chairman of the proceedings.

'Dr. Drexler, I think the stage is clear if you are ready. Thank you.'

As Lee made his way towards the stage, someone interrupted the muffled hush that had descended upon the delegates: "A pity Copernicus is not here for this one." Others were heard to titter at this and mutter remarks of a similar derisory nature, but Lee offered little indication or acknowledgement that he himself had heard anything.

After spreading his papers on the podium, he checked the projector by flashing up a photo of a disrupted galaxy for a quick test then turned it off and waited for the audience to settle down.

'Good afternoon, ladies and gentlemen. I want to present today some observations that appear to suggest our belief in the cosmological theory, commonly known as the "big bang," may be misplaced. That perhaps there never was a big bang or, at least, not a single one that resulted in the expansion universe—a belief that has become very widely accepted today.'

'One stormy night last September at Mt. Palomar, I made a careful check of the positions of all the double-lobed radio sources so far discovered against a number disrupted galaxies from an atlas I have been compiling over the past few years. To my surprise, I found that several of the radio sources lined up across some of the most disrupted galaxies from my atlas. As you know, several of these radio sources have been identified visually with the high-redshift star-like objects known as radztars.'

Lee stood and surveyed the hushed delegates crowding the hall for a moment then continued.

'Because of their high redshift, radztars are thought to be the most distant objects ever discovered—situated billions of light years from us. If my observations are correct, and I believe they are, then at least some must associated with relatively local galaxies. Indeed, some appear so close to erupting galaxies, they seem to have originated from them. The implications of this, if it is true, are very far reaching and cast serious doubts over our present cosmological assumptions—particularly the Hubble redshift/distance relation, which, as you know, is the cornerstone of our belief that the universe is expanding. I have a slide here I would like to show you.'

Lee flicked a switch on the projector, and a sky chart illuminated the screen. Below it were aligned radio source positions and a photo of a galaxy that appeared to have been severely disrupted.

A ripple of voices conferring in hushed tones spread rapidly around the hall as the delegates took in the implications of the image on the screen.

'As you can see from this display, when we plot the position of the radio sources against galaxy M82 here, three radztars appear to align closely with the disrupted galaxy. Now, two things appear rather obvious from this observation. Firstly, if the radztars were thrown out of the galaxy by the explosion that has clearly taken place, we might then expect to find them situated close by. Secondly, if we calculate the observed background count of all known radztars, the chances of actually finding the three examples I have observed here amounts to a 1 in 100 chance of it being accidental.'

Lee continued his presentation by flashing two other slides of galaxies associated with radio sources, which had been identified as radztars when their spectrum had been analyzed, and followed by summing up the latest evidence he'd had been able to assemble both photographically and statistically. Finally, he fielded a number of questions from the crowded hall. Lee knew there wasn't exactly a mountain of evidence to support his thesis so far, but he felt if only one of the examples he had shown were confirmed, it should be enough to convince his colleagues that the observation was valid and should be taken seriously.

A delegate from the front row rose, clutching at a bunch of rolled-up papers.

'Dr. Drexler, Mark Lazerby, Smithsonian Institute. You have made some rather remarkable and provocative assertions in the claim that the radztars are not really at the distance indicated by their redshift. As much as one doesn't wish to, er, impugn the observational expertise of one's fellow astronomers—especially those working at the prestigious Mt. Wilson and Palomar facilities—are you sure there is no error in this survey you have presented? I agree that superficially there *appears* to be an association between the high-redshift radztars and the low-redshift galaxies as you present them, but this could be a simple artifact of perspective, a line-of-sight effect, could it not?'

Lee was a little taken aback by the implication his colleague was making—that his observations were the result of a professional error—but he let it pass and attended to the last part of the questioner's point.

'As I said in my presentation, Dr. Lazerby, from the known background density of radztars across the sky, we calculate the chances of a coincidental background projection to be exceedingly small, but more tests are planned which should refine the error window. Also bear in mind we are not finding the radztar associations aligned with normal galaxies. We observe them clustering preferentially around the most disrupted galaxies in my atlas. As the galaxies look like they have ejected matter during their explosions, it seems natural, to me at least, that this is the reason we are finding the radztars so close to these particular galaxies.'

Dr. Drexler looked around the hall and selected one of the several raised hands. 'Yes, in the middle there, you have a hand up.'

'Dr. Drexler, Vince Marsden, Lick Observatory. If the radztars are shot out of the galaxies, as you suggest, we should see as many displaying a blueshift as well as a redshift. In other words, we should expect to find as many coming towards us as there are receding. As no blueshifted radztars have been found, doesn't this rule out your ejection hypothesis?'

A murmur of approval followed Dr. Marsden's comment.

'Not necessarily, Dr. Marsden. If most of them were shot out at high speed and sufficiently long ago from the nearby galaxies, they may have passed beyond our galaxy by now and be receding on the other side. I don't subscribe to this argument myself, but it could, theoretically, be put forward to account for the lack of observed blueshifts. One also has to bear in mind that the redshift may be some kind of intrinsic effect, one that overwhelms any radial velocity the ejected object may have. At this stage, it is not clear. Perhaps their redshift is the result of a massive object's extreme gravitation or the relativistic motion of gases contained within it. There are several theoretical possibilities to consider.'

Vince Marsden raised his hand again. 'Can I press you on that, Dr. Drexler? I wonder why you don't subscribe to this 'no blueshift' argument.'

Lee poured a little water into a glass and took a sip before continuing.

'Well, really, because of the radztars so far observed, their angular separation from the disrupted galaxy is only a few degrees. If they had been shot out of the local galaxies and the redshift was due to high velocity, they would long ago have moved well away from their host galaxies. We should expect to find many turning up in empty space, but that is not the case.'

Lee turned and pointed to a hand held aloft on the left side of the hall. Lee recognized the small bespectacled man in the gray baggy suit as an astrophysicist from the University of Chicago cosmology group.

'Yes, Dr. Stockton, you have a hand up.'

'Dr. Drexler,' the little man said in a strained voice, barely able to conceal his indignation, 'it is difficult to believe that the Hubble redshift law, which has served us so well for so long, should suddenly be violated by your claim. Every galaxy that has been measured over the past forty years has followed his redshift-distance relation. Surely these star-like radio sources must obey Hubble's Law and lie at the distance prescribed by it? No, they are simply extremely energetic, luminous galaxies receding at velocities close to the speed of light...er, I believe the radio emission is synchrotron radiation, is that right?'

'Yes, that's right, Dr. Stockton. But it is also another reason why they cannot realistically be at their presumed location. Because of their small size, they must be radiating *so* intensely that if they are out at the edge of the universe, the radiation they emit would disrupt any fast-moving electromagnetic particles, such as electrons, which would normally give rise to synchrotron radiation. But, as you correctly point out, Dr. Stockton, synchrotron radiation is exactly what we do observe. The intensity of the sources cannot therefore be as great as would be necessary to disrupt it. If they local objects, the problem doesn't arise.'

A huddle of three figures, toward the back of the hall, lowered their heads and conferred in conspiratorial whispers.

'I don't understand this at all. It is a clear violation of all that has been achieved over the past forty years. Goodness! If we let this crazy claim go unchallenged, who knows what other crack-pot idea will be thrown up next.'

Dr. Ravindra Pondrabhann, editor-in-chief of the prestigious *Astrophysical News*, was a committed member of the conventional view and used his stewardship of the journal to campaign vigorously in support of the standard cosmology. He and his two companions, Dr. Dick Dickson, editor of the *Harvard Observatory Report*, and Ronald Pinnger, an astrophysicist from Colorado State University, were troubled by the wild assertions coming from the podium.

Dick Dickson's face cracked a smile. 'Absolutely, Ravi! I think poor old Drexler has been reading Velikovsky's *Worlds in Collision*.'

'And we know what they did with his crazy ejection hypothesis!'

Ravi Pondrabhann had been pleased with the way the scientific community had so vigorously responded to Velikovsky's attack on mainstream ideas and had little sympathy for those who would try again to upset the established order of how things evolve in the cosmos.

'Yes, and his books!' chimed Ron Pinnger in support of his two colleagues. 'Next thing you know, he'll try and get the notion into print so the whole world can read about it. Fortunately, thanks to the strict referral system the journals employ, there are checks and balances to safeguard against excessive…er…speculations of this sort.'

Ravindra Pondrabhann's well-oiled balding dome resembled a polished chestnut in both color and contour, and his face now creased with a little gratuitous laugh as he whispered, 'There certainly are in my journal! Of course, you can't stop them, but they can be…er…delayed.'

Ron Pinnger quickly shot the editor of *Astrophysical News* a knowing glance. 'Not that we'd expect *your* referees to act in any way other than with the utmost objectivity, impartiality, and rigor, Ravi!'

Ravi needed little encouragement. He spread wide the stubby fingers of one hand, twisted impatiently at a heavy jewel-encrusted ring with the other, and delivered a pious impromptu editorial edict for the benefit of his friends.

'It is our duty to communicate the latest discoveries, gentlemen, but...' He stopped to emphasize the point. 'At the same time, we must be most vigilant in preserving the sanctity of the established foundation.'

'*And* the distinguished reputations of our illustrious forbears,' Dick Dickson offered. 'Why is it the young and radical always think they can jump in and upset the most carefully laid plans?'

'We owe it to the taxpayer too, Dick,' Ron Pinnger whispered. 'They shoulder a considerable burden to enable us to continue our astronomical investigations. It is our job to make sure they get their dollar's worth and are not misled by wild and unsubstantiated claims.'

The three friends broke from their good-humored banter to listen to another question from the floor.

'Dr. Drexler, Paul Reddish, Massachusetts Institute of Technology. My question follows up on Dr. Marsden's. In my view, the standard explanation may be preserved if radztars are remnants of some past explosion in our own galaxy that shot material out in all directions at velocities close to the speed of light. Do you not think this is a viable explanation and one that may save the conventional belief?'

'Well, Paul, I'm not here to defend any particular belief. I try to assess the facts from the observations and build upon that. But with regard to your question, my answer would have to be similar to the one I gave to Dr. Marsden: It looks like an attractive idea, but I believe the close proximity of the radztars to the disrupted galaxies is telling us they are associated with these relatively nearby bright galaxies.'

Dr. Drexler turned and prodded at the screen with his thin wooden pointer.

'Further, bear in mind, matter emitted by the radio galaxies tends to be ejected symmetrically, in two lobes, on either side of the central nucleus. As I mentioned before, the angular separation between the lobes is small, so whatever is shot out is short lived. If it wasn't, then we should expect to see radztars turning up in relatively empty space, far from the disrupted galaxy. We do not. Another phenomenon supporting the local claim is the observed rapid variability in radztars' brightness. This puts an upper limit on the size of the region from which their energy can be emitted. In the case of 3C 328, examination of Harvard Observatory photographic plates has shown that over the past seventy years, this radztar has varied significantly. Some bright flashes have lasted less than a month. Recently, Arnold Blackman and his colleagues at Lick Observatory observed a twofold change in brightness in twenty-four hours. This means that the emitting region of 3C 328 cannot be much greater than the diameter of our solar system—tiny compared to the size of a galaxy. The problem from the conventional perspective is to explain how an object so small could emit enough energy to be seen at a distance even more remote than the farthest galaxies.

'Well,' Dr. Drexler looked at his watch and then conferred with the conference chairman, 'I believe we are just about out of time. I must make way for the next speaker. In summary of what I have presented today, let me say that, in my view, the correlation between galaxies and radztars strongly suggests that they are local objects and not as remote as their large redshift implies. One way to test this will be to use the most powerful telescopes to take long-exposure photographs to find evidence of any visible connecting material between the two. This is a program I have already embarked upon at Mt. Palomar with the 200-inch. Some very faint nebulous material has shown up in one or two cases, but we need to wait for the new high-sensitivity emulsion being developed by Eastman-Kodak. Hopefully, this new film will have the sensitivity required to capture any connecting material, if it is there. Thank you.'

There was only one speaker to follow Lee, who gave a short talk on lunar geology, a subject that wasn't of immediate interest in the present context. Lee decided to make his way out of the hall and wait for Erikson to come out. He turned off the projector, collected his papers, and headed out of the hall through a side entrance.

It wasn't long before the meeting broke up and delegates started filing from the hall. He soon spotted Professor Erikson; he went up to the guest speaker and introduced himself.

'Good of you to come and give us your views on the companion galaxies, Professor Erikson. I was impressed with your presentation. You know, there's a lot of resistance to the idea that small companions may originate from the larger, more dominant galaxy. Not sure exactly why it should be so frowned upon as a scientific concept.'

Professor Erikson shook Lee's hand and responded with a light-hearted laugh.

'Probably something to do with the big bang, Dr. Drexler, and how everything is supposed to have formed early on, at the beginning of it all, with nothing much changing since then.'

Erikson lowered his voice, looked around furtively, and drew Lee to a corner, out of earshot of the departing delegates.

'One of the reasons I accepted the institute's offer to come and give a talk was to get a first-hand account from you on the association between radio sources and radztars aligned across disrupted galaxies. I read your paper in *Astrophysics Today* and thought this might provide an opportunity to meet up with you here. By the way, how did you think my report went down today?'

'Well, they can't argue with the evidence, Professor Erikson. It's the *interpretation* of the evidence that they might use to try and refute it. It's the implications that seem to scare the pants off the big bang pundits. To suggest the companions are somehow formed from the pre-existing galaxies is to suggest that galaxy formation is not a one-time event that happened way back in the early universe—it may still be going on today.'

'I know, Lee. That's what I think. It's the only sensible conclusion to draw from the observations. You know, Ambarzumian suggested in the early 1950's that companions to active galaxies most likely formed by either ejection or division, but very few listened. They believed it to be quite impossible.'

Professor Erikson was your archetypal academic. Now in his early 60s, his full head of wavy gray hair was complemented by an equally gray goatee. He wore a checked flannel shirt, baggy green corduroys, and a tweed jacket that had leather patches stitched to the elbows. His footwear was, of course, the obligatory pair of well-worn brogues.

'Yes, I've got a lot of admiration for Victor too. The clear, logical way he reasoned out what was happening just by looking at the small-scale photographs way back in the fifties. He certainly was a pioneer. But when you think about it, it seems natural that galaxies might eject matter from time to time to form new sibling companions—like cells dividing in the plant and animal world here on Earth. It happens on a different scale, of course, but who knows? The analogy, in principle, might hold up. *As below, so above*, to invert a sagely wisdom.'

'Victor actually went further. He believed that entire chains of galaxies were ejected this way. He reasoned that condensed lumps of matter are ejected from super-dense states in the nuclei of active galaxies. A revolutionary idea for the time, but now, with your evidence, it looks like he might have been right all along!'

They moved to a recessed semicircular alcove and sat down. Lee took a number of black-and-white photographs from his briefcase and handed one to Erikson.

'Look, this is one of the images I presented in my talk. You can see clearly, here, that the two radztars are aligned symmetrically across the disrupted Seyfert galaxy 1C 767. These two radztars are the brightest two radio sources in the field and are so conspicuous that it is difficult to believe the alignment is an accident. The natural explanation is that the radztars have been ejected from the central galaxy. That, again, suggests the reason why it is disrupted.'

As Erikson took the photo and studied it, Lee added, 'Your research is of course supportive of this evidence too, Oluf.'

'Well, yes.' Erikson's face turned into a worried frown, 'but I'm not prepared to go quite as far as you are and say publicly that the companions have been ejected from the dominant galaxy. You know, my work mainly deals with the companions' alignment along the rotational axis. This seems to suggest a possible ejection axis, but there might be other explanations, such as gravitational attraction or collisions of some sort. I'm not sure I want to upset the applecart.'

Although their research seemed compatible, Lee wasn't sure how much support Professor Erikson would be willing, or indeed able, to offer. Because he needed to gather as much support for his claim as he could find, he threw both caution and discretion to the wind and decided to find out.

'You know, it would greatly support my argument if you would bring it up as a theoretical possibility, perhaps during your stay here. We need all the help we can get in view of the implacable opposition to any kind of ejection theory. Sure, it's a provocative claim, but if we don't heed the observations and make it, who knows when the opportunity will arise again? It has already been raised once and passed over. With the new observations of galaxy/radztar associations *and* your companion alignments, we would be in a better position to have the idea taken seriously.'

'But Lee,' Erikson lowered his voice and looked nervously up and down the corridor, 'I would be inviting ridicule if I openly supported such an unconventional claim—and besides, it would be seen as most discourteous to my hosts here. I really don't want to offend anyone. Lee, what you are suggesting goes very much further than merely associating galaxies with radztars. You are hacking away at the very foundations of established cosmology. I'm afraid I've never been much of a gambler, especially when the stakes are that high.'

Lee was trying to be as diplomatic as he could. 'Well, let's just say that radztars are ejected from galaxies and later evolve into the companions; we could keep it that simple while you are here—'

The professor cut Lee short. 'Wait a minute, wait a minute. Are you saying the radztars *evolve into the companion galaxies?*'

'I believe so, Oluf. I don't know why it didn't dawn on me sooner; it's been evident in the photos since the 1950s. The radztars are being ejected like seeds, which grow into the companions, grow into new galaxies. One can assume this is a natural process that goes on throughout the entire universe all the time, though we see only the nearer examples. It's like a key fitting into a lock. And do you know what's terrifying to the conventional position?'

'What's *behind* the door the key might open?' he offered meekly.

'Exactly! But why should it be terrifying? It would surely only amount to an admission that we took a wrong turn somewhere along the way. I mean, if you take a wrong turn on the highway and realize you are not headed toward your destination, you make a U-turn and head back toward some previous turning point. It's the same with cosmology: we "thought" we were on the right track, but we have just passed a sign post that indicates clearly that we are not. The problem is that today, the driver's asleep at the wheel—or he is not paying proper attention to the road signs.'

Erikson recovered a little of his composure and issued a light laugh at Lee's depiction of contemporary cosmology.

'That's putting it very diplomatically, Lee. That car might also have been hijacked!'

'Either way, it's important we wake the driver or take control, or we could wake up in no-man's land and not have a clue where to go. It could end in a long wasted journey that someday will have to be reversed, Oluf.'

Lee sensed he was pushing his new acquaintance too far too quickly, but he was convinced, following the skeptical reaction to his announcement in the hall, that he must enlist the help of anyone who seemed to harbor similar conclusions to his own.

'What's so difficult about changing course and admitting we've been heading down the wrong road? I mean, there's no one around to witness the U-turn but us. It is surely better to live with the truth, no matter how bitter a pill it might be to swallow, than to blunder on dogmatically with a mistaken belief.'

'Lee, believe me, I understand what you are saying, and I sympathize with you, but I don't want to do anything while I'm here to antagonize my hosts. I'll see if I can do anything when I get back to Denmark. I'll see what I can come up with then, Lee.'

'Well, every bit of support would help, Oluf.'

Professor Erikson got up, explaining that his wife was waiting in the lobby, and took his leave with a friendly shake of the hand.

Lee crossed to a window and looked out on the sun-lit, palm-tree-lined patio. He considered awhile the prospects of gaining support for his thesis and was about to make his way back to his office when a figure with a heavy northern English accent called out his name and approached with an outstretched hand.

'Great presentation, Lee! You know that kind of thing is going to get you hauled over the coals though.'

Lee turned to see the short, stocky figure of British cosmologist Professor Ted Howell, accompanied by a pretty young woman in a floral dress and a portly, heavy-jowled fellow who was in the process of stuffing a wad of tobacco into the bowl of large wooden pipe.

'The expanding universe is sacrosanct today. Look at what happened to my continuous-creation theory. For some reason, they won't countenance anything whose origin does not support the first page of Genesis: "In the beginning, God created the big bang."'

The pipe smoker torched the wad of tobacco with the flame of a silver lighter, blew a large cloud of blue smoke in the air, and then surveyed the glowing embers. 'And in the end, all astronomers came to believe in it!'

'Well, almost all' Professor Howell added. 'There're still one or two skeptics around. Welcome to the club, Lee. May I introduce you to two of my accomplices: Monica and Jim Bainbridge from Cambridge, UK.'

'You know, we didn't know about your results, Lee, but Jim and I have come to a similar conclusion.'

'Oh, really?'

'Yes. Actually, we've just submitted a joint paper to one of the journals saying basically the same thing: namely, that radztars need not be the most distant objects but might originate from nearby galaxies.'

Lee Drexler shook hands all around and reflected a moment on the presentation he had just given.

'Well I certainly felt some opposition to my presentation. I don't understand it. I would have thought as scientists they would have been excited to follow up some new observation and see where it might lead. The majority seem to be more interested in preserving the status quo than evaluating new and unexpected insights.'

'Lee,' Monica Bainbridge said as she fondled a string of fine pearls around her neck, 'Jim and I have made a rather interesting discovery concerning radztars that we thought might be of interest to you.'

'Oh! What's that, Monica?' Lee looked at her intently.

'Well, we are not in a position yet to make any kind of formal announcement—we need to study the effect more thoroughly—but it seems as though the radztar redshifts are not spread out continuously. It seems they tend to group around certain discrete or preferred values.'

'Are you sure?'

Jim Bainbridge opened a window and flapped his hand wildly for a moment to evacuate the dense smoke then he turned to elaborate upon his wife's announcement.

'Yes, fairly early on in the measurement we noticed too many were occurring very close to the redshift value of $z = 1.95$. They seem to prefer certain other periodicities too. We don't understand what this means, but the effect seems to stand up, at least in all the analyses we have carried out so far. We are enlisting the help of others to verify it. The point is, these periodicities, these groupings, in the spectra of the redshifts just shouldn't be there if the universe is expanding uniformly.'

Professor Howell turned to Lee. 'Look, Jim, Monica and I are having dinner together this evening in Santa Monica. Why don't you join us? We're meeting at The Mayflower. It's a highly recommended New England seafood restaurant right by the old harbor.'

'They also keep some of the best chilled Spanish white wines!' Monica Bainbridge added by way of encouragement.

Lee didn't need a sell on either the wine or the dinner. Relishing the prospect of spending the evening with the author of the continuous-creation theory *and* the chance of learning more about the radztar redshift groupings from the professor's two accomplices, he readily agreed.

'That would be marvelous! This periodicities business sounds important. Look, I'll have to call home first; it's my youngest daughter's birthday tomorrow. Can I call you to confirm?

'Sure, Lee.' Professor Howell scribbled down a telephone number and handed it to Lee. 'We could meet up at the bar around 8:30. The restaurant is on Ocean Drive, just past Marina Quay. You can't miss it.'

Lee returned to his office and called his wife to inform her about the negative reaction to his presentation and that he'd be home a little later than planned. After checking his mail and seeing to some other clerical duties, he drove out to Marina Quay and located first the restaurant and then the bar, where he found his friends taking a pre-dinner cocktail. A table had been reserved for them in a secluded corner of the busy restaurant. After an excellent meal and two bottles of Spain's finest whites, the party relaxed over coffee.

'Excellent restaurant, Monica!' Lee dabbed at his mouth with a table napkin 'I bet this beats your famous English fish and chips!'

'Not those in Yorkshire, Lee.' Professor Howell interjected in his thick northern accent. It's one thing the Americans don't seem to be able to get right. They have chips with everything, but they forget the fish—isn't that right, Monica?'

'Oh stop it, Ted! Jim, dig out those histograms. We didn't invite Lee along to be the butt of Ted's jokes all night!'

Jim Bainbridge withdrew a couple of charts from a battered leather briefcase and handed them across the table to Lee as the waiter set down two large cognacs and poured more coffee all around.

'You see here, Lee. The tendency for different radztars to have the same redshift is clearly evident in this log.'

'Phew! I see what you mean.' Lee ran his finger down the column slowly. 'I was aware that Brandon Stoppard at Griffith Observatory was getting results that suggested differential redshifts of galaxies in the Coma cluster appear to indicate a certain preference for grouping, but I wasn't aware that our radztars also showed this effect. Do you have any indication yet what it might mean?'

'Not yet. It's almost as surprising as your discovery that radztars appear to be aligned across the disrupted nearby galaxies—perhaps it is some kind of intrinsic effect.'

Ted Howell took a sip of cognac and placed the glass back on the table, a thoughtful look on his face. 'Lee, did you say Brandon Stoppard has found evidence of galaxies in clusters following this apparent periodicity?'

'*Is* finding, Ted. I don't believe the result of his survey is complete at the moment, but according to a colleague of his I ran into the other day at the Faculty Club, he seems fairly confident that the effect will hold up.'

'From the conventional point of view, this is quite nonsensical, Lee. If the whole cluster is participating in the expansion of the universe, the effect ought not to exist—it *should* be smeared out.'

'Exactly, Ted!

Monica Bainbridge brushed at one or two crumbs of bread then neatly folded her napkin. 'You are going to publish the results of your radztar associations with nearby galaxies, Lee?'

'Oh yes, sure. As soon as I complete one or two more configurations, I'll send it to the *Astrophysical News*. That's the one really big news stories are broken in. This might be a challenge to the orthodox paradigm, but they'll have to publish it, because the observations are there. The observations support it, Monica.'

'Well, one would hope so.' Jim Bainbridge threw back his head, draining the last drop of fiery cognac. 'But let's not be too hasty on that score. Galileo surely believed that the observations vindicated his claims too, but that got him into a heap of trouble!'

Ted Howell straightened himself, patted at his tie, and uttered proudly, 'Yes, and I got into a spot of bother too, for proposing an alternative to the established cosmology. Having apparently survived that challenge, they are not going to be blown off course by a few discordant redshifts.'

'Well, yes,' Lee conceded, 'but surely we've learned from mistakes made 300 years ago. This is the twentieth century. And besides, Ted, they didn't actually stop you from publishing your alternative theory. What I'll be doing is presenting the observations. I'm not pushing a theory. No one can object to that.'

Lee looked at his watch. 'Well, anyway, we'll see. It's early days yet. Heck, I'd better be heading back or I'll be in trouble. I promised I wouldn't be home too late.'

After settling the bill, they collected their coats from the cloakroom and filed outside.

Lee rolled down his car window and turned the ignition key. 'Let's keep in contact on this; it'll be interesting to see how it develops.'

Jim Bainbridge rested his hand on the open door and lowered his head. 'I've been seconded for the post of director at Kit Peak, Lee. Don't mention it to anybody else, but the committee is going to vote on it next month. Just thought I'd let you know.'

'Great! That's good news, Jim. I have a feeling we are going to need all the observing facilities we can get our hands on if the reaction to today's conference is anything to go by! Keep in touch. Most Friday afternoons I'm in the Athenaeum at the faculty club. If you have anything, give me a call; we could meet up there.'

Ted Howell jangled his car keys impatiently as he watched Lee's car disappear into the night traffic. 'You know, Lee is one of the best of the new breed. He knows how to look at the observations without bracketing them into a preconceived perspective.'

Jim Bainbridge nodded in agreement. 'Lee certainly is one dedicated professional—and he's worked with the greats. Hubble enlisted his support when he stepped down as chief observer at Palomar. Not everyone gets that kind of break when they start out.'

Monica took her husband's arm and laughed. 'And he'd probably be turning in his grave if he thought Lee was about to undermine his concept of an expanding universe.'

5

1970: Storm Clouds Brewing

Dr. Lee Drexler did what he did most Fridays when he wasn't toiling at the 'Monastery.' He had a lunch date at the Caltech faculty club, the Athenaeum, an old pre-war Spanish building consisting of tiled courtyards, columned gardens, fountains, and palm trees. As he entered the building this Friday, he was particularly thankful to be out of the bright midday California sun and walking along cool marble corridors en route to the dining hall.

By now, Lee was used to the teasing wit and the jibes of various acquaintances and colleagues. He was gaining a reputation as a bit of a maverick, an *astroheretic*, amongst the club's members, and his reception was no different today.

'Hi, Lee, did you hear the news? Jodrell Bank has found a radztar just outside the orbit of Jupiter.' That was Barney Newday from the Cosmic Ray Lab passing hurriedly the other way. 'They want you to check the redshift.'

Lee had long since developed a supply of stock answers to counter such banter and whipped one out now as Barney disappeared down the hall.

'Must be some mistake, Barney. They're at the edge of the universe; we all know that. They're probably picking up on Io!'

He pushed at the glazed swing door of the dining hall and stood a moment surveying the diners, some queuing at the long stainless steel and brass serving counter, others carrying trays of food and drinks back to trestle tables.

His preferred method to avoid the minefield of wisecracks and whispered innuendos that usually accompanied his entrance was to spot a table taken by a friend or colleague at least partially sympathetic to his views and make straight for it. Now, as he made his way to a table in the corner occupied by Oscar

Olitsky and three others, whispers of 'Look out, here comes the Lone Ranger' and 'Well, I wonder what surprises Lee's got for us today—maybe he's found a radztar in the Milky Way!' were just audible as he passed between the rows of diners. Though he expected these lighthearted quips—and in some ways thought they could be construed as a back-handed acknowledgement of the importance of his research—they still irritated as he felt they elevated him to a position of notoriety quite unjustified by the nature of the observations he had made.

Lee slapped Oscar on the shoulder, found a free spot at the table, then went to the counter and returned with a tray containing a slice of prawn and mushroom quiche, a salad, and a small bottle of Catalina Valley Chardonnay.

'Hey, guys! It's busy today.'

'Hi, Lee. How's the big bang demolition job going?'

Martin Smallbrook looked up from his plate as Lee sat down and unloaded his tray.

'Terrific! Martin, haven't I convinced you yet with all the statistics I've compiled? You don't still go along with that expanding universe stuff do you?'

Martin Smallbrook picked uninterestedly at the remains of his meal.

'Well, I *was* warming to your claims Lee, then I went and read that your galaxy/radztar associations paper in *Nature* got slammed in *Astrophysical News* by several guys who put your stuff through the statistical mincer. They found only one chance in a hundred that radztars weren't a background projection.'

Lee poured some wine and picked at the quiche. 'Well, just depends on where you want to put the emphasis, Martin. I said there was about one chance in a hundred that it *would* have been a coincidental association using the known distribution of radztars on the sky. They are just doing the sums backward.'

'You mean arguing from the conventional point of view?'

'Sure. Their claim that there was *only* a one in a hundred chance of the claimed association being accidental amounts to little more than saying that in order to make extraordinary claims against the standard theory, you've gotta have extraordinary evidence.'

Oscar shot him a glance as he dangled a piece of bread over a bowl of soup.

'What's wrong with that, Lee?'

'Well, nothing, except that you could add "In order to make basic changes to conventional assumptions, there is no evidence which is extraordinary enough."'

'So you're not convinced, Lee?' Martin Smallbrook threw a crumpled napkin onto his plate and leaned back.

'Well one can argue about numbers all day long. Perhaps it is in the very nature of statistics that they can't show the real picture, but these can.'

Lee fished into a briefcase, withdrew a bunch of photos, and passed one across the table.

'So what's new, Lee?' Martin Smallbrook leaned forward and peered at the photo. 'Looks like a more distant version of M51 to me.'

'Well, it may look like that, Martin, but it is actually NGC 3067. I got this after four hours in the prime focus cage of the 200-inch. Last week, I went back into the cage on my following run to get a spectrum of the small companion. You know what I found? The companion has a redshift twice that of the main galaxy: z =17,000 km per second for the companion, z = 8,700 km per second for the larger galaxy!'

'That's because it's a good deal further away, Lee. Basic Hubble law: the higher the redshift, the greater the distance of the source from the observer.'

'It's no good, Dr. Drexler. You'll not convince us around *this* table.' A studious-looking fellow with tightly drawn lips and a strained expression, wearing alarmingly large square-framed tortoise-shell glasses, had leaned forward. 'We are all convinced that the redshift, as a Doppler effect, is very firmly established, *thank you very much!*'

Melvyn Rutter—Lee privately dubbed him 'Melvyn the Nutter'—was from the University of Nottingham in the UK and following up a post-grad research project at Caltech on the quantum fluctuations of spinning black holes. He was considered by some as Nottingham's answer to Albert Einstein and, though barely into his early thirties, his professors held that his fertile 'number-crunching' brain would soon unlock the very mechanism that triggered the big bang itself. Indeed, Melvyn Rutter had assured the public only recently in *New Scientist* that he had 'tracked back fifteen billion years and was now within the first two and a half minutes of detonation—and closing.' When asked what came before the big bang, Dr. Rutter declined to be drawn, saying this was a trick question—he only dealt with certainties.

'Melvyn, you sound like something out of the Mad Hatter's tea party. Will you ever be convinced of anything other than the proclamations coming from your peers?'

Lee decided to play his trump card. He selected another photograph and handed it to Martin Smallbrook.

'I knew this would be the reaction from most of my colleagues, so I went back another night and got the deepest photo possible. Here, you can actually see a bridge of material connecting the large galaxy to the small one.'

Dr. Andy Seymore, sitting next to Smallbrook, took the photo and studied it for a moment.

'It does look like the two are connected there. I think you've got a point, though because of the difference in redshifts, it would seem unlikely. The large galaxy is a Seyfert, isn't it?'

'Yes, it's a Seyfert.'

'It would be interesting to see if it were possible to find more examples where the companion is connected visibly to the main galaxy, Lee. You're only using your atlas of disrupted galaxies, based on the Palomar Northern Sky Survey done in the 1950s, right?'

'Yes, we really need to go and have a look in the Southern Hemisphere next. Now that the new generation of 'scopes are coming on line in Chile and Australia, we should be able to make a start on that.'

'Lee, I've been given a grant from the Science Research Council in the UK to start just such a project using the new Schmidt telescope at Siding Spring in Australia. I'm going to need an expert observer to help out on this project. Would you be interested when you get time from your research?'

The giant pair of tortoise shells peeped forward again in urgent protest, but Lee ignored the 'Nutter's' complaint that 'this would be a flagrant waste of the tax payers money' and responded with enthusiasm.

'Sure would, Andy. I'm going down to Chile soon to test the new 4-meter at Cerro Tololo. Word has it they're nearly finished installing the mirror. Maybe we could make a start on a Southern catalog.'

Andy Seymore made a move to get up from the table.

'Look, can I call you next week, Lee? I've got to catch Doug Myres over there. Maybe we can discuss it further and plan something definite?'

'Sure, sounds great! Look forward to it, Andy.'

The others took their leave too, offering apologies, saying that it "was time to get back to work confirming the expansion of the universe." The 'Brain of Britain' took his leave also and went off now crunching numbers of a fiscal nature. He would soon know the exact cost to Her Majesty's Treasury for funding such a foolish project.

Lee contemplated his half-finished meal then pushed his plate to one side and took out an *Astronomy* magazine.

'Goddamn skeptics.'

*   *   *

Dr. Ravi Pondrabhann, editor of *Astrophysical News*, scrutinized the research paper in his trembling hands.

'Well, Edward, if it wasn't bad enough being obliged to publish this Drexler's claims a couple of years back, *now* I am supposed to entertain his latest fantasy that companion galaxies are being ejected like…like *popcorn* from ordinary galaxies! Well, here are some *key* words for you, Dr. Drexler!'

Ravi Pondrabhann snatched up a pen and scribbled angrily across the top of the page, "This exceeds my experience!" and threw Dr. Drexler's research paper into the 'out' tray.

Edward Dahlman, a small, frail man rapidly nearing retirement age, who looked as though he had spent his entire life sifting through papers in a darkened attic somewhere, had been Ravi Pondrabhann's editorial assistant-cum-secretary since the start of the *News* in 1965, and he knew how to offer moral support when a particularly crackpot paper tested his chief's patience.

This moment, he sprung to his master's aid while nibbling on a sandwich and almost choked as he offered his own indignation at the thought that a previous 'offender' should try again to slip a paper past their vigilant defenses.

'Like popcorn! You are quite within your rights, Ravi. Like popcorn indeed! What does he think we are editing here, a science-fiction comic?'

The editorial office was a model of conservative decor. Its walls, crowded with dark wood-paneled shelves, heaved with bound copies of journals and scientific dictionaries. The only window was covered by a Venetian blind, and two heavy tables, separated by a worn Persian carpet, stood facing each other at opposite ends of the room. The grander of the two was the one at which the editor-in-chief now sat, in a gold-embossed throne-like chair. Amidst its piles of papers, a typewriter, two telephones, and wire 'in' and 'out' trays, a jumbo-size plastic Coca Cola mug proudly displayed a paper flag heralding the stars and stripes of America An ancient electric bar heater—which, from the discolored surface of its ceramic tiles, looked like it served a secondary role as makeshift a toaster—stood against the far wall. In a corner by the door, a wooden coat stand held a heavy, long red cloak and what appeared to be a scarlet pillbox hat.

'Edward, would you be so kind as to find me Professor Hayman's number at Palomar. I must try to put a stop to this stream of phantasmagoria before it is allowed to go too far. Not just for our journal's sake, but for the sake of oth-

ers who are working so tirelessly and responsibly in the field and would themselves not wish to be impeded or denied the opportunity of having their own
reports evaluated for inclusion in our journal.' He paused. 'We are so far along
the road to understanding our place in the universe, and of how exactly it is
evolving, that we must not let our guard slip now.'

Edward flipped open a plastic telephone index and fingered the pages.

'We owe it also to our founding fathers, Ravi,' he said, hurriedly hunting
down his master's request.

Dr. Pondrabhann crossed to the window and peeped through the Venetian
blind just as a throng of long-haired hippies, en route to a downtown Vietnam
War demonstration, happened to be passing along Mt Palomar Drive. One
particular protester caught sight of the editor, pulled a face, and made a
threatening gesture. Pondrabhann quickly pulled back and let the blind snap
shut again.

'Perhaps it is just symptomatic of these "liberal" times, Edward, where the
young and revolutionary believe they can sweep away everything that we hold
dear, everything that has been built and accomplished through exacting professional commitment and painstaking expertise over the centuries.'

Pondrabhann crunched a string of wooden beads in his clenched fists.
'Well, *our* foundation is not so easily swept away, Edward! It has been put to
the test by the greatest intellects of the day and has measured up to every challenge. No! If you want to test the mettle of our foundation, you must have very
solid proof for your assertions! *Very* solid proof!'

'Yes, yes, Ravi, you are quite right. We must hold firm to our chartered
course. We are nearly in port. And we must not forget that the public also
shares the burden of our labors. They must be rewarded with a convincing and
profitable return on their investment. There is so little respect from the young
today for all that has been accomplished. You are quite right, you are quite
right!'

Edward was delighted and filled with admiration for his editor's tough and
uncompromising stance.

'Our readers hold you in the highest esteem, and it goes without question
they have the utmost confidence in you as custodian and guardian of the highest and most exacting academic and professional standards.'

Pondrabhann looked suddenly tired; he put his arm out and clutched the
back of his gilded throne.

'Thank you, Edward. It is a responsibility that weighs heavily on my shoulders, but in the interests of maintaining those high standards to which we are

so committed we must hold firm to our policy of filtering the unsubstantiated claim from the genuine article.'

Edward passed the telephone number to Pondrabhann then held up a copy of the journal.

'This is not a comic!'

Pondrabhann slumped to his chair, dabbed at his brow with a handkerchief, and dialed the number.

'Professor Hayman? Pondrabhann here…yes…*Astrophysical News*…very well, thank you…and very busy trying to keep abreast of the volume of papers flowing from your marvelous research institute. Your telescopes are proving a veritable gold mine. Under your guidance, we shall soon have answers to astronomy's oldest and most profound questions.' Pondrabhann shifted down a gear and offered cautiously, 'But it is becoming increasingly difficult to find the space to publish everything of importance. Our filtering mechanism has to be implemented most vigorously.'

Huber Hayman's response crackled back through the earpiece. 'Thank you, Ravi. We are endeavoring to do our best. You know, I believe our research into the cause of the big bang and the subsequent evolution of our expanding universe is going better than we had dared hope. The 200-inch is performing magnificently. It is a marvelous instrument and well worth the enormous expense and effort employed to build it. In the skilled and dedicated hands of our young astronomers, it really is proving a most powerful eye on the universe. But you didn't ring to congratulate us on that!'

Ravi Pondrabhann eased forward, resting his elbows on the edge of the table, and adopted a confidential tone.

'Huber, you know how we strive here at the *News* to maintain the very highest standards of professionalism, editorial integrity, and impartiality.'

Mt. Palomar sensed a chill in the wind. 'Of course, Ravi. I sometimes think you have a harder job than any of us. Your editorial leadership is most highly regarded, and the *News* is *the* flagship for the communication of our research reports—'

Pondrabhann snapped.

'But we can only make progress along this exciting road of discovery, Huber, if we all pull together and in the same direction. Now, it is not my business to advise you on the best way to guide your flock, but it is my duty to let you know when I receive submissions from a member of your staff who seems not to look at things from the…er…common perspective.'

Hayman responded with a note of alarm. 'Oh, who do you have in mind? Don't tell me old Olitsky's being provocative again! I did have a quiet word in his ear after the shooting incident, and he assured me he wouldn't cause any more trouble.'

'Drexler! Dr. Drexler!' Pondrabhann crushed the beads in his left hand. 'He appears not to heed your rallying call, Huber. From what I can discern from the increasingly bizarre nature of the submissions received at my office, he appears to be suffering from some form of hallucination.'

He changed tones again, this time to one of resignation. 'We do our best at this end to adjudicate fairly and objectively, and we strive to offer our readers a forum for the publication and debate of the newest and most important discoveries, Huber. But Dr. Drexler appears to be a very loose cannon in your arsenal, a very loose cannon. He appears to be harboring independent ideas that, quite frankly, Huber, I am not sure it is our job to...er...underwrite.

'Indeed, I have before me his latest submission, and I can tell you that I have had to return it without even bothering my referees for a second opinion. It is quite nonsensical, and I have indicated this to Dr. Drexler in no uncertain terms. It was bad enough when he tried to claim the radztars were not at their correct Hubble redshift distance; now he has the temerity to offer us his latest speculations, which claim companion galaxies are attached to the end of spiral arms and that they have been put there as a result of being ejected like "popcorn" from the principal galaxy!

'It makes our work so very much more arduous, you know. I cannot continually delay publishing research reports from members of your staff. That would not look good, and it would reflect badly on the esteem and competence of your acclaimed observatories if I did. We can, of course, subject them to *vigorous* refereeing; this usually discourages all but the most persistent offenders. But in the end, we cannot reject everything, and the offending submission can always be withdrawn and submitted to other less scrupulous, less *professional*, journals.

'No, Huber, an ailing plant must be treated at the root. In my view, you need to have a word with your Dr. Drexler and see if he can be shepherded back into the fold. He appears to be a black sheep and in danger of straying very far from the flock with his independent flights of fancy. I will mail you today his most recent "imaginings" so you may evaluate them yourself and see if my concerns in this matter are warranted.'

Professor Huber Hayman was indeed aware that some of Lee's recent claims had become more persistent, and his papers were turning up in some of the more independent journals. He had several astronomers under his wing, and he couldn't keep track of them all or check on what and with whom they were publishing. He relied on his team to inform *him* when they put forward something they felt was important. He felt it best to err on the side of caution here and try to console Pondrabhann.

'Ravi, I do my best to inspire in all my staff an awareness of the necessity of pooling our efforts if we are to reach our common goal. What you have told me today distresses me greatly, but you are right to bring it to my attention, and I respect your discretion in doing so. I will await your written report. Then, if I judge as you do, I will have a word with Dr. Drexler and urge him to consider the negative consequences his claims will have on our collective enterprise. Telescope observing time is a very valuable commodity here at Palomar, and I will not, I assure you, have it frittered away on independent, non-officially sanctioned programs that do not support our objective. We cannot stop members of our team from proposing certain areas of study, of course, but we do reserve the right to deny funding on a proposal if it is deemed unproductive and not in the best interest of our research aims here.

'Thank you for letting me know of your concern, Ravi. We are so close to putting the finishing touches to the big picture, we must all be thoroughly vigilant that we do not let deluded or misguided notions undermine or weaken our resolve to see this great work completed. To think that a member of my staff was pulling at the very foundations…the very *foundations*. I will get back to you on this. Good day, Ravi.'

6

A Shot across the Bows

Lee tossed some papers onto the back seat and put his travel bag and several carefully wrapped glass photographic plates in the trunk of his Datsun Bluebird. He returned to his office again briefly to call his wife and tell her that he would be home around 7 P.M., then he went out to meet Mike Durran, who was waiting by the car as arranged. Lee had just wrapped up a five-night observing run and was heading back down to the Palomar offices in Pasadena. He planned to drop some things off at his office on the Caltech campus, but before that he had to call in to see the director in his office on Mt Palomar Drive.

'Hi Mike, you ready?'

Mike Durran usually took the observatory shuttle, a minibus that ran between Pasadena and Mt. Palomar twice a day, but he had learned Lee was heading down by car that morning and had eagerly accepted the offer of a lift.

'Thanks.' Mike jostled a rucksack into the back and slid into the passenger seat next to Lee. 'Did you have a successful run?'

'Can't really complain. Had a small patch of cloud Tuesday night, but it passed in twenty minutes or so. Wasn't much of an inconvenience. It was a three-and-half-hour exposure I was working on, so it didn't make any real difference.' Lee released the handbrake and moved off. 'How's the black hole search going?'

'We're doing some more observations on Cygnus X-1. All the evidence seems to point to a black hole—it's the intensity of the gamma-ray flux that makes it difficult to imagine it could be anything else—but still too early to be absolutely sure. A neutron star doesn't quite fit the bill somehow. We've got a paper on the initial findings due to come out in the *Astrophysical News* next month.'

Lee followed the winding lane that led through the observatory's manicured gardens, rattled over the cattle grid that bridged the perimeter gate, and then joined the road that would take them back down to sea level.

'Good for you. I'm having a real tough time getting *anything* in there now since my infamous paper on galaxy/radztar associations a couple of years back. Check this!'

Lee reached back with one hand, pulled a paper from a folder on the back seat, and passed it to his passenger.

'The editor didn't even bother to have it refereed! Can you believe that! Sent it straight back with that scribbled across the top: "This exceeds my experience!" What does that mean? Any new observation, by its very definition, is going to be beyond one's previous experience, for Christ's sake. That's no reason to summarily reject it!'

'Yeah, it must be frustrating.'

'It is, Mike, because *we* are the people doing the observing, and in my view, the journals should be guided in what they publish by the data, not the theory. It seems like the current belief is so goddamn cast in stone, any observations that contradict it are blackballed. Fortunately there are other journals one can try.'

Mike studied a photograph accompanying the paper.

'What's this, Lee?' Mike pointed to the photo.

'Oh, that's one of the photos from my atlas: no.65. I enclosed a copy with the paper. It supports my thesis that small companion galaxies, often seen on the end of spiral arms, are the result of their being ejected from the central galaxy.'

Lee reached for the folder again while keeping one eye on the road ahead and handed it to Mike. 'Check no. 49—it's from my atlas. That's another example of the same process, except that the ejected material hasn't got so far along the ejection tube yet—the arms are not fully formed.'

'Sure looks like something, Lee, like lumps of matter are being thrown out or breaking off there. Do you have any idea why galaxies would be ejecting material like this, assuming it is being ejected?'

'The only answer I can see, Mike, is that new galaxies are being born from old ones. It's as simple as that—and why not?'

Mike Durran looked at Lee for a moment. 'Why not? Because current theory claims that galaxies formed early on in the evolution of the universe and that no new ones have appeared since then—that's why not, Lee. To have new galaxies forming all over the place, even now, would really screw the redshift relation. We wouldn't know where anything was anymore. You would destroy the big picture, Lee.'

Though Lee was becoming used to such predictable skepticism, he was pleased that his colleague at least appeared to understand the point he was making.

'Exactly! And that's why I'm getting a hard time with the journals. Nevertheless, I believe it's what the observations are indicating. Furthermore, it might mean that we would see two galaxies physically connected. That's the trail I'm following now. If we could find visible bridges of material connecting back to the disrupted galaxies, it would be persuasive evidence that they were born recently, through ejection. You know, I have a hunch that the high-redshift radztars and the companion galaxies are somehow related, like they are both manifestations of a single object that evolves from one state into another.'

'Wait a minute, are you suggesting radztars are like some kind of cosmic seed that grows into a new galaxy?'

'That's exactly what I'm thinking, Mike. Most things in nature are born from the inside—they are ejected from the mother figure—so why shouldn't the same process be going on in the cosmos?'

Lee continued excitedly, 'It's been obvious all along from the photographs. The only reason it's not accepted is that it conflicts with the "once only" approach to galaxy formation.' He paused, then reflected, 'It would tend, also, to favor the alternative cosmological theory proposed by Professor Ted Howell and his colleagues at Cambridge, where new matter is constantly being created in a cyclical rain of continuous creation.'

Lee and his passenger spent most of the journey weighing the pros and cons of the claim, and though Mike Durran appeared not to reject Lee's assertions outright, he harbored reservations.

'You need more data, Lee,' he concluded.

They were now finally approaching the suburbs of L.A. At Santa Ana, Lee pulled into a gas station to fill the tank. After getting back in the car and rejoining the flow of freeway traffic, Lee continued their conversation.

'I plan to do some spectrographic studies on these companions and check the redshifts. If my hunch is right, I wouldn't be surprised if the companions turned out to have a redshift different to that of the central galaxy.'

'You mean higher?'

'Yeah.'

Mike Durran laughed. 'Lee, you sure like stirring the hornets nest!'

'Yeah, I'm developing a pretty tough skin. Hey, we're nearly there, where can I drop you?'

'Oh, anywhere near the Robinson Faculty, corner of Santa Monica Blvd. will do fine.'

Lee pulled off the freeway, took a right turn after getting a green at a busy intersection, and then followed the signs to Pasadena.

'I've got a meeting with Hayman at Mt Palomar Drive; that's close by.'

Lee pulled off at the requested stop and let Mike Durran out.

'Thanks for the lift, Lee. See you at the club, maybe, or back up at the Monastery next week. Don't go upsetting Hayman with your radical proposals, now.'

Lee laughed and replied with a friendly crossing of his fore and index fingers for good luck.

The Mt. Palomar Drive offices were only a couple of blocks from the campus. After parking the car, he knocked on Professor Hayman's door in good time.

'Dr. Drexler, please come in. Just a moment. Please sit down.'

Professor Hayman returned to his desk and picked up the phone. Yes, yes, Dr. Evans needs the plates urgently. Well, I've got to go over to Lick sometime next week. I could bring them along then. OK, Dan, I'll do that then…yeah, you too. So long for now.'

Hayman replaced the receiver with a thoughtful frown.

'Sometimes I wish I'd stayed on the observational side. Administration is a necessary task, but it adds greatly to the responsibility of keeping the whole enterprise moving along toward our goals.'

Huber Hayman perched himself on the edge of his desk, took a silver cigarette case from his pocket, withdrew a cigarette, and tapped it against the case.

'Dr. Drexler, do you *know* what our goals are?'

Lee got to his feet, and as he did so he noticed a copy of his rejected paper lying on the director's desk. Instantly he knew the reason he had been summoned to see his boss. A shiver of apprehension shook his frame.

'I believe they involve understanding how the universe all hangs together, Professor Hayman. How it all got started, how it evolves, and how it might end.'

'Exactly!' Hayman raised a hand and adjusted his thin metal-framed glasses. 'We have, in fact, already established how it all got started, and we have a pretty clear understanding of how it is evolving. The only missing piece of the puzzle right now, Dr. Drexler, is how it might evolve in the future—whether it will continue expanding forever or perhaps one day collapse in on itself: the big-crunch scenario.'

He slid off the desk and now began pacing the room.

'I say "we," Dr. Drexler, because you also are a member of our research institute and are here to participate and help facilitate this grand quest toward cosmic enlightenment.'

'Now, it is my responsibility to make sure this voyage of discovery, this grand enterprise, is carried forward with the utmost conviction, the utmost proficiency, commitment, and professionalism.'

Hayman picked up Drexler's paper by the corner and dangled it as though it were something to be dropped into the trash can.

'I have had communication with the editor of *Astrophysical News*, Dr. Drexler. He is of the opinion that you harbor an agenda that is not entirely in accord with the shared aims and objectives I have just spoken of. He seems to believe your are caught up in some form of "hallucination" and that as a result, your submissions are incomprehensible.'

Hayman waved the paper gently between his fingers then offered it to Lee for his positive identification. 'See here, I believe this is one of your latest submissions?'

'Yes, that is my most recent paper, Professor Hayman, but it wasn't accepted. In fact, it wasn't even refereed, which is a little unusual—'

Hayman cut him short.

'It wasn't accepted or, indeed, refereed, I have been assured, Dr. Drexler, because it is quite beyond the editor's comprehension and, may I add, the remit of our present agenda. To remind you again, this is the confirmation of the expanding universe.'

Professor Hayman returned to rest on the edge of the desk and brushed at an errant hair off the arm of his jacket.

'Dr. Drexler, the task we have, by general consent, put ourselves to is the refinement of the present picture, a picture painstakingly and convincingly drawn by many of astronomy's most brilliant and creative minds. Dr. Drexler, you appear to be pulling in the opposite direction! This makes our work so much more difficult. I have read your paper, and I have to say it troubles me to find a member of my staff pursuing independent observations that seem designed to undermine the work our illustrious mentor, Dr. Hubble, set us to and to which we are all so energetically toiling to complete.'

Lee sat down again. He would receive his chance to reply, but it hadn't come yet.

'It is one thing to claim that some of the radztars appear to lie close to galaxies on the sky. It is perfectly valid to claim that some radztars are identified with certain strong radio sources. But it is quite another matter to claim that they are ejected from nearby galaxies and form a physical union with them.'

Hayman leaned forward.

'In short, that they are not at the location assigned by their redshift *and* to try to make this revolutionary claim in the world's most prestigious, widely read, and respected astrophysical journal.' Hayman reassumed a more upright pose and adopted a more regretful tone. 'This is not only a great personal embarrassment, Dr. Drexler, it also undermines the reputation and prestige of the institute as a leader in observational astronomy. That, I imagine, is why the editor, Dr. Pondrabhann, feels unable to accept or comment upon your submission.'

Drexler sensed the director had finished his opening attack and now moved to shore up his defenses.

'But the photographs appear to show evidence of a connection between the disrupted galaxies and their companions, Professor Hayman. If this contradicts the conventional picture, so be it. It would be improper of me, both ethically and professionally, if I attempted to suppress what I consider to be a genuinely important observation, an observation that has only come to light as a consequence of improvements in observational technology. I don't believe it serves anyone's best interests, especially those of our hallowed institute, to suppress results simply because they don't support the conventional picture.'

Professor Hayman waved a hand. 'Well, the conventional picture is the one the Institute, under my guidance, is most interested in confirming, Dr. Drexler. He got up and moved towards the door.

'As you appear unwilling to alter your views and seem determined to pursue your own agenda, you might need to think about finding a more independent-minded research establishment in which to continue your studies. I regretfully have to inform you I will not be recommending renewal of your tenure next year. I cannot support those who are not 100% committed to the principles and research goals we are committed to at this institute. If you wish to question the foundations of our present understanding of the universe, you will have to do it someplace else. When we welcomed you aboard the ship a few years ago, we did not expect you would attempt to intentionally sabotage our voyage.'

Hayman twisted the brass handle and opened the door. 'Thank you, Dr. Drexler. That, for the moment, is all I have to say.'

Lee picked up his coat and made for the door. He stopped as he went out and turned to the director.

'Professor Hayman, I have no wish to undermine the present cosmology. If it is correct, then it will stand up to the most rigorous tests and embrace the newest discoveries. But at the same time, I must defend my observations. I believe they have been made carefully, that they are good observationally, and that the interpretations are based on sound scientific reasoning. I was under the impression that my tenure here was of a permanent nature. If you intend to alter that arrangement, I would be grateful if you gave me notice of this change in writing. Good day, Professor Hayman.'

*   *   *

Kay Drexler looked at her watch. It was nearly nine, and she had just begun to clear the dinner dishes away when car headlights illuminated the drive and she heard a door closing. A minute later, Lee entered the hallway and stripped off his coat.

'Hi, honey, you're late. Everything all right?' She took her husband's coat and gave him a peck on the cheek. 'Hey, you look worn out. You said you'd be back around seven. Did you have a breakdown or something?'

'The car or me?'

'The car.'

'No, but I almost felt I was in the middle of one.'

'Honey, what do you mean? Was it something to do with Hayman? You said you had a meeting with him this afternoon.'

'Yeah, it was Hayman. You know what the meeting was about? He wants to get rid of me for following up my companion galaxies. I couldn't believe it. Pondrabhann, the editor of *Astrophysical News*, complained directly to him over the paper I submitted last month. You remember, the one he sent straight back with "This exceeds my experience!" scrawled across the top.'

'You're kidding.'

'Wish I were, Kay. This is serious. I always thought my tenure was permanent, but Hayman seems to think otherwise. He told me he was not going to renew my appointment next year. Apparently, I'm researching things that undermine the institute's position. He's clearly being influenced by the editor of the journal. Hell, it's not their job to interfere with research projects. It's a flagrant violation of academic rules of tenure and freedom of research. It's a journal's goddamn job to report the research results—to encourage further study and debate, not to act as censor. To go behind a researcher's back and appeal to the director to try and have the research altered is unheard of—it sets a very dangerous precedent.'

Lee slumped onto the settee. 'Sorry, honey. I'm mad, real mad. When I came out of the meeting with Hayman, I was so stunned I just dumped some stuff over at my office then went for a wander to collect my thoughts and try and figure out what to do. I guess I just lost track of the time. I should have called you.'

'Oh, Lee. This is so unfair. Why would the *News* take this attitude? They should be supporting your research, not trying to cut it off. What is it with this desperate effort to preserve the prevailing view at all costs?'

'I don't know, Kay. Seems more like an effort to preserve the reputation of those who have contributed to the establishment of the present cosmology than any genuine interest in establishing new observations. Seems like they are only interested in observations that support the conventional belief. In the past it was the church that complained that their authority was being undermined by science. Now it's science itself that complains observations undermine its authority. Seems like nothing has changed.'

Kay gathered up her husband's coat from the back of the settee and hung it on a peg in the hall. She then returned to the settee and sat Buddha-like opposite Lee, resting a cushion over her knees.

'But this is not about science, Lee; it's politics.'

'Yes, I know. And that brings another element into the equation. I'm not a politician, I'm an astronomer. I can only deal with the research, the observations, and their implications to our understanding of the universe. Now, if the people who run the show say I'm spoiling the fun and they want to expel me, what can I do?'

Lee stretched out his long legs, threw his head back, and studied the ceiling a moment before offering an answer to his own rhetorical question.

'I'm gonna call my lawyer—that's the first thing I'm gonna do. No, that won't help at all. Hayman's the director, and if he says I'm wasting time on unproductive research and that I'm not an asset to the projects the big 'scopes are to be used for, it's his word against mine.

'I can complain to the editorial board of the *News*, of course, but I don't know what good that would do. I suppose I could at least remind them of their responsibility to communicate research results to other astronomers and not act as censors.'

'That'll probably just make matters worse, Lee. It'll just exacerbate the situation.'

'Well, maybe. But there is a principle at stake here, Kay. Even if my claims turn out to be wrong—and this will emerge, eventually, if they are—it is not justifiable to dismiss them, and me, because they question the sanctity of the prevailing wisdom. That sets a dangerous precedent that will lead to censorship and the persecution of dissident opinion in the future.

'I need a drink!' Lee got up and strode to the kitchen.

'Could be difficult to find another observatory or institute willing to allow me the use of their facilities too,' he called over his shoulder after taking a bottle of wine from the refrigerator. 'At least here, in the U.S. Who's going to take on someone thrown out of Palomar? We might have to consider leaving, Kay, moving overseas.'

Lee came back with two glasses and handed one to his wife.

'Well, I guess that's something we might have to think about.' Kay sipped the wine then let her forefinger trace the ridged pattern of the cut crystal thoughtfully. 'You're used to all the traveling, living in different places. But it would be a big break for me and the girls. I have my friends and family here. Then there would be the problem with finishing the girls' education—and there might be a language problem too, if we didn't move to an English-speaking country.'

Kay let out a sigh and placed her glass on the small side table.

'Why do people have to make life so difficult sometimes?'

'Well, you can't do anything more today, Lee. Better sleep on it and see how you feel tomorrow. You feel like a bite to eat? I can heat up something.' Kay got up, took a bunch of letters and a magazine from the writing desk, and passed them to her husband. 'Oh, these came.'

'Thanks, honey. Yeah, I'll have a little something. I could also do with a stiffer drink after today's drama.'

Lee poured himself another drink then returned to the settee and checked his mail while his wife set out some dinner on the kitchen table. He opened two of the letters and discarded them. After reading the third, he called out with a note of satisfaction, 'Well, it's not all bad news, Kay! You, remember Oluf Erikson, who gave a talk at the Caltech meeting some while back?'

'Was he the one who supported some of your proposals. Danish, wasn't he?'

'That's it! He's sent me a copy of an article he published in a Danish journal. Listen to this! "Physical satellites of spiral galaxies favor systems which have predominately young stellar nuclei and contain large amounts of gas. The results—" listen to this "—seemingly point to one interpretation: that the satellites have been formed from gas ejected from the central galaxy."

Lee picked up his glass and raised it in a toast to Erikson. 'Thank you, Oluf. You've made my day!'

'There you go. Every cloud has a silver lining. Oh, somebody called Matt Mellencamp called. Said he was expecting to meet up with you next week. Said give him a call when you got back. You know Matt?'

'Yes, he's from JPL. Says he's interested in helping me out on some image processing with the big computers they've got there. I've arranged to meet up with him next week so I can get a better idea of what his particular skills and interests are. Now, with this cloud hanging over my future at the observatory, he might be better off finding someone else to work with.'

Lee poked at his food with little enthusiasm then pushed the plate to one side.

'Sorry, Kay, my stomach's in no mood for this. I'm gonna turn in, see how things look in the morning.'

He got up from the table and gave Kay a lingering hug.

'Go on up, Lee. I'll put the stuff away and be along soon.'

After Lee had gone upstairs, Kay cleared the table, turned the lights low, crossed to the window, and stared silently at a crescent moon. She reflected awhile on the implications of Lee's confrontation with the scientific establishment. Could the same moon she was looking at now—the very same that shone upon Galileo as he attempted to defend his observations three centuries ago—now be bearing witness to a re-run of the same drama? Kay dismissed the notion. No, it wasn't possible, not in today's secular and enlightened world.

*   *   *

Lee rose late, but all the more refreshed for it. He had some breakfast then remembered to call Matt Mellencamp. The big new IBM supercomputers were being used to clean up the images coming down from robotic space probes, and Matt thought this might be useful in helping to extract the maximum amount of information from ground-based photographic images too.

They arranged a meeting at Matt's office for the following Wednesday and Lee looked forward to meeting up with his potential new assistant.

He hadn't visited Mt. Palomar in the intervening five days. He had worked in his office at Caltech, arranging the atlas, writing reports and proposals, and applying for travel grants to attend two international conferences on galaxy formation, one in France, the other in Mexico. He hadn't felt too enthusiastic about any of this, however. *What's the point if the work is not welcomed?* he thought. By the time Wednesday came around, he was ready to try something different.

After getting directions from the inquiries desk at JPL reception and negotiating a maze of corridors, Lee found Matt's office and knocked on the door.

'Dr. Drexler? Hi! Matt Mellencamp. Pleased to meet you. Come in, come in.'

Lee was met at the door by a slightly-built sandy-haired man in his mid-thirties with an easy, lop-sided, welcoming smile. He noticed that Mellencamp's right eye blinked nervously as he smiled. He was dressed with typical Californian informality: a light-blue open-neck denim shirt, baggy off-white slacks held at the waist with a striped canvas belt, and brown leather 'yachting' shoes. Lee had the impression of someone carefree, confident, and relaxed about his work.

Lee shook the extended hand and followed Matt Mellencamp into a neat modern office, the walls of which were plastered with photographs of the planets and satellites of the solar system. A wide trestle bench ran around two walls, and Lee noticed this held a large light box for viewing photographic plates and slides, a computer console, and various other pieces of modern electronic equipment for processing and printing out digitalized information.

'Pleased to meet you, Matt! I'm both flattered and heartened you want to join forces with the heretical school of astronomy. I hope you know what you are getting yourself into! You know this line of research is not exactly the most popular at the moment. I could certainly do with some research assistance, but getting involved with me will probably be the kiss of death as far as your future prospects are concerned. Not trying to put you off, but it's only fair to be brutally frank about it, Matt! I'm getting a pretty rough time from the establishment, you know.'

Mellencamp brushed some magazines from a chair and gestured for Lee to sit down.

'Is that so? Well, I'm aware your research is controversial, but I also happen to believe that the present picture simply doesn't add up. That's why I'm interested in helping with your radztar research. It's the star-like appearance of radztars that convinces me that they are comparatively local objects—that and the fact that they 're aligned across the disrupted galaxies.'

'What exactly is your particular field of interest now, Matt? By the way, call me Lee. Most of my colleagues do—' Lee settled himself in the chair and added with a note of resignation "—those that I have left, anyhow."

'Well, as I explained briefly on the phone, Lee, my main interest is computer-animated projection and image processing, but I can use the 'scopes too. I did my doctoral thesis on interacting galaxies. For the past two years, I've been working with Harvey Mendelson at JPL. He's the real expert in the field. We clean up the images coming down from the Mariner and Surveyor probes, filtering out the extraneous background, applying color correction, that kind of thing. Might be useful in extracting the maximum information from your observations, especially low-intensity emission background material between galaxies and companions or radztars. We can do some pretty amazing things with the latest high-speed IBMs.'

Matt crossed to a computer, quickly tapped in some numbers, and then waited a moment as a high-speed printer spewed out a roll of print. He scanned this quickly and turned back to Lee.

'Excuse me, data from Landsat. Seems to be running smoothly. So what if your observations run counter to the prevailing view, Lee? It wouldn't be the first time in the history of science that the established picture has needed an adjustment.'

'No, it wouldn't, Matt. But it seems they are so convinced of the present picture, there's nothing for them to do now but join up the dots.'

Matt Mellencamp looked at the controversial astronomer sitting across from him and was struck by the colorful art-nouveau tie that contrasted Drexler's otherwise sober appearance. The tie, he thought, stood out from the dark suit and New England hand-stitched navy blue shirt, and it gave Matt the impression that Dr. Drexler wore it as a deliberate statement of nonconformity or protest.

'You know, Lee, one day when the dust has settled on this radztar controversy, we are going to have to go back to square one and try and figure out where and what went wrong in the historical chain of arguments leading to our present distance measurements. If redshift doesn't give us a reliable measure of cosmic distance, as your research suggests, then the whole cosmological picture suddenly changes.'

'I agree, Matt. But first we have to build on the present observations, continue the research, and mount a water-tight case for the alternative picture, the alternative explanation for the redshift of radztars. There must be one if they are connected to low-redshift galaxies. I'm convinced we can do it. It just needs a bit of a push.'

Dr. Drexler tucked the end of his colorful tie under the last button of his jacket then picked up a leather briefcase.

'One of the images I am particularly interested in following up on at the moment, Matt, is one of Trenchman's galaxies.'

Lee pulled a large photograph from a folder and handed it to Matt. The photograph, printed in the negative, showed what appeared to be the blackened image of a spiral galaxy with a smaller black blob, almost touching, below it.

'This is something we might start to work on. This picture will soon be famous. The extraordinary thing about it is that this small star-like image, just below the large Seyfert galaxy, has a redshift measured at 21,000 km per second, but the galaxy has a redshift of only 1,700 km per second.'

'Phew! That's a lot of kilometers per second, Lee! Is it a radztar?'

'Yes, I captured it recently during a four-hour exposure with the 200-inch, using Eastman-Kodak's new high-sensitivity film. When we developed it, I found this luminous connection between the radztar and the galaxy.' Lee leaned over and pointed with his finger to a faint bridge connecting the two.

'I guess you've ruled out any kind of emulsion defect or a blending together of the image due to light distortion from a background source?'

'Yes, that would be unlikely with this very fine grain film. In any case, it would almost certainly produce an hour-glass effect and we don't see that here. I'm currently checking other interacting examples for bridging material. If we can establish evidence of material connections beteen the two, then the claim that radztars are ejected and that they evolve into companion galaxies would be pretty near impossible to deny.'

Matt saw immediately what Lee was suggesting.

'And consequently, that redshift is not a measure of cosmic distance!'

'Yes, absolutely.'

Matt Mellencamp picked up a brass magnifying glass and studied the image closely.

'Look, I can work on this stuff. If there is connecting material, we should be able to enhance it by filtering, adjusting the brightness parameters.'

'It's a real pity that we have to go to all this extra trouble, Matt. I mean, most ordinary folk would see, just by looking at the picture, that the two are physically connected, but not, apparently, your average astronomer, who is *supposed* to be an expert at grasping the implications of such an image. No, he will argue that it is impossible because we *know*, based on established evidence, that the higher redshift of the compact object indicates that it is much further away. This way it *automatically* becomes a background projection, one that just happens to line up with the galaxy, because the viewer has subconsciously edited the visual information to agree with previously-established assumptions. It's an astronomical *Catch 22*, a no-win situation.'

Matt put the magnifying glass down and looked at Lee.

'I'm reminded of those early Italian paintings, before perspective was discovered, where they represented everything in the two-dimensional plane. It didn't represent reality, of course, but that wasn't the point.'

'Yes. They didn't have a need to represent things in a three-dimensional space, because that wasn't the primary concern. They were simply illustrating metaphysical concepts, the spiritual and religious teachings of the day.'

Matt interjected, 'In fact, Islamic art still uses only this two-dimensional plane and forbids any realistic representation of nature, believing only God has the power to create such images.'

Lee picked up the photograph and held it aloft. 'It's the same way, in reverse, in which most modern astronomers are looking at the pictures we have here. They don't see the connection we are interested in, because it doesn't support the present belief.'

'You know, this aspect of visual perception is of fundamental importance to artists. They are constantly challenging and redrawing the parameters of visual cognition. Revolutions spring up with almost every generation and go on to question the perceptions of the school or movement that went before. The surrealist painter Magritte, and M. C. Escher, the Dutch graphic artist, in particular, were very successful in exploring the way we perceive visual images, how reality is often filtered by the senses to reflect collective cultural and conventional imperatives. We see things not as they really *are*, but as they *appear* through repetition or familiarity. The mental picture we build up often defines the way the brain reads or processes visual information.'

Lee put the photo back into the folder and searched through a number of others.

'In many ways, especially in our profession, the camera is a more reliable recorder of an image than the human observer, who may produce a very different version, or interpretation, of reality. People will swear the world is flat; see flying saucers when very often they are clouds; they see the face of a man on the moon; canals on Mars; animals and things in the patterns of the stars; people see and believe what they want to in images. It's all relative to society's cultural, intellectual, and philosophical imperatives.'

'Interesting that both Magritte and Escher were exploring a visual form of relativity in the decades immediately following Einstein's scientific theory,' Matt added. 'It's sure fascinating how the brain filters and manipulates information received by the senses, and how we consciously, or unconsciously, construct a picture of reality.'

Lee Drexler leaned back in his chair and doodled with a pencil.

'It's a pity that art and science have become so separated. It wasn't always like that. Up until about the eighteenth century, Nature was seen to be imbued with a creative spirit; it was "Mother" Nature. Since the rise of rational thought, Nature has been reduced to the workings of a machine, and everything, except humans, is seen as soulless, with the universe grinding blindly toward oblivion, without any apparent meaning or discernable purpose.'

'Sounds like you are pretty disillusioned with science today, Lee?'

'Well, I don't think much of what passes for science today really *is* science. Science seems more concerned with preserving the reputations of its historical patriarchs.'

Matt went over to a small sideboard, filled an electric kettle, and called over his shoulder.

'People who have become accustomed to a certain way of doing things, and the rewards and privileges that go with all that, are reluctant to change, Lee. You know, they form a collective structure—a mass—that becomes difficult and slow to change. It's like the force of inertia in physics. The more massive, the more rigid, established, or crystallized a structure becomes, the more difficult it becomes to effect change.'

Lee laughed. 'Yes, it does look that way. I guess it would be nice if things stayed the same—if we stayed young forever, or whatever—but change seems to be a basic law of nature, and probably the only one that can be relied upon not to vary.'

Matt Mellencamp laughed at the paradox implied in Lee's analysis, dropped a couple of tea bags into a pot, replaced the lid, and set two mugs and a carton of milk down on the table.

'Well, Matt, I have a feeling it's gonna be tough to get the new observations accepted, because they're deemed to undermine established concepts. But if you believe the actual observations should be the defining criteria in this debate, not theory or historical precedent, then your help will be an asset to the few of us dissidents who are trying to persuade the mainstream to accept the new observations.'

Lee pulled some more photographs from the folder and handed them to Matt. 'Here are some other associations I'm studying for possible material connections.'

'See here, NGC 3842; there are at least two radztars close to the central elliptical galaxy, though there doesn't appear to be any evidence of connective material so far.'

Lee shuffled the photos and passed Matt two more. 'See here? NGC 1073 has the typical double-arm structure seen in many other ejecting spirals where radztars have been found nearby. Now here, in NGC 622, we can actually see a filament of bright, knotted material leading out of the arm and ending on the bright, compact, star-like objects—this would be a good candidate for radztars as well. We need to observe this with ultraviolet filters and check them as bona-fide radztar candidates, then get a spectrum and check the red-shift. This will take time—and then there'll be a lot of statistical backup work. If you can help on both the spectrum-analysis stuff and the computer-imaging side, it will relieve some of the pressure from my own observing schedule.

'Maybe we could make a start with these and then go on to check further likely candidates from my atlas later. You'll need the original plates. Maybe you could come by in a couple of days to pick them up.'

Matt poured tea and slid a cup across to Lee.

Lee continued, 'I'm going to be collaborating with Andy Seymore from the UK on a southern sky version of the northern atlas. Hopefully, we'll find many more radztar pairings across disrupted galaxies from our southern observations, but we certainly have enough here to be going on with.'

Matt Mellencamp leaned back and ran fingers of both hands through his wavy hair. 'Do you have many other collaborators, Lee, that are…uh, willing to put their professional reputation on the line?'

'Well, Jim and Monica Bainbridge at ULCA are committed and Professor Ted Howell at Cambridge is a firm supporter, as he sees it as vindication of his continuous-creation theory. Ted is our biggest asset. Together with his Indian colleague, Jiri Rappannipan, they form a very creative pair of theoreticians. Actually, Howell is over here on sabbatical from Cambridge. I'll organize a meeting one Friday at the faculty club. I'll let you know when we get something fixed up.'

'Look forward to collaborating with you, Lee! This stuff looks interesting—it's going to be fun.'

'Oh, it's fun all right, Matt!' Lee finished his tea and got up, adding ironically, 'if you like witch hunts. Well, Matt, I'd better get moving. Call me in a couple of days and I'll give you some plates to make a start on.'

*   *   *

Dr. Drexler kept his promise and arranged the rendezvous with Professor Howell at the faculty club two weeks later. When he and Matt arrived at the Athenaeum, they found him sitting alone, picking at his meal while leaning over and reading some papers.

'Ted, sorry we're late. Had some last minute business with—'

Professor Howell looked up as they slid a couple of trays onto the table. 'Hello, Lee! No problem. Haven't been here long myself. Pull up a chair.'

Lee had come to learn Ted Howell possessed a boyish, mischievous nature; it was as though he had spent his school days playing constant pranks on the other boys and had never really grown out of it. This effect was enhanced by a round, dimpled face and a pair of wire-framed pebble-lensed glasses that rested on a button nose. Now in his early forties, he gave the impression of someone who disdained authority, pomp, and ceremony.

Lee and Matt Mellencamp unloaded their trays and sat down. Lee removed his jacket and slung it over the back of his chair.

'Another week over.'

'Have you come straight from Palomar?'

'Well, yeah, I did come down this morning. I had to dump some stuff at the office and then stop by JPL to pick up Matt. Ted, this is Matt Mellencamp. Matt, Ted Howell.'

'Pleased to meet you, Matt. Lee tells me you want to join our little band of saboteurs. Welcome aboard! What's your specialty?'

'Computer imaging. We are working with the large IBMs over at JPL, processing the data coming down from Mariner and Surveyor. I also do computer animation.'

'Like Walt Disney?'

'Ha ha!' Lee shot Matt a wink. 'You'll soon get used to Ted's sense of humor, Matt.'

'Seriously, that could certainly prove useful, Matt. When one is working at the limits of instrumental capacity, as Lee is, techniques to enhance low-level photon counts, and filter signal-to-noise differentials can be invaluable.'

'How's the hunt going, Lee? What's the latest?'

'We're checking some radztar candidate fields around galaxies in ultraviolet on the Schmidt. It's proved to be a great way to spot them now that we've found them to be much more numerous than the radio-loud radztars. We're looking for direct visible evidence of material connecting them and compact companions to disrupted galaxies.'

'That sounds like a good idea. Have you found anything positive?'

'Sure have. Matt has enhanced some very exciting images of what appears to be trailing ejecta linking back to the main galaxies.'

Ted Howell looked suddenly interested. He gave Lee his full attention.

'If we could find evidence of this sort, Lee, it would certainly help to strengthen our case that radztars are ejected. How much evidence have you got so far?'

'We're looking at four possible cases from the sample we are studying at the moment. The two most obvious are NGC 9134/502 and NGC 3067. I've just gotten the photos back from the lab of those two, and we think they show pretty incontestable proof of ejection even though, in both cases, the measured redshift of the small companions is much greater than the parent galaxy.'

'How's the statistical analysis you, Jim, and colleagues are carrying out coming along?'

'There seems to be pretty strong evidence of a relation in the graphs we have plotted so far; the radztars associated with the more remote galaxies appear closer to the galaxy of association—'

Matt Mellencamp cut him short, 'As would be expected if the whole partnership were viewed from a greater distance.'

'Exactly, Matt! Basically, it is simply a result of perspective—but it is a very important relationship, because it is what we would expect if we view associations through a range of distances, some close by, others more distant. If the radztars were scattered randomly throughout space, the effect certainly wouldn't be expected to show up.'

Professor Howell studied Matt through his thick lenses as he continued.'This result tends to disprove the conventional assumption that radztars are the precursor of the earliest galaxies, because, if that were true, they should increase in numbers as we look back further in time toward the big bang. They should tend to clump together in clusters, as galaxies are seen to do. This doesn't appear to happen.'

Lee put down his fork.

'Yes, at the very least, we should expect to see the clustering that characterizes the distribution of galaxies on the largest scale.'

'Lee, Jim and Monica Bainbridge and colleagues have just analyzed one of five pairs of radztar/galaxy associations in the 21-cm band, and the radio contours clearly connect the bright nearby spiral galaxy NGC 3067 to the radztar 3C 232. They are going to check the other candidates, but they expect that these associations will show radio connecting contours as well. Who knows what the X-ray contours will show when we get the planned X-ray satellites airborne. I wouldn't mind betting that we'll see evidence of connective material reflected in that wavelength too.'

Lee pushed aside the now empty plate, stuck a teaspoon into a trifle, and twisted at it thoughtfully.

'It wouldn't be so bad if the journals published the results of all this work promptly, Ted. It's one thing to move forward prudently and with clear verifiable results, but it's quite another to drag their feet on the publication of research papers because they don't support the orthodox picture. That's not science, it's censorship.'

'Yes, I'm against this form of editorial censorship. Always have been, Lee.'

'Speaking of editors, I see your old sparring partner at the *Astrophysical News*, Pondrabhann, has just been honored by the Nobel committee for his services to science. Did you get anywhere with your complaints to the editorial board after he refused to publish your paper on companion galaxies?'

'No, not on that particular occasion. Fortunately, it was accepted by the new European quarterly, *Astronomy Review*, which has made things a little easier.' Lee let out an ironic laugh. 'Now, instead of the papers bouncing straight back, they are just delayed for a year or two by interminable refereeing. At least my observatory director, Huber Hayman, hasn't so far carried out his threat not to renew my appointment for next year. Looks like that, at least for the moment, was a shot across the bows. But I feel kind of hunted, watched, like I'm doing something that is not welcomed.'

Professor Howell loosened his tie, removed his spectacles, and gave the lenses a wipe with a pocket handkerchief.

'I guess it's human nature to try and maintain a certain advantage for one's own position, or the position of the dominant majority, the orthodox view. We would all be hopeless idealists to imagine that editors are completely neu-

tral in what they publish, Lee. The problem is, the system operates in anonymity.'

Howell held his glasses up to the light to check that he had cleaned them
thoroughly and continued.

'That's good for the editor, of course, because it saves him being personally
confronted by an angry author who might have had his research paper
rejected, but the system is open to abuse. The establishment can safeguard
itself from unwanted challenges to its authority.'

'So what's the answer, Ted—more and more independent journals?'

'Don't know, Lee. That could be a slippery slope too, because quality can
suffer as one lowers the editorial threshold. In the end, one could end up publishing anything, with no editorial control at all, a sort of academic tabloid
press full of articles by complete cranks!'

Howell looked up and saw Pondrabhann entering the dining hall.

'Talk of the devil! The object of our discussion has just entered. Keep your
head down, Lee. Oh no, the old warrior's coming over to sit at our table. He
can't have seen you.'

Lee glanced over his shoulder and was dismayed to see the editor of the
Astrophysical News heading towards them.

'Keep talking, Ted. We'll have to try and ride it out.'

Pondrabhann pulled out a chair opposite them with a brusque, 'Hello Ted,
I hope you are not plotting anything subversive with the young and revolutionary around here.'

'Oh no, Ravi. You know me. Wouldn't think of such a thing. I'm just passing through, enjoying my retirement from the burden of administration at
Cambridge.'

Pondrabhann put down a bunch of papers and looked askance at Professor
Howell over the top of his glasses. Without further comment, he started to eat
and scan the pages of a journal at the same time.

Lee felt distinctly edgy. He flicked back his hair, loosened the knot of his
tie a little, and endeavored to lighten the conversation.

'Are you pleased with what you achieved at Cambridge, Ted? It must have
been very satisfying molding that institute into a major research center. I guess
you could call it the UK's answer to Princeton's Institute for Advanced Studies. Is that a fair comparison?'

'Well, it's a bit more of a balance between observation and theory. Princeton is more a theory-driven institute. But, yes, I think it was a necessary and
ultimately successful development for UK astrophysics, Lee. We badly needed

a purpose-built center for theoretical research to back up the observational side. Can't say I'm sorry to give up running the place though. I have more time to follow my own research interests now.'

Lee leaned back in his chair and inquired politely of Pondrabhann, sitting silently opposite. 'You too, Dr. Pondrabhann, must be looking forward to the day when you finally hand over the reins?'

Pondrabhann's face stiffened. He rose a few inches from his chair and replied angrily, 'And not a moment too soon when people like you constantly complain about me!'

Lee was unprepared for such a reply but managed to remain calm and replied coolly, 'Well, I would hope, in spite of our professional differences, we could remain cordial in public, Dr. Pondrabhann.'

He looked at Ted Howell. 'Ted, Matt and I have to get over to JPL by three…er, stop by my office on Mt. Palomar Drive before you head off back to La Jolla. I'll give you the latest radio isotope maps of the candidates we are planning to follow up. Oh, if you and Barbara are still into that hike in the San Bernadin's on the weekend, Kay said to fix a time to meet up.'

'Sure. I'll drop by later, Lee.'

Ted Howell watched them leave the dining hall, then turned back to Pondrabhann.

'Drexler's not so bad, you know, Ravi. He's just 100% committed to his research. You must admit, he was right about the radztars lining up with the radio positions back in—'

Pondrabhann cut him short. 'He is a very loose cannon, Professor Howell. An idealistic revolutionary who will not listen to reason. People like Dr. Drexler just want to tear down and start all over. Subversion is the name of their game. He is possessed of some kind of phantasmagoria, *phantasmagoria*, Howell!'

Pondrabhann knocked over a glass of water with his flailing arms. 'I am troubled, Howell. He is tearing at the very *foundation*; he's going to be the cause of much unnecessary contention unless he can be made to see the error of his ways. *Mark my words, mark my words!* He is hell-bent on revolution and the destruction of our beloved institutions.'

At that moment, particle physicist Rudi Steinmann came in and beckoned to Howell from across the hall. He looked back at Pondrabhann, who was dabbing at the spilt water with a paper towel. Should he leave Pondrabhann to his convulsions or call for emergency medical aid? He eased himself out of his seat.

'Ravi, I'm afraid I have to go; have to discuss some technical stuff with Steinmann over there. I'm sure things will work out. Don't let Drexler trouble you so. At least you soon won't have the responsibility of editing his papers.'

Pondrabhann's red face now indicated he was close to meltdown. He began pulling wildly to loosen his tie so as to better breathe and shouted at Howell so loudly several people in the hall looked in their direction to see what the commotion was about.

'We all have the responsibility, Howell. We all have the responsibility!'

Howell shrugged with embarrassment, backed slowly away from the table, and made his way over toward Steinmann.

'What the hell was that all about? Ravi looks like he's real mad about something. What's he doing down here anyway. I thought he'd retired?'

'Hi, Rudi. No, not quite. He just had a close encounter with Lee Drexler. He went apoplectic when Lee inquired how he felt about the prospect of stepping down as editor-in-chief of the *Astrophysical News*. I didn't think things got so personal in astronomy these days!'

7

From Siding Spring to Soggy Edinburgh

One year later, in the fall of '71, saw Dr. Lee Drexler take up Andy Seymore's offer of help in cataloging the planned *Southern Sky Atlas* of peculiar galaxies. The new Anglo/Australian telescope was nearing completion, and Dr. Seymore was soon to start trial observation runs to check out the telescope's performance.

Lee had phoned to say he would be arriving in late September, and now Dr. Seymore scanned the passengers filtering through the arrivals hall at Coonabaraban Airport, twenty-five miles north of Siding Spring Mountain Observatory. He eventually saw the tall figure of Dr. Drexler come through the automatic doors and hurried forward to greet him.

'Lee, welcome to Coonabaraban, Outback Australia!'

'Hey, Andy! How're doing? Good of you to pick me up.'

Dr. Seymore took one of Lee's bags and led the way out to the car park.

'No problem, Lee. At least we don't have to drive all the way out from the Sydney offices now they've extended the airport here to facilitate the new AAT.'

'Yeah, I called into the offices on the way out. Seems crazy to have located the offices so far from the 'scopes. I gather the Australians insisted on it over the wishes of the Brits. Howell was pretty mad that the Aussies vetoed the Brits' wish to have the offices here. Apparently, he and his wife were willing to move out here to become telescope board members if they had sited the offices here. But, it wasn't to be.'

After stowing Lee's bags in the back, they climbed aboard Andy's pick-up and threaded their way out of the airport parking lot.

'Yes. It was a puzzling decision; all it means is that they'll have a lot more traveling to do. Still, now that one can fly out, I guess it's not too bad. This last bit doesn't take long.'

'How was the Sydney meeting, Lee?'

'Oh, the usual jamboree, with everybody doing their best to justify the conventional view. Mostly they tried to show how objects with very different redshifts can't be physically close together in space; sometimes I wonder why I bother. It got so bad I had to show a short exposure photo of one of my galaxies that didn't show connecting material, just to prove I could take a picture as good as theirs and my results weren't due to my being a bad photographer!'

Lee surveyed the clear blue sky and flat, red-earthed landscape.

'Clear out here, Andy. The nighttime seeing must be good.'

'About as good as it gets, Lee. The air's steady and it doesn't get any darker. We'll soon be running some initial tests on the 4-meter AAT. It's supposed to be getting the royal send off in November.'

'Oh yeah? Is the Queen coming?'

'No, Charles, I believe.' He lit a cigarette and eased the window down a little. 'It's amazing that we can build these things in about three years nowadays. The Palomar 'scope took decades to construct. But then, I guess, the technology and designs were new. Now we just basically copy what the pioneers worked out.'

Lee reached searched for a lever under his seat, found and pushed the seat as far back as it would go, and stretched his long legs.

'Yeah, the new 4-meter at Kit Peak in Arizona is the same design as our 'scope in Chile and the AAT here. Together with the wide-field Schmidt, it's like having two lenses for your camera: A wide angle for the broad landscape and a zoom for close-ups. The big difference, except for the 'scope in Chile, is that we don't have to freeze our butts off riding the cage all night. A remote camera can now do the observing for us.'

Andy Seymore laughed. 'You're not complaining, are you, Lee?'

'No, I guess that's progress, but somehow you become insulated from what you are observing sitting in a comfortable office. When you're up there riding it out in the cage, you feel closer to the stars—it's a special, mystical kind of experience. Today's astronomers just don't know the feeling we had in the old days.'

Lee knew advances in telescope design meant that modern astronomical research could be carried out in relative comfort, but he felt that remote observing denied much of the sheer human excitement one got from operating the giant 'scopes manually. Participating in the actual loading of the photographic plates, controlling the exposures—'being' there. Lee was a product of the old school; those pioneering loners who had to overcome physical obstacles as well as conceptual and philosophical ones in order to push back the frontiers of knowledge.

'How's the technical backup, Andy?'

'Excellent! Grant Sampler from Caltech is here to get things off to a fast start. He is strong on the technical side; he's currently in the process of designing a new type of spectrograph that should allow us to identify fainter spectral lines. We're going to test it on the AAT.'

Andy reached into a plastic drinks cooler and chucked Lee a can. 'Here, you want a beer? Jeez, these roads get dusty. Not far now.'

They headed into hillier country, eventually ascended Siding Spring Mountain itself, and reached the observatory at around four in the afternoon. Dr. Seymore led Lee to the office of Grant Sampler, the director.

'Grant, I think you've met Dr. Lee Drexler from Caltech. He's come down to see the setup and compare notes with me on our *Southern Sky Survey*.'

A lean, crew-cut man in his late forties, wearing jeans, a pair of logging boots, and a red checked lumber shirt extended his hand.

'Welcome to Siding Spring, Lee. I think it was the IAU Berkley Symposium on Active Galactic Nuclei when we last met, wasn't it?'

'Hello, Grant. Yes, I believe it was. I was presenting early evidence of associations of radztars and radio sources with the disrupted galaxies from my atlas.'

'Andy tells me you are putting together a *Southern Sky Atlas* to complement the one Hubble compiled. As soon as we get the AAT commissioned in November, we should start making very detailed observations. I think this is going to be a major new facility in the Southern Hemisphere, Lee. A part of the sky that has been largely overlooked until they started to build these new 'scopes.'

Sampler's tanned face broke into an easy grin. 'Looks like the days of Mt. Palomar's monopoly are coming to an end.'

Lee knew that advances in computerized technology were beginning to make very large mirrors less important. There was even talk of designing a segmented mirror composed of many small ones fitted tightly together to make a smooth tiled surface.

'Sure does, and with the light-gathering capacity of the CCDs that are being installed in the cameras of these new 'scopes, they end up with virtually the same light-gathering power as the 200-inch, even though the mirrors are smaller.'

'Yeah, the CCDs are going to be a powerful new aid in optical resolution, Lee. A good emulsion might capture about 5% of the photons; the CCDs pull in around 50–80%. The 4-meter AAT here will be equipped with one.'

'Hey! Why don't you let Andy show you where to stow your bags and then call back. We can go take a look around. It's a bit of a mess—we've still got the construction people here—but the main gear is in place.'

The sun was low by the time they got back to meet up with Grant Sampler. The three of them picked their way through a maze of construction equipment that surrounded the nearly-completed telescope. Large cranes, trucks, metal shipping containers, and cement mixers surrounded the site, though at the moment there did not appear to be any human activity taking place.

'Did you come straight from the U.S., Lee?' Grant Sampler inquired as they made a circle around the large domed building.

'Not quite. I attended the IAU meeting in Sydney last week. I was presenting some new images of NGC 9134/502 and tied that in with a visit here to confer with Andy.'

'Lee, I know you are having a hard time convincing the establishment, but I'm pretty convinced myself that your observations are to be taken seriously. Give me a call if I can help in any way, OK?'

The director stepped through the doorless entrance of the unfinished telescope building and beckoned for them to follow.

'I'm working on the design of a more sensitive spectrograph at the moment which might be useful—'

'Yeah, Andy mentioned that.'

'It should allow us to measure much weaker spectra, and many more redshifts as a result. I'm gonna call it the "Samplertron."'

'Hey, I like that! The Samplertron. Should be very useful, Grant.'

Sampler pushed at a heavy chain hanging from a metal beam and watched it slowly swing forwards and backwards for a moment.

'If it works!'

Lee looked up at the girdered metal structure of the 4-meter telescope. It was a far smaller instrument than he was used to using at Mt. Palomar, but the most obvious difference was that it had neither an observing cage nor the two huge metal 'pontoons' that supported the Palomar 200-inch mirror. The tube of this instrument swiveled between large, flat semi-circular mounts.

'How come the AAT has an American director?'

'Oh, that's just to get the site up and running quickly. We've got a lot of experience with these types of 'scopes. Once they are fully operational, the directors here will rotate between the UK and Australia, Lee. I'll be going back to Caltech when it's commissioned.' These types of telescopes are springing up like mushrooms on mountaintops all over the world now. The European consortium is constructing a 4-meter reflector down in Chile too.'

Lee followed the director and Andy back outside, where, in the now-gathering dusk, a swarm of brightly colored birds were screeching loudly as they jostled for position amongst the peeling branches of a tall gum tree.

'Yes, I'm looking forward to trying that out when it's completed. The director, Victor Oscuro, has asked if I would perform some initial trials when it is completed next year. I think the seeing will be superb because of the altitude and colder climate.'

Andy Seymore couldn't resist muttering a cheap joke, 'Chilly in Chile,' as Sampler continued.

'It involves a lot of extra travel, though, Lee. By the way, what about your old buddy, Scott Ferris—he doesn't seem to do much traveling.'

'My ex-buddy, actually. He doesn't talk to me now—says I'm making a big fuss about nothing. But yeah, it's true, he doesn't like to stray too far from the Monastery. If you fixed him an apartment, he'd live in the thing. Thinks the 200-inch is his very own instrument, handed down to him for safe-keeping by Edwin Hubble!' Lee laughed. 'He's very possessive about it.'

'Mind you, it is still the original and the biggest—the jewel in the crown,' Andy added as they headed back towards the administration offices. 'One day it will be preserved as a UN World Heritage site. People will make a pilgrimage to it like they do Stonehenge or the Pyramids. I doubt the others will be accorded that status.'

Lee agreed. 'Yes, There's something unique about the 200-inch…it's like holding Galileo's original telescope in your hands. You just know something historic was involved with the making of that great instrument. It was a milestone in astronomical observation that will probably never be equaled.'

After they made their way back to the administration building, the director paused at the entrance of his office.

'Well, guys. I have some paperwork to attend to. Lee, Andy will show you our other facilities here. I'll catch up with you tomorrow.'

Dr. Seymore caught Lee's arm. 'First stop, let's go and check the canteen. I've got an observing run tonight and should get something to eat before I get started—you'll probably want to grab an early night too, Lee. We can meet up at my office tomorrow, say, around midday? I'll dig out some of the photos I've taken with the Schmidt wide-field camera.'

'Sure, fine with me, Andy. I've pretty well had it for today.'

*   *   *

Lee awoke to the intoxicating smell of eucalyptus and the excited chatter and screech of a multitude of colorful birds: cockatoos, parakeets, and rosellas. Although it was still early, the tinder-dry air was already primed by the early morning sun and humming with all the activity that heralded the beginning of a brand new day in the Southern Hemisphere.

After a leisurely breakfast in the observatory canteen, he made his way to Andy Seymore's office at the prescribed time and knocked on the door.

'Hey! G'day, mate! Andy playfully affected an Aussie accent. 'Did ya' get a dinkum night's sleep?'

Andy stepped back to allow Lee to enter, holding a large mug of coffee in his right hand.

'Slept like the proverbial log—except for being woken at about 5:30 by some animal banging about on the roof. I don't know what that was, but it was sure running around up there.'

'Oh, that would be the possums. They seem to get in everywhere. We found one asleep in the focusing tube of the ATT awhile back. Don't know if it was trying to do some observing.'

'You're kidding!' Lee caught the joke and smiled. 'Probably wouldn't do any worse than some of the observers I know!'

'You get used to them; they're quite harmless. They just like to come out at night and play around—bit like us, really. Hey, you want a coffee?'

After fixing some coffee for Lee, Andy pulled open a large filing cabinet and selected several black-and-white photographs.

'Here, these are some of the best examples of compact, close-connecting companions we've taken so far, Lee. Most of the others have been forwarded to the UK headquarters in Edinburgh.'

Dr. Drexler examined the photos carefully, one at a time.

'Andy, do you have any slides of these we can blow up on the screen?'

'Yes, sure.' Andy crossed to the window, closed the blind, and switched on the projector. He then loaded a cartridge and flashed the image of a galaxy up on the screen.

'They are pretty good examples of companions on the arms of spirals, I think. I thought you'd like these.'

Lee moved closer to the screen. 'They sure are. How many of these have you got?'

'Oh, around a dozen so far. I just made some copies to show you when you said you would be coming out here. You'll be able to view the rest on your way back to the States—you're booked to head back via the UK Friday night, right?'

'Yes, I want to do some scans on the wide-field plates and mark some of the more interesting candidates for closer visual inspection while I'm in Edinburgh.'

'Give me the coordinates when you've made a list of what you want to observe. When we're fully operational, I'll have a look.'

Lee reached into his briefcase and brought out some photos of his own. He passed them one at a time to Andy.

'These are from the Carnegie 2.2-meter at Las Campañas, in Chile. I've made a preliminary classification here as to whether the spectra have emission lines and whether the absorption lines are characteristic of young or old stellar populations.'

'AM 2054-221 here, in particular, is very similar in appearance to NGC 3067—you remember the companion I photographed last year at Palomar?'

'Phew! Sure is, Lee. The arms are a little more tightly wound, but the one stretching out to the companion here seems obviously real to me—they are very similar objects. You have a redshift for the companion?'

Lee pointed to a figure next to the image. 'Yes, 36,460 km/second excess!'

Dr. Seymore stared at the photograph. 'That's heavy!'

'Yes, startling isn't it? Every one of the small companions I've checked so far has a large-excess redshift compared to the galaxy it appears to be connected to. Unlike the case of the radztar/galaxy pair, NGC 9134/502, no one's questioned the reality of the luminous arm of NGC 3067. What little debate that has taken place centers on whether the connection to the companion is real or only an apparent line-of-sight effect. Of course, most people dismiss it as merely apparent, because if it were real it would violate the Hubble law.'

'Well, they look clearly connected to me, Lee. And look here, at this line of objects curving away to the NW—they look like they're the result of objects that have emerged from the opposite arm!'

'I would say there's little doubt about it, Andy. You know, if we could prove the reality of just one of these examples, it would blow a gaping hole in the conventional picture. The difference in redshifts is so enormous, it would be bound to. If they are at the same distance it must mean the redshift is caused by something other than the expansion of the universe. It must be some kind of intrinsic effect. The trouble is, the standard interpretation has become so institutionalized, the companion *must* be at its Hubble redshift distance. The "law" may not be violated.'

Andy laughed out loud. 'Sounds more like Murphy's Law to me! It's a ridiculous way of going about astronomical research. I don't know why we don't just scrap the Hubble law—or mothball it for a while—and see if the alternative explanation makes more sense.'

'Yeah, I get mad, Andy, because you can clearly see that these objects are physically connected, so why not try and prove it rather than disprove it? It just makes the whole exercise so much more difficult. At the Sydney meeting, they actually showed a number of photos of NGC 9134/502, taken with short exposures that failed to show the bridge of material, just in order to preserve the standard perception.'

'I don't know how you manage to keep up this constant battle, Lee. It must sometimes get you down when your colleagues won't face the obvious, no matter what evidence you present them with.'

'Can't see any alternative, Andy. It's a matter of principle. These people are simply not looking at the photographic evidence. They don't *want* to look at it objectively; they only see what *they* want to see.'

'So you didn't exactly convince them at Sydney?'

Lee laughed. 'Convince them! I think they'd burn me at the stake if that form of punishment was still an option. No, I'm afraid they've convinced themselves that Hubble's Law, like Moses' Ten Commandments, is cast in stone and cannot be altered.

'Mind you,' he added as an afterthought, 'they did graciously offer, for the sake of the honor of science, to allow that I had been misled by some transient effect, thereby attempting some all around face-saving so everybody could go home satisfied.'

Andy clicked the remote control of the slide projector and another image flashed up. 'But you are not leaving it like that?'

'No, I plan to use the new 4-meter 'scopes at Kit Peak and Cerro Tololo to get a better enhancement of the bridges. Maybe my image-processing collaborator, Matt Mellencamp at JPL, will be able to bring out the connections more clearly. It'll take time, but I believe this is the best approach.'

Andy studied the photo of NGC 3067 again. 'What do you think it means if companions on the end of spiral arms are ejected from the nucleus of the parent galaxy?'

'Looks like we are seeing some kind of evolutionary sequence, Andy. First. a small, compact, high-redshifted object is ejected. This then quickly expands, the redshift decays to more normal galactic levels, and you end up with only a slightly excess redshifted companion on the spiral galaxy's arm.'

'Kind of like seeds being scattered from the pod in the plant world,' Andy reflected.

'Exactly! The seeds then grow into companion plants—or galaxies, in this case—to repeat the whole process in an endless cycle. I believe we are witnessing a steady-state universe, constantly regenerating matter from many points within itself. This is similar to Professor Howell's continuous-creation idea, except that we don't, in this picture, see the galaxies moving apart on the large scale. I don't see this as any less interesting or convincing than the standard picture. Perhaps the only difference is that it might be difficult to establish a first cause—what brought it all into existence. But even the big bang shrugs that little problem off by deferring to the biblical notion of divine intervention.'

Lee checked the electric clock over the door and was surprised to see it was now twenty past six. 'But who's to say it had to have a beginning anyway? Notions of beginnings and endings are derived from our own sense of mortality. They are human concepts. Did God have a beginning?'

Andy thought a moment then added, 'Time doesn't pass—we do!'

He laughed at the thought: 'Why couldn't the universe always have existed in a timeless dance between creation and destruction as the Eastern mystics have always maintained? There's certainly something philosophically more satisfying about a system that has evolved the intelligence to reproduce itself; one can see in such a cyclical system the process necessary for the continuous development and reproduction of life.'

'And also don't forget, Andy,' Lee continued seriously, 'if we are right, it only requires *one* explanation to account for the excess redshift of both radztar *and* companion galaxies.'

'You mean if there is a continuous physical evolution between the two…then the same mechanism for non-velocity redshifts could explain both?'

'Yes.'

'Well, we'll certainly be using the ATT when it's commissioned to follow up on these bridges, Lee. You can count on that from our side. Send me the coordinates of anything you would like checked when you get back to the States.'

*   *   *

Lee arrived back at Heathrow with little more than an hour to spare before catching a shuttle flight up to Edinburgh and the headquarters of the Anglo/Australian Telescope. After checking into his hotel and getting a good night's rest that helped to alleviate the worst effects of his jet-lag, he located the offices of the Schmidt imaging team the next morning and quickly started a search for evidence of connective material between galaxies and their companions by systematically scanning the Schmidt plates the Australian side had sent over.

He was busy at the viewing machine when there was a knock at the door followed by the entrance of Jim Palmer, one of the technical staff.

'Hi, Jim. Got some great photos here. The light-gathering power of these CCD chips is sure making a big difference.' Lee gestured to a stack of glass plates. 'I've put these aside for future observation. They all show traces of low-level surface brightness between the disrupted galaxies and their close compact companions. I'm gonna have to get some spectral data on these when I get back to the States.'

Jim Palmer crossed to the viewing machine and handed Lee a photograph.

'Here's one taken by our team down under from a different part of the sky. We're not sure what to make of it. It looks like a very low surface brightness jet coming out of the galaxy NGC 7901 and ending in a curious right-angled "dog-leg." Do you see this faint marking here?'

Lee examined the photograph carefully.

'Hmm…well, yes I see it…but it doesn't look like the kind of ejecta material I've been observing so far. I'm not sure it's part of the actual galaxy. Maybe it's some transient intervening material, an optical effect. We'd probably need to go to deeper resolution to be sure, emphasize the contrast. Who noticed this?'

'Roger Dandby and Duncan Mayhew. They've already asked colleagues at Siding Spring to get a higher-contrast image. Check with Roger to see if anything has come up. He's down at the institute in Cambridge at the moment, but he's due back on Wednesday. It might be worth asking him if he's got anything more positive on it.'

'I'm here until Friday. I'll check with him. Thanks, Jim. The galaxy looks like a Seyfert; you never know.'

*   *   *

It was pouring with rain when Dr. Roger Dandby hailed a cab upon his arrival at Edinburgh Railway Station late Wednesday afternoon, and he now folded his umbrella and shook it vigorously as he dashed from the cab into the entrance of his office.

'Goodness, what weather, Doreen! It was lovely down in Cambridge.'

'It's been raining all day up here, Dr. Danby.' Doreen Southerland, Roger Danby's secretary, took his coat and hung it on the back of the door.

'Your wife phoned to remind you she's going to the local Lion's Club charity do this evening. Said that since the weather's so awful she'd like you to pick her up around 9:30. Also, Dr. Drexler from Palomar rang. He wants to know if you've got any more plates back from Australia on the galaxy you passed on to him to have a look at. He needs to check before returning to the States—he's booked to go back to Friday.'

Dr. Danby pulled a tissue from the box and dabbed at his rain-flecked glasses. 'Oh heavens, I'd completely forgotten about the Lion's meeting. Thanks for the reminder, Doreen. I'll pick her up. Do you have Dr. Drexler's number? It sounds urgent.'

Dr. Dandby laid a briefcase on his desk, released the two catches by pressing with his thumbs, took out some papers, and then dialed the number his secretary had given him and waited.

'Dr. Drexler? Roger Dandby. You called this morning…yes, yes, I've just got back. I gather you would like to see me before you go back to the States…yes, we do now have some higher-res images. They came in a couple of days ago…yes, indeed…yes, come over and have a look at them. I'm over at Blacketts Lab…yes, come in by the Raglin Hall entrance, office number 3. Thirty minutes? Yes, fine. I'll get the photos ready.'

Lee found the building as indicated and, brushing rain off his coat, knocked on Dr. Dandby's door.

'Dr. Drexler, pleased to meet you, come in. Sorry about the weather. We're used to it, but you Californians must find it a bit tiresome? Bet you can't wait to get back home!'

'Well, at least I don't have to try and do any observing in it, Dr. Dandby! I must say I am rather looking forward to getting home though. Been away now for nearly two weeks. First to Australia, where I attended an IAU conference, then up to Siding Spring to confer with colleagues, then here to spend a few days checking out the Schmidt Southern Sky plates. I wanted to check the higher-resolution plates of NGC 7901 to see if the marking on the earlier photos Jim Marshal showed me were confirmed. He said you were expecting some others in soon. I'm very interested in anything that shows evidence of a jet-like activity.'

'That's why I asked Jim to show you NGC 7901, Dr. Drexler. It's a most unusual jet—if that is what is.' Roger Dandby handed Lee two large photographs. 'Here, these are the new photos. Looks like more than one jet lines up across the nucleus on these...'

Lee examined the photos with the small tube-like magnifying lens.

'Phew! Well spotted, Roger. I thought I was the one who was supposed to discover these erupting jet-like features! I told Jim Palmer I thought it might be a transient optical effect, but I think you've proved me wrong!'

'It took our team quite an effort to bring out the low-surface brightness on these. Here, you can just make out an oppositely-directed jet that appears to have punctured the south arm.'

Lee traced the faint line emanating from the nucleus. 'I think you are right. It's likely the optical jets may be related to the decay of high-energy radio-emitting material expelled in opposite directions from the central galaxy's disrupted nucleus. This is just the kind of place where we would expect to find radztars.'

'Can you give me a couple of copies of the best images, Roger? I'd like to take them back to Pasadena and get some colleagues at JPL to do an image processing-job on the latest computers they are working with.'

'I can get some copies made by Friday morning. What time do you leave?'

'I should be at the airport by around 7 P.M. at the latest. I could call by here midday?'

'I'll have copies ready for you by then. I'd like to follow up on this jet. Let me know if we can do anything here.'

'Thank you, Roger. Good work! At a time when so many astronomers are shying away from these kinds of observations because they don't conform with the standard picture, we welcome all the help we can get to push on with the research. There are a lot of candidates to follow up. I've a young post-doc student, Xin Lin, from Beijing University helping us. He has an uncanny knack for picking likely radztars just by studying their spectra.'

Dr. Dandby made for the door.

'I can liaise with our people in Australia. You know, Lee, I'm not convinced that radztars are at their supposed redshift distance either. If we can help in anyway to topple this myth, just let me know. It's an exciting quest!'

Lee hesitated a moment in the doorway then turned and shook Dr. Dandby's hand warmly.

'It could change everything we have come to believe about the structure and evolution of the universe. It has very wide ranging and important implications, Roger.'

'See you Friday.'

8

1973: A Hike with the Howells and a Rumble in the Andes

Dr. Drexler dropped his travel bags in the hallway, thrust a large bunch of daffodils at his wife, threw his arms around her and smothered her with a kiss.

'Hi honey, welcome home! Didn't expect you 'til this evening.'

He stepped back and held her, by the shoulders, at arm's length. 'I managed to get on an earlier flight; there was a cancellation. Didn't think it was worth phoning; thought I'd surprise you!'

Lee threw his overcoat on to the settee, opened a holdall, and whipped out a tee shirt that had a picture of Ayers Rock printed on the front. He thrust it at Kay with the mock flourish of a bullfighter.

'Souvenir number one!'

Kay took the tee shirt and held it up with pleasure.

'Hey! Thanks honey, that's neat. I've always been fascinated by Ayers Rock. Seems like a real special place.'

'Yeah, the aboriginals consider it a spiritual site. Kinda looks like an asteroid to me, or one of the moons of Mars.'

Kay laid the tee shirt carefully over the back of a chair.

'How was the trip, Lee?'

'Long, long, long. But the site in Australia is very impressive; should be a big feather in the cap of the Anglo/Australian astronomical community when they finish the new 'scope. Somebody in Edinburgh showed me what looks like a jet galaxy, which will be interesting to follow up when I get a chance to try out the new 4-meter in Chile. I'm going to collaborate with one of the discoverers to see if there are any radztars close by. It looks like the kind of Seyfert where we might expect to find them. Hey, are the girls coming home this weekend?'

'They've gone to a concert in Monterey with some friends. Neil Diamond I think. They said they'd make it home Sunday afternoon.'

'That'd be nice. Any mail or calls, honey?'

Kay picked up a bunch of mail from the desk and started to shuffle through it.

'These came in. Oh yes, and Ted Howell called. He's over for his half-yearly visit to Caltech and wants to meet up with you. He wanted to know if you fancied another hike in the San Bernardin foothills on Sunday. Barbara's with him and she is keen to come along as well. I said you'd phone as soon as you got back.'

Lee looked pleased as he kicked off his shoes, loosened the knot on his tie, and sank back on the settee. After so many hours cooped up in airplanes, he was enthused by the prospect of getting some exercise and fresh mountain air.

'Hey, I'm into that. I want to talk with Ted. He's been working on some new gravitational theory with Rappannipan. What about the girls, though?'

'Oh, they'll be fine—they'll stick around if they get home before us.'

'I'll ring Ted and confirm it then.'

'Hey, I'd better freshen up and slip into something more comfortable.'

*   *   *

Sunday morning saw Lee and his wife turn into the parking lot at the starting area of the mountain trail they were to follow with the Howells, a little early. Lee cut the motor, got out, and looked around.

'No sign of them yet. It's going to be warm, Kay, at least until we get higher up. That won't bother Ted, though; he's a real mountain goat.'

'Well, if you two want to go charging ahead, you can forget about me and Barbara. We'll make it up at our own pace and meet you at the halfway rest area. You two will have plenty to talk about anyway.'

A loud beep of a car horn interrupted Kay's preemptive strike at any thoughts of a rapid climb up the trail and, as they turned in its direction, a green MG convertible—circa 1930—crackled and popped into the parking area.

'Here they come. Jeez, what the heck has Ted gotten hold of?'

He went over and rested his hand on the side of the open car.

'Where'd you get this buggy, Ted? I didn't know you were allowed to drive museum pieces on the highway!'

Lee looked over the car and at the attire of its two occupants. Professor Howell and his wife were dressed identically, in stout green corduroy gaiters, buttoned just below the knee, woolen socks, heavy mountaineering boots, crew-necked sweaters, and hooded nylon anoraks. The back seat of the car was loaded with serious climbing equipment that included coiled rope and maps, a powerful flashlight, a large brass compass, and two large rucksacks. A large plastic bag appeared to contain bottles of water, bread rolls, and an assortment of fresh fruit.

Howell turned a key on the dashboard that immediately cut the cacophony of crackling and popping emanating from the car's exhaust, pulled at a cable to open the door, and stepped out laughing. 'If you think this is ancient, you should see what I drive in the UK. I borrowed this from a friend, actually.'

Lee went around to the other side of the car and opened the door for Barbara Howell.

'Ted,' he winked at Barbara good naturedly, 'we're not climbing the Himalayas. Are you sure you are going to need all this gear? We've only packed a couple of bottles of water and some sandwiches.'

Professor Howell pretended not to hear Lee's quip and pulled the coiled rope and rucksacks from the car.

'In my experience, Lee, you must have the right tools for the job—and besides, better safe than sorry! I've had some close scrapes on the Scottish highlands. The fog on the Cairngorms can descend suddenly without warning. Without my trusty survival kit it could have been nasty on more than one occasion, believe me.'

Lee felt the weight of a rucksack. 'Well, sure, but this is sunny California, Ted.'

Barbara Howell got out and shrugged helplessly at Kay then gathered up the bags from the back seat.

'I told Ted we didn't need all this paraphernalia, but you know what he's like.'

Kay moved to give her a hand. 'Well, I've warned Lee that if they want to go rushing ahead, they can forget about us. We'll make our own pace and see them at the top later!'

After persuading Ted Howell he likely wouldn't need the mountaineering equipment on this particular climb (particularly the rope and flashlight), Lee pulled two small nylon backpacks from his car and pointed to a wooden signpost that indicated the start of the trail. With a "Well, if we're all ready?" they picked up their gear and moved forward.

The menfolk did indeed soon leave the women behind and after climbing for nearly an hour came within sight of a grassy plateau where someone had thoughtfully constructed a roughly-hewn wooden table and two long bench seats for hikers to rest at.

'I can see the ledge where we rest up—just a bit further up the track, Lee.' Professor Howell was panting under the weight of his equipment. 'Hey, this is a bit tougher than the walks I do back in the UK. It's the damned heat, Lee!'

He scrambled up on to the flat ledge and took in the view. 'Great view. Can you see the girls?'

Lee scrambled up beside him and set his backpack down on the table. 'I think they've stopped for a breather. We'd better wait here until they catch up. I don't think they are far behind.'

Professor Howell surveyed the valley stretching below them.

'You know, once, on a visit to Mt. Palomar, I walked back down the old Mt. Palomar trail. Took five hours, but what a great walk.'

'Phew! You were moving, Ted. It would take me a week and a half to walk down that trail!' He paused a moment, taking in the scene.

'You never thought about observing, Ted?'

Ted Howell laughed. 'Oh goodness, no! The practical side of it doesn't interest me. I prefer to leave that to the professionals like you, Lee. Don't get me wrong,' he added quickly, 'I'm in awe of the patience and dedication you guys have, but I think it's safer to leave the observations to people with better eyesight.'

Professor Howell removed his spectacles and tapped at the thick glass.

'Look at these lenses; they're almost as thick as the 200-inch mirror! No, I prefer the theoretical side. I'm more interested in how things fit together, in the grand design. That's why I'm interested in your observations. It looks as if the radztars might be the site of new matter creation. It supports the on-going birth of matter, which is the cornerstone of our continuous-creation theory.'

Lee picked up a small stone and sent it rolling down the slope.

'Radztars are certainly ejected from the exploding galaxies, no question. But why the high redshift? That's the big mystery. Ted, I'm moving toward the idea that radztars and compact companion galaxies are the same objects, just viewed at different epochs.'

Ted Howell looked momentarily bewildered. 'You mean the radztars start out small, with high redshift, evolve into the compact companions, and then become fully-fledged galaxies?'

'Yes.'

'Then…you're suggesting that the redshift changes…decays to more normal levels as the object evolves…as it grows.'

Lee squatted and brushed at the leaves of a plant growing from the ledge. 'Yes. Like this plant here. It grows from a seed, reaches maturity, then produces seeds itself to continue the life cycle.' He rose and looked up. 'It must be the same up there. I'm convinced we are observing the same principle at work in the cosmos, only in this case, it's the very subatomic particles that grow, becoming more and more massive with the passing of time.'

Professor Howell sat down at the log table. 'That's an interesting angle, Lee. And one that more closely mirrors what goes on here than we perhaps realize. You certainly have to have a system that constantly recycles, regenerates itself, for life to flourish, or you get no life. The present theory predicts just the opposite and has the universe winding down and eventually running out of steam.

Lee levered himself onto the bench seat opposite the professor. 'I wanted to talk to you about this new gravitational theory of yours, the one you're developing with Rappannipan.'

'Well, we are not there yet, Lee. But it might offer a theoretical explanation for the initial high redshift difference between radztars and galaxies. We are basing this work on Dirac's idea that the mass of elementary particles, such as the electron, may not always be the same—as has been assumed since Newton formulated his theory of universal gravitation in the seventeenth century.'

Lee cut in quickly: "And which has led directly to the belief that redshift is a result of the expansion of the universe.'

'Exactly. But if we relax this constraint on particle masses having always to be the same, we can imagine the possibility that, in certain situations, the mass of particles might be less than it is today or, at least, when compared to the adjacent galaxy. If the mass varies, then so does the frequency, or energy, of the oscillating particle that we receive as electromagnetic radiation.

Again, Lee cut in.

'In other words, they will be shifted towards the red, less energetic, end of the spectrum compared to the lab reference and, presumably, the older parent galaxy from which they evolved.'

'Yes. So you see, Lee, though I'm not an observer, I can use theory to support or explain an unexpected discovery. In some ways the continuous-creation theory predicted the existence of radztars way back in the early '50s, when we first proposed it. Back then, though, we didn't foresee exactly what form the newly created matter would take, but it was a necessary aspect of continuous creation—something had to appear in the gaps left by the receding galaxies. It looks like you may have found it in the form of radztars.'

'Heck, those girls are taking their time.'

Lee rose and looked back down the trail. 'I thought I heard voices. Yep, here they come, just crossing the wooden bridge down there.' He waved as Kay looked up and pointed to the ledge he was standing on.'

'Yes, Lee,' Professor Howell continued. 'We originally thought the new matter would appear as a slow drizzle of particles—imperceptible to observation—but your observations may change that. It now looks as though new matter may spring into existence as a coherent lump in the form of a seed galaxy. This is exciting, since this form can be experimentally observed.'

Barbara and Kay scrambled unsteadily into view.

'Ah, here you are. Lee and I were just about to send out a search party!'

Kay slipped a strap over her shoulder and dropped her bag on to the table. 'Oh, so you stopped to wait for the Sherpas to bring up the refreshments!' She turned to Barbara Howell and added, 'I expect these two are dying of thirst, Barbara. Have you got the drinks?'

'I thought you picked up that bag, Kay.'

'Sorry guys, looks like one of you will have to run back.'

'Hah! We're not falling for that!'

Ted Howell fished through his wife's rucksack and tossed Lee a plastic bottle of water.

'Lee, we'd better take charge of the refreshments or we'll never make the "Buena Vista" mirador. Still only about halfway there, girls!'

Kay sat down on the bench, dabbing at her forehead with a handkerchief. 'Hey, this is some climb, Lee. Are you sure we're on the right track?'

'We are, aren't we, Ted?' He winked at Ted Howell.

'Sorry, honey, referring to cosmology there. Ted and I have just formed an alliance. I do the observations and he explains them. Pretty neat partnership—piece of cake.'

'Well, I don't know about cake, Lee, but there should be a sandwich in the bag there somewhere.' Kay pointed at her rucksack.

Professor Howell dug into his bag and broke open out a round of sandwiches and spread them on the bench. They sat and ate, admiring the view. It was completely quiet in the warm sunshine, save for a background hum of bees and the occasional chirp of small birds flitting excitedly amongst the shrubbery.

After finishing their refreshments, they repacked the bags and prepared for the final leg of the ascent, which would take them to the mirador: a point affording a 180-degree vista of the distant coastline, stretching from L.A. to San Diego, and the valley below them.

On reaching the mirador some thirty minutes later, Lee leaned heavily against a wooden guardrail that cordoned off the viewing area and threw off his backpack. 'Made it! Just look at that view! Look way over there; you can just make out the white dome of Mt. Palomar. Must be fifty miles at least.'

Professor Howell came over and joined him.

'That's some view, all right. You know, if I hadn't gone into science, I think I would have been a mountaineer. You get such a different perspective on things—it clears the mind. I've had some real insights while walking in the mountains.'

'You're right, Ted. I'm off to the Andes soon . You should see those peaks!'

'Is that to the new 4-meter at Cerro Tololo?'

'Yes, Victor Oscuro, the director, has asked me to check out the optics now that the mirror's in place. I also want to have a look at a particular object that's only visible from the Southern Hemisphere. Somebody from the Anglo/Australian Schmidt team recently brought a galaxy to my attention that has faint jet-like trails of material shooting out of it. Just the kind of disrupted Seyfert that should be a candidate for radztars.'

The climb had been tough, but the spectacular view more than compensated for that, and they lingered a good half-hour taking in the panorama that stretched before them. Professor Howell broke out his camera and screwed it to a small tripod, then told everyone to line up for a shot. He programmed the self-timer then stepped back to join the others for the group photo.

After a while, Lee looked at his watch. 'Well, gang, we better head back down—it'll take a good hour and a half and our two daughters, Connie and Alicia, are coming over this afternoon. We don't see so much of the eldest, Connie, now that she's working up in 'Frisco.'

They picked up their things and headed back down the trail.

*   *   *

Delays in the construction of the 4-meter telescope meant Dr. Drexler's visit to the observatory in Chile was postponed until the last two weeks of January 1975. He used the time afforded by the delay to make a careful list of the objects that needed special attention and to organize travel arrangements for the trip. Having applied and received by post the required visa from the Chilean embassy in Washington, he finally booked a flight with the Spanish carrier Iberia. This stopped in Los Angeles en route to Santiago from Madrid. It was a fourteen-hour flight, after which he had to board a domestic twin-prop aircraft for a one-and-a-half-hour flight to Serena Airport, situated some fifty miles west of the observatory.

Lee now looked out of the aircraft window at the white mushroom-like dots perched atop the mountain range below, and knew he was reaching the last leg of his journey: the two-hour drive by jeep to Cerro Tololo mountain observatory. He felt buoyed not only by the elevated, aerial perspective of his new research center, but also by the thought that he would be using the very latest facilities to further his research. If the new telescope was as good as the designers expected, he would test it to the very limits of its light-gathering power and, hopefully, resolve the material connections between the galaxies and the star-like radztars.

He had been met at the airport by an observatory employee and now bounced along a dusty, potted, unpaved road in an open Toyota Landcruiser. There was little evidence of habitation, save the occasional stone dwelling, llama, mule, or colorfully-dressed peasants carrying bundles of sticks and other items of vegetation on their backs. There seemed a marked absence of any kind of machinery to aid their meager existence—mules, llamas, and man himself seemed to bear the brunt of physical hardship here.

They arrived shaken, hot, and dusty in the late-afternoon sun. After Lee had been introduced to Director Victor Oscuro and shown his cabin, where he took a thankful shower, he was given a tour of the facilities. The following day had been designated a rest day to compensate for any jetlag he might have incurred (though traveling north-south didn't usually put the clock out too much). It also gave him time to familiarize himself with the equipment and go over the telescope's operating procedures. He was scheduled to start an observing run the following day.

Fernando Perez, a small, bespectacled, timid-looking young technician on a post-grad course from Santiago University's astrophysics department, was to be his assistant for the night's run, and he and Lee met inside the domed building after sunset the following evening.

After Lee had climbed the metal stairway that led up to the observing cage, settled himself, and arranged his charts and photographic plates, he picked up the intercom and gave some instructions to Fernando below. Though this telescope could be operated remotely from the comfortable office, it still had the traditional 'hands on' observing cage, and this was better used when testing the limits of the optics.

'Hello, Fernando. Can you guide me to right ascension 2 hours 45 minutes; declination 31 degrees 23 minutes. I need a 4-hour run on NGC 7901. We need to track very accurately on this one; she's pretty faint, and I want to get a look at the low-surface brightness of those spikes. We should get something with this 3J Kodak emulsion.'

'OK, Dr. Drexler, let me check the computer setting. OK, I'm punching in the coordinates now...should start tracking automatically...now! Hey, you want some nice music?'

Lee fiddled with the plate holder and adjusted the finder microscope. 'Yeah, give me some nice music, Fernando, nothing too loud—no Jimmy Hendrix, OK?'

After a minute or two, the tube of the telescope tilted slowly upward while the widening slit in the dome swiveled into the correct position, accompanied by a low mechanical hum and the muted strains of Herb Alpert and the Tijuana Brass.

Fernando's stilted English crackled up to the domed roof via the intercom. 'OK, two minutes, pleeze then I lock you on. OK, should be there, Dr. Drexler.'

Lee bent low over the finding microscope and fixed the guide star steadily under the crosshairs.

'Contact! Thank you. I've got a sighting. Could you turn down the music a little, I need to concentrate on this image for a while? OK, that's fine—you can take a siesta for a while, amigo. I'll call you later.'

Lee continued for some minutes, peering intently at the guide star while making small adjustments to focus the image coming up to him from the 4-meter mirror down in the base of the skeletal metal tube.

'Damn it!' He suddenly noticed the tiny star wobble out of position. Lee leaned back a moment, rubbed his eye slowly, then peered into the eyepiece again. Suddenly, the image wavered wildly and he became aware of a loud cracking sound coming from the dome above his head.

Dr. Drexler recoiled abruptly, dropped the intercom, and then flailed wildly with his hand to retrieve it as it swung to and fro on its coiled lead.

'Jeez! What the heck are you doing, Fernando?'

Suddenly a siren began wailing and things started falling from the sides of the dome. The cage lurched drunkenly to one side as Lee grabbed the guard-rail with one hand and snatched at the swinging intercom with the other.

'Fernando! What the heck's going on? Have you got a motor malfunction?'

'Dr. Drexler! Dr. Drexler! I do nothing. Go out, go out! We have *temblo*! *Terremoto*…QUAKE…get out!'

'A what!'

'Earthquake! Dr. Drexler, come down! Come down! Go out! I go out, eez not safe here in dome.'

'I can't come down, Fernando. This thing's like a bucking bronco. Stay at your post, do you hear! That's an order, Fernando!' Lee did indeed feel like he was riding a bucking bronco as he grabbed the safety rail now with his two hands as the dome started screeching with the sound of twisting metal.

'Cut the power; cut the power or you'll damage the tracking rail and motor. CUT THE POWER, Fernando!'

Fernando was clearly now thinking about saving himself, the panic in his voice confirming *his* only intention was to cut and run.

'I can do nothing! I go out quick, Dr. Drexler!'

The sound of a metal door slamming caused Lee to turn his attention from the spectacle of the starry heavens swaying through the slit of the heaving blackened dome to the floor below. As he peered over the edge of the swaying cage, he saw Fernando running terrified across the dome floor, scattering barrels and boxes as he went.

The siren continued its wail of alarm, chains swung wildly from metal beams, lights flickered on and off, and in the semi-darkness, the metal dome shrieked in demonic pain as metal strained against metal.

After a minute or two of this pandemonium, the tremors stopped as suddenly as they had begun. The siren fell silent and the music, which Fernando had programmed for Lee's run, abruptly switched to the lulling sound of Glen Miller's 'In the Mood.' Out of sight, a barrel rolled to a standstill somewhere on the concrete floor below and the chains too slowly stopped swinging. Lee decided to call for help.

'Fernando, Fernando, get me down from this thing! Oh, jeez, where's the override button?'

He fumbled around in the dark, eventually found it, and moved the platform over to dock with his cage. Lee waited a minute to reassure himself there would be no more shocks, and then he clasped the rails of the platform and climbed unsteadily out. He reached the safety of the metal stairs as a voice called out from below.

'Dr. Drexler Dr. Drexler! Are you OK?'

'Get the emergency light on, will you. I can't see a thing up here. I dropped my flashlight.'

The voice echoed back, 'Hang on, hang on. Don't move.'

After a minute, the lights flickered back on and Lee made his way down the metal stairway to terra firma.

'Heck, that was an earthquake!'

He was met at the foot of the stairs by Arturo Calero, a member of the observatory staff, and hurriedly led outside.

'Yes, Dr. Drexler. A big one. We sometimes feel a few minor shocks up here, but I haven't experienced one like that before. We can't go back inside; there might be aftershocks. I hope it hasn't damaged the 'scope.'

Lee noticed Fernando lying on the ground, some distance away, looking up at the stars.

'The dome tracking rail might be OK; we had just stopped positioning when it started.'

'It must have been pretty scary, Dr. Drexler, suspended up there in the cage.'

'It sure was swinging around. I hope it hasn't damaged the tube.'

Fernando got up upon hearing Dr. Drexler's voice and came over, wringing a colorful Chilean woolen hat in his hands contritely.

'I very sorry, Dr. Drexler. I can do nothing. I run out!'

'Oh, don't worry, Fernando. I guess I would have too, if I hadn't been trapped up there in that birdcage! Phew! Not the kind of observing situation I want to experience again. These 'scopes are designed to withstand quite severe shocks, but...'

The technician directed the beam of his flashlight up to the silhouetted dome. 'Won't be any use trying to continue with your observations tonight, Dr. Drexler. There're bound to be aftershocks. We'll have to let things calm down until tomorrow.'

'Yeah, well that's certainly ruined tonight's plates. I've experienced one or two tremors up at Palomar, but that was something else. I was just beginning a 4-hour run.'

Fernando pulled the colorful Chilean hat low over his ears and pushed the technician toward the dome's open door. 'We must to close down the system. After you, Arturo, please!'

As they stepped inside they were joined by the director, who hurried up and shone a powerful beam across the assembled faces and then up to the telescope.

'That was nasty! Is everyone OK? Anything damaged?'

The four of them entered the building and stood there looking up at the telescope for a moment. The muted strains of Glen Miller and his band, apparently still stuck in a groove, filtered down from the dome.

Lee turned to the director and offered an ironic laugh.

'Well, I guess that's one way to test the telescope—for structural rigidity, at least.'

'Yes! Can somebody cut the music. Makes this place sound like a dancehall. Did you get far with the observations, Lee?'

'No. Luckily, we had stopped positioning, and I was only just starting. I think it's cracked some of the plates though. I guess the gods don't want me to see what they're up to tonight!'

There was indeed little they could do that night apart from cutting the 'scope's main power and picking up the boxes and drums that had been scattered by the force of the quake. After securing various other loose items to prevent damage from aftershocks, it was nearing 2 A.M., and they decided to leave a more thorough inspection until daybreak. Bolting the iron door to the main entrance, they jumped into the director's pickup and headed back to the dormitories.

The report from the technical staff the next day was good news. The rails, roller bearing, and motor that turned the dome luckily hadn't been damaged, and the slit seemed to open and close correctly. Mechanically, at least, the telescope seemed in good shape. If the alignment of the mirror and tube hadn't been affected, it would be possible to try a second test run.

The following night, Lee went back to the cage and managed to complete his 4-hour exposure without further incident. He was studying the plates in the photographic lab when the director entered.

'Hello, Lee. Everything alright? Did you manage to get anything last night?'

'Dr. Oscuro! Yes, it looks OK. The mirror and optics don't seem to have suffered any damage. Look at the imaging in this 4-hour exposure!'

Lee held up a plate to the light.

'This galaxy is one of those observed by the Anglo/Australian Southern Sky Survey. A colleague in Edinburgh pointed out to me that it appears to have jets of material shooting out from the nucleus—they show up quite clearly on this shot. I've taken it with different color filters and will give them to a colleague at JPL's computer-imaging lab to see if he can stretch the contrast.'

Victor Oscuro studied the black-and-white negative image with interest. 'It looks like a Seyfert, right?'

'Yes, it's just the kind of active Seyfert galaxy where we would expect to find a number of radztars close by. It's beginning to look like these particular galaxies are rather like radztar factories.'

Lee continued thoughtfully. 'In fact, spectroscopically, a radztar looks much like a small portion of a Seyfert nucleus. That, and the evidence of the jets we see here, supports the conclusion that they have been ejected in opposite directions from the central core.'

The director carefully handled another plate.

'Perhaps when we get the proposed X-ray satellite in orbit, we should observe the Seyferts in this part of the spectrum too, Lee. See if there are X-ray traces from the ejection cone.'

He checked his watch. 'Good work, Lee. Look, if you need to use the facilities here, let me know. One or two people have criticized me for even offering to let you be one of the first to test it. I don't know why people have to take such offence at your line of research, I really don't. As far as I'm concerned, it is simply a matter of choosing the most experienced optical astronomers I can get to test its performance. Who else am I going to get, some young kid fresh out of college? You are one of the most experienced observers we have.'

Victor Oscuro stopped at the door. 'Let me know as soon as you've got a specific observing program sorted—oh, and let me know if you find any radztars associated with your Seyfert here!'

'I certainly will, and I look forward to returning. Maybe,' Lee added wistfully, 'I'll check with the seismologists first though!'

9

On the Road

Dr. Matt Mellencamp tugged at the ends of a tartan scarf hanging loosely around his neck and looked out on to the slush-filled street as the black Mercedes taxi splashed its way toward the conference hall.

'How do you think our presentation will go down today, Lee? We are putting forward some pretty radical observations.'

Dr. Drexler crossed his outstretched legs and stroked his chin before replying, as he reclined in the back of the spacious taxi.

'Maybe, but they *are* the observations. We are simply presenting the photographic evidence, Matt. A picture is open to different interpretations, but if we can convince them of the reality of the material connections between the galaxies and the radztars, then half the battle is won. The second half might be more difficult, but the statistics clearly back up the fact that radztars tend to group more readily around the active galaxies.'

'Well, I hope we won't be accused of spoiling the party.'

Dr. Lee Drexler and his collaborator, Matt Mellencamp, were in Germany to present their latest evidence at the 1978 Texas Cosmology Symposium. It was called the 'Texas' Symposium because that was where it had first taken place, organized by world-renowned expert on cosmic waves Professor Frank Stoorman.

'We've got the 4:30 slot, right?'

'Yeah, 4:30 in Lorentz Hall.'

Lee paid the taxi after they reached the conference building and then both he and Matt joined several other delegates making their way into Lorentz Hall. They had some twenty minutes to wait before they were due to give their presentation and they spent the time huddled in a corner going over their papers and readying a series of slides to illustrate the talk.

Finally, the time of their presention neared. As the previous speaker stood down, they gathered together their papers and slides and mounted the rostrum. Lee surveyed the lecture theatre, filled with an excited buzz from the murmuring delegates, checked his watch, then glanced toward his colleague.

'Looks like we're ready, Matt.'

Lee tapped the mike to check that it was on and cleared his throat.

'Good afternoon, ladies and gentlemen. It's a pleasure to be back once again amongst our colleagues in Europe. This afternoon Dr. Mellencamp and I want to show you some very surprising new evidence we have recently compiled, which, we believe, strengthens the case for the association between radztars and nearby galaxies.'

'We will first show a number of slides and then discuss some statistics that we have computed to back up the observational picture. This is recently collected data from an ongoing research program looking for radztars around disrupted active galaxies.'

Lee turned a moment to confer with Matt Mellencamp, readying some slides at the projector, and then continued.

'Over the past few years, we have presented extensive evidence of this association between nearby galaxies and radztars. Several papers have appeared attacking this evidence, and much private opinion has been circulated claiming that the associations are meaningless accidents, chance associations, or effects of perspective. We want to show some examples that we hope will go some way towards convincing the doubters of the reality of the associations.'

The image of a galaxy flashed onto the screen.

'Thank you, Matt. We start by showing the large low-redshift galaxy NGC 3842, with three radztars, ringed here.' Lee picked up the wooden pointer and indicated three encircled black dots near the edge of the galaxy.

A ripple of thinly-disguised incredulity and gasps of amazement spread quickly through the hall as Lee continued.

'We calculate the chances of three radztars falling this close to the central galaxy is about one in a million.'

Lee looked back to the screen and then at his papers.

'Matt would you show slide number two, please? Ah yes, here we have a photograph of NGC 3701, which, again, is found to harbor three radztars: two projected near the edge of the spiral and one, apparently, embedded in its spiral arm.' Lee went to the screen and raised the pointer. 'As you can see,

NGC 3701 is a very beautiful barred spiral galaxy, and here we have arrowed and numbered the three radztars. Ironically, this galaxy was photographed by Dr. Scott Ferris and is featured in Hubble's atlas of galaxies, compiled in the '40s and early '50s. This enabled me to make the pointed joke to my friend Scott, editor of the atlas and co-discoverer, with Marty Schwitters, of the first radztar, that his atlas seemed to contain many images of radztars before they were discovered!'

A tide of muted laughter spread through the hall.

'Now, we calculate the chances of finding three radztars this close to NGC 3701 at about 1 in 50,000. On top of this seemingly unlikely event, NGC 7901 is only *one* of 176 galaxies in the Hubble atlas and only one of 1,246 in the more recent Shapley-Ames catalog of bright nearby galaxies. The vast majority of these have never been searched for radztars. It was only out of curiosity, after a small radio source was discovered near the galaxy, that I searched for radztars and found the three shown here.'

Lee lowered the pointer and returned to the lectern.

'Well, the three radztars sit there, apparently in the arms of NGC 3701. Where did they come from? That is the $64,000 question. What can we learn about these mysterious highly-redshifted objects, if they indeed are intermingled in the filaments of gas and young stars in this spiral galaxy? The most direct way to answer this question, as well as to confirm the reality of the association, was to find further examples of such associations.

'Matt, could we have slide number three? Thank you.'

'Yes, it was helpful, therefore, that at about the same time the three radztars were discovered in NGC 3701, a pair turned up very close to NGC 622, our spiral galaxy here.'

Lee turned to look at the galaxy Matt had flashed up.

'We calculate the chance of finding two radztars this close to the galaxy at less than 1 chance in 100,000. I discovered this system during the inspection of plates that registered ultraviolet objects over about 100 square degrees of the sky. There should be from ten to fifty galaxies as bright as this in the region searched, therefore this is a very significant confirmation of direct physical association.'

'However, the especially significant aspect of NGC 622 is the filament of material that comes out of the galaxy and reaches the radztar, R1. It appears quite similar to the gas and dust in the spiral arm of the galaxy, except that it does not curve around the edge of the galaxy. It comes straight out and ends on the radztar.'

'The chances of this unusual filament ending almost exactly at the position of the radztar by accident is vanishingly small, unless the filament is physically related to the radztar. It also suggests ejection, from the galaxy, as the origin of the radztar.'

'Matt, could we have the next slide please? Thank you.'

Slide number four showed a photograph of galaxy NGC 3067.

'Here we have another example of a bridge of luminous material, apparently connecting two objects with very different redshifts. Now, although this bridge of material doesn't end on a radztar, the small, compact companion does have a much greater redshift than the galaxy—8,100 km per second for the main galaxy, 17,000 km per second for the small companion. Now, no one, to our knowledge, denies the obvious physical connection between the two, so how do we account for the enormous difference in redshift between them? This photograph will be submitted as evidence in addition to the other famous duo, NGC 9134/502, which Matt will show us now.'

Lee turned and looked at the screen.

'The star-like object just below galaxy NGC9134 is a radztar with a redshift indicative of 21,000 km per second. The galaxy, on the other hand, has a redshift of only 1,700 km per second. Now, a tantalizing question arises. Are perhaps both NGC 3067 and its companion *and* NGC 9134/502 related in an evolutionary way? Could the radztar NGC 502 evolve into an object like the small, high-redshift companion to NGC 3067? Could NGC 3067's companion have started out as a radztar?'

Lee looked up at the audience. 'These are important questions, and it seems amazing to us that more astronomers are not following up these important clues.'

'We come to our last slide in this presentation. 'Matt? Thank you. Yes. Here we have the galaxy NGC 473. Marked with arrows are two recently-discovered radztars apparently buried in the remnants of this bright spiral's arms. It should be emphasized that the probability of finding two radztars like the fainter one here, this close in a given point in the sky, is about two times ten to the minus four. Since one radztar is considerably brighter, and therefore less common, the probability of finding two so close together is even smaller.'

'Matt, could we have the tables, please? Table 1-1 here summarizes the properties of galaxies with multiple radztars, as we've just discussed; it is apparent that the radztars have a tendency to be fainter if the redshift is higher. It is also apparent that certain preferred redshift values appear more frequently than one would expect by chance. Some years ago, Professor Bainbridge noticed that too many redshifts occurred too close the value of z = 1.95, and several others have confirmed this early result since then.'

Mat flashed up another chart.

'Table 1-2 here tabulates the most complete analysis of those preferred red-shifts to date. It is immediately noticeable from Table 1-2 that the redshifts of the three radztars associated with NGC 3701 follow this magic formula very closely indeed.

'Let me, finally, point out that from my initial discovery of radztars aligned across disturbed galaxies, and the similarity to radio sources—whose align-ment *is* caused by ejection from the nucleus—the implication has always been that radztars are ejected from the nuclei of active galaxies. I hope we have demonstrated that this view is supported by the recent observational evidence we have presented to you today.'

Matt Mellencamp turned off the projector, put the slides back in a box, and moved to join Lee at the rostrum.

'Perhaps second only to the question of what causes the redshift, if it is not a result of movement away from the observer, the *method* of the ejection of material from disrupted galaxies seems to be the most significant puzzle. Ejec-tion from the nuclei of active galaxies raises the question of whether condi-tions in the innermost core involve the kind of physics we observe around us today. Could the redshift of radztars be related to the nature of the material they are composed of in the nucleus? That seems to us the most pressing prob-lem in astronomy today. Thank you. Any questions?

'Yes, at the back there!'

A figure rose and held a rolled paper aloft.

'Dr. Mark Glasby, Princeton Institute for Advanced Studies. Dr. Drexler, you emphasize that radztar redshifts tend to prefer only certain values. Do you have any idea why this should be so, or could it, perhaps, be a selection effect on the part of the observer?'

Lee brushed at his hair and fingered the bunch of keys in his pocket.

'Oh no, it's not a selection effect—it's real all right. The redshift measure-ments are extremely accurate. It might have something to do with the quanti-zation of matter at the subatomic level; it might have something to do with the time of new matter's birth. We are considering these and other possibili-ties from a theoretical point of view with colleagues Professor Ted Howell and Dr. Rappannipan. Yes, over there?'

The question-and-answer session lasted longer than the presentation, with most of the delegates expressing strong reservations about the validity of Lee and Matt's evidence. Finally the symposium drew to a close and Lee and Matt elected to take the courtesy bus back to their hotel. They found themselves entertained on the journey by an exchange of similar skepticism between the science correspondent of the *New York Times* and one of the conference participants sitting a couple of seats in front of them.

So, Dr. Armstrong, you don't agree with Drexler and Mellencamp that radztars are really local objects ejected from the nearby galaxies?'

'No, I'm afraid Drexler has got this all very wrong. It may *look* as though they are, but I can assure you that it is simply an optical illusion. There's really no need to look further than the formula discovered by Hubble in the 1930s and tried, tested, and refined to a very high degree of precision since then. This is what really decides where the radztars are to be located in space. I really don't understand why Dr. Drexler continues his relentless and fruitless quest to find filaments and material bridges between these distant radztars and the nearby galaxies. I think he would be most wise to give up his improbable claims and join with the rest of his colleagues in helping to refine the established picture.'

'The expanding universe?'

'Yes.'

The *Times* correspondent bit at the end of his pencil and tried another tack.

'I must say I was rather intrigued by their presentation—but then I suppose I am just a reporter and not professionally committed to either side of the argument; however, they do seem to have a point. What exactly do you have in *principle* against the possibility that radztars might be ejected from galactic nuclei, Dr. Armstrong?'

'Well, apart from the fact that it would be most unlikely to happen from a physical point of view—and we have no evidence that it happens, despite Drexler's claims—the enormous redshift proves that radztars are at the furthest reaches of time and space. No question!'

'But if I could push you on this. In *principle*, Dr. Armstrong?'

Dr. Armstrong heaved a sign of resignation.

'Well, I suppose elephants *might* fly. Anything is indeed possible if you put it like that. But realistically, no. It's a non-starter—period!'

Lee Drexler and Matt Mellencamp shook hands in a private show of mock irony, closed their eyes, and pushed their seats into their maximum reclination mode.

*   *   *

Lee removed his Ray-Bans and rubbed his eyes. In the sweltering midday heat, the distant mountains shimmered purple, and, in places, the ribbon of black asphalt, cutting through the Sonoran Desert of New Mexico, seemed to buckle and levitate clean above the ground.

'Sure good of Jim to fix us some more time on the 4-meter, Matt. There's a heap of people waiting to use the new CCD camera.'

He and Matt Mellencamp were on their way to Kit Peak National Observatory and a couple of nights testing the light gathering power of the new camera that had been installed in the 4-meter telescope. Matt was eager to test it on the faint bridge that appeared to connect NGC 9134 and the star-like radztar 502. He believed that by photographing in different colors, he could image process the plates and bring out the lower-surface brightness if the CCD camera lived up to expectations.

They had left Pasadena around 10:30 and were now passing through a flat, desolate landscape littered with cacti and occasional crumbling sandstone Indian dwellings on Interstate 12, en route to Tucson, Arizona.

'Yeah, it's a real advance in the photon gathering stakes, that's for sure. They'll probably be fitted to most telescopes before too long—might even be used in conventional cameras eventually' Matt cupped a hand over his eyes to better focus on a distant figure sitting beside the road.

'Hey, should we give him a ride, Lee?'

'Yeah. Looks harmless enough. He's not going anywhere fast out of here if we don't.'

Lee slowed the car as they approached the figure sitting patiently on his rucksack, strumming a guitar. He looked up and stuck a thumb in the air as they approached.

'Hey, friend, where're you headed?' Matt wound down the passenger window and surveyed the figure, who could have passed for a member of the Confederate side during the American Civil War. He could certainly have doubled for Willy Nelson if Hollywood ever needed an actor to play the part of the country music star.

'Willy' scrambled to attention and wiped his mouth with the back of his hand.

'Hey! Thanks. I'm headed to Tucson if you guys are headed that way.'

'Sure, we're going to Tucson. Well, actually, we turn off just before for Kit Peak. Climb aboard.'

The hitchhiker bundled his possessions onto the back seat and slammed the door shut as Lee released the handbrake and continued their journey.

'What's Kit Peak? Is it a mountain or something?'

Lee took a swig of water from a plastic bottle and offered it to their hippy passenger.

'Yeah, it's a mountain with a telescope on top. You going to Tucson for something special?'

Willy leaned forward and returned the bottle. 'Going to see Bob Dylan. He's doing a concert there. Gotta see him if I have to hitch all the way from San Diego!'

Lee replaced the bottle between the front seats and looked in the rearview mirror.

'He's one hell of a poet, that's for sure. I saw him one time at the Philmore in 'Frisco. Just blew everybody away. Loud though.'

Willy was impressed that he'd gotten a ride with a Dylan fan. 'Hey that musta been a while ago. He's into country now! Are you guys astronomers or something?'

Matt gestured towards Lee. 'Lee here is. I'm mainly into computers myself.'

'Hey! I saw some program by Carl Sagan—you guys know Carl? He said we all started out from a big explosion millions of years ago. He said it's all now expanding. Is that what you guys think?'

Lee shot Matt a glance. 'Actually, we have a problem with that. We don't believe that it is expanding.'

'Carl Sagan says it is! He said so on TV, so I guess it's gotta be true.'

'Well, you can't believe everything just because it's on television. What did Carl say about the radztars?'

'What stars? Oh, those galaxies at the end of the universe? Yeah, he said they are so far off because of the red light we measure, or something.'

Their passenger bit the filter off a cigarette and crumbled the tobacco onto a cigarette paper. He then unwrapped something from a piece of silver foil and put the flame of a lighter to it. Without looking up from what he was doing, he continued, 'I love that stuff, man, but I don't understand how you guys can measure things so far off. Seems kinda esoteric to me. I mean, I don't know what's happening at the end of the universe, but I know Bob Dylan's gonna be in Tucson Saturday night, if you know what I mean. It's, like, what's happening here and now, if you get my meaning. Like, reality is here and now, not something we *imagine* is happening a billion light years away.'

Matt looked back in alarm as the hitchhiker suddenly exploded into a fit of coughing and the back of the car filled up with thick blue smoke.

'Hey, you on fire back there?'

'Willy' fell sideways across the back seat and felt blindly through the cloud of smoke for a window winder; he found it and lowered the window. After struggling to regain his composure, he leaned forward abruptly and proffered a large joint toward the front seats.

'Hey, sorry, you guys smoke?'

'Oh, that's OK. We'll pass—we have some technical stuff to attend to when we get to Kit Peak. Is that stuff legal?'

'I guess if God provides it, it doesn't need a license does it? Maybe some people in the government say it ain't legal…' Willy paused to take another draw '…but then a lot of things they do might be considered illegal too, like dropping bombs on foreign countries and people they ain't never met. I mean, that would be kind of illegal in a legal world, wouldn't it? Dropping bombs on people you never met because you don't like the way they dress or something—'

'Hey, sorry, what's your name?' Matt turned to the back seat.

'Seth. That's the only name I got.'

Matt reached back and offered his hand. 'Matt Mellencamp. This here is Lee Drexler. Pleased to meet you. You have a point there.'

'I thought you said you didn't want it…'

Seth realized he had misheard 'point' for 'joint' and then continued, 'I dropped out, man! Couldn't take the laws. There's too many holes in it. Bombing people you never bothered to say hello to—it's like saying you know what's at the end of the universe when you ain't never been there to see. It don't add up; it ain't convincing, if you know what I mean.' Seth cupped his hands over the end of his joint and drew heavily to rekindle the glowing embers. 'They say this is a democracy, but it's all corrupt, man! Step out of line and try and change the American way and you end up on the slab. You guys be careful if you want to change the system. The system is controlled by the Mafia, man—and you know how the Mafia operates? Survival of the fittest, law of the jungle.'

Matt looked a little startled at this tirade against the system coming from the back seat.

'We understand what you're saying, Seth.'

'They wanted to send me to Vietnam. Can you believe that! They called me up and said, "We want you to go to Veee-et-naam and kill as many Veee-et-naam folk as you can." Hell! I never met no Vietnamese people, man!'

'What did you do about that, Seth?'

Seth fell sideways again on the back seat, choking with laughter. 'I said, "Fuck you! Go fight your own wars, man! I got nothing against no Vietnam people." So I went over the border—went up to Canada—and kept my head down till it was all over. I got no problem with the Asian people, man. I got some real good Chinese friends from that part of the world—mostly living in 'Frisco now—some real good friends.'

Seth started strumming on his battered guitar in the back seat, improvising a song.

> *Big Bang, Big Bang, it started with a bang.*
> *Big Bang, Big Bang, I'm ridin' the Big Bang.*
> *Ain't never been to China, ain't never been to Nam.*
> *Only place I'm a headin' is Tucson to see my man.*

Lee eyed Seth in the rear view mirror. 'Hey, that's terrific! Did you just make that up?'

Seth lay the guitar across his knees and looked around proudly. 'That's what I do, I write songs. After a moment he picked up the guitar and broke into song again, effecting this time a high nasal whine that sounded remarkably like the Bard of American counter culture, himself.

> *Jewels and binoculars hang from the head of*
> *the mule.*
> *But these visions of Johanna, make it all*
> *seem so cruel.*

Lee turned to Matt. 'Hey, I could use that as my epitaph!

'Did you write that too?'

'No, that's one of Bob's. That's why I was singing it the way he does.'

So you guys have a problem with the big bang. Hey, that's far out! I mean, cool. I like that. What's the problem with the big bang, guys?' He leaned forward, resting his elbows on the backs of Lee and Matt's front seats, mouth frozen, eyes glazed and bloodshot, staring vacantly into the middle distance of nowhere.

'Well, Seth, you know the story about how Galileo got into a whole heap of trouble with the authorities for contradicting what the church said about the Earth being the center of the universe?'

'Hello, Seth!' Matt passed a hand in front of Seth's vacant gaze and triggered a temporary return to consciousness.

'Sure…er, they burned some guy who agreed with Galileo or something. So, you guys are like Galileo? You heading for the barbecue too?'

Matt turned around. 'Well, we don't expect to be burned at the stake! But yes, I guess you could say we are discovering some things that contradict the big bang, Seth, and it is getting us into some trouble with the authorities.'

'Is that where you are headed now, to do some more observing that will get you into more trouble?'

Matt pulled the sun visor down, eyed Seth in the mirror, and laughed. 'Yeah, probably.'

'Hey, revolution, man! I'm a-ridin' with rev-o-lution-aries. I thought all those big problems got sorted out way back when. Now you guys are stirring it all up again!'

'Well, we hope it'll blow over, Seth, but you never can tell. Hey, Tucson's coming up. Can we drop you on the bypass, Seth? We don't exactly go through the center of town.'

'Perfect. Thank you very much, guys.'

Lee pulled over at the intersection and Seth stumbled out.

'Take care now, and have a good concert!'

Seth gave them a peace sign as they drove off. 'Take care there, guys. Don't follow leaders, watch the parking meter!'

Matt waved his arm out of the window and looked across to Lee.

'Phew! Some weird folk out on the road, Lee.'

The rest of their journey to Kit Peak proved rather less eventful, and when they finally arrived at around five, they located the director, Professor Bainbridge, in his office.

'Hey, Lee! Matt! Did you have a good drive out?' Professor Bainbridge ushered them through the door. 'I used to do it, but now I prefer to fly.'

Lee accepted a seat and sat down. 'Yeah, picked up some anti-war draft dodger hitching a ride to see a Bob Dylan concert in Tucson. Felt like we were in the movie *Easy Rider*! Gee, there are some characters out there!'

Matt crossed to the window and looked out across the range of blue mountains.

'Great that most of the important telescopes around here are within a day's drive of Pasadena, though.'

Lee cut in, 'And located in the most isolated places. It always seems to amplify the mystery and remoteness of what we are observing.'

Professor Bainbridge rested his portly frame on the edge of the desk. 'I never get tired of the place. For me, it's the center of the universe!'

'And good to have friends in high places! It's good of you to fix us some time on the 4-meter, Jim. Things are getting tough at Palomar. People are trying to squeeze my observing time. I'm getting a lot of resistance to my proposals, and the post-grads all want to do things that support the conventional picture, so they wind up getting the time now.'

Lee lit a cigarette and threw the match into a glass ashtray.

'Still, with these new 'scopes coming online here and in the Southern Hemisphere, it helps to distribute the load. Palomar probably won't be much use in the next few years anyway; the light pollution from San Diego is increasing.'

'That's true, Lee.' Jim Bainbridge shifted his weight onto the other foot. 'I think we should be safe out here for a few years. So, you want to try the CDD cam on NGC 9134?'

'Yes. We want to follow up on the image-processing work Matt did with the best of Mt. Palomar plates and the ones you took here. We've brought an image that Matt made by processing the best of seven plates.'

Matt Mellencamp took a photo from his briefcase and handed it to Lee, who passed it to Professor Bainbridge.

'Matt was able to filter the information contained in the best plates with JPL's supercomputer, and—'

Matt pointed to a section of the photograph. 'Yes, we've managed to bring out this very narrow central spine within the broad bridge of luminous material connecting the two.' He ran his finger over the connecting line between the galaxy and the radztar. 'Here we can trace well back towards the nucleus.'

Bainbridge stared at the picture. 'Yes, I see what you mean. Good work, Matt! It must have been an incredibly delicate operation playing around with the filters and image intensifiers without altering too much of the information contained in the original image.'

Matt looked pleased at the positive appraisal of his work.

'Yes, it is a new science. I think the digitally-enhanced capability of your CCD camera will allow us to take this image-processing technique further and filter at the source rather than wait until the photos are developed. We should be able to correct for unwanted foreground stars, just by amplifying the weaker photons we want to capture.'

Professor Bainbridge lowered the photo to the table. 'Did you guys see the picture of NGC 9134/502 in *Telescope* magazine recently? It was rather amusing, because the authors maintained the bridge wasn't real in the article, but in their computer-enhanced pseudo-color image, the connection appeared stronger than in your original black-and-white photos.'

Lee laughed. 'Yes, I did see that. If you held the magazine at arm's length, the connection virtually jumped off the page! Matt and I thought about making up some tee shirts with a superimposed outline of the Golden Gate Bridge linking the two objects.'

Matt interjected. 'Yeah, but we abandoned the idea when we considered how little humor there is among the participants in this controversy!'

'So things are not altogether hunky dory over at Caltech, Lee?'

'Hunky dory! I'm thinking of taking up an offer of temporary refuge at AstroNet in Germany. Some friends there have indicated that I could use their computer facilities and access their satellite X-ray data that's now coming on-stream. You know, until recently, I thought we were beginning to win the battle. Just one more clear example of a galaxy/radztar association, just one more convincing statistic that showed radztars fell closer to disrupted galaxies than would be expected by chance, and we would start winning over the skeptics and the fence-sitters. Then this paper appears in a British journal criticizing the way I did the calculations on a search for radztars around predefined candidate galaxies. Even though I redid the calculations another way and came up with the same result, most people now use this erroneous claim to discredit my results.'

The director got up, paced the room, then returned to his desk. 'Was that the paper in the *Observatory*, where you outlined a section of the sky and picked out a number of likely candidate galaxies where you thought radztars might be found?'

'Yes, that's the one! We found thirteen cases where the radztars fell so close to the galaxies, the chances of it being accidental was about 1 in 100. But, all to no avail, everyone goes off and sides with the skeptics!' Lee stopped, then added reflectively, 'I guess if you believe that the conventional redshift interpretation explains everything, no amount of statistics is going to change your mind.'

Matt picked up the photo idly. 'Yeah, it would probably annoy you even further.'

Lee levered himself out of his chair, picked up his briefcase, and replaced the photographs.

'Jim, as I mentioned on the phone, the other thing I wanted to check was NGC 3701. You know, Matt and I found three radztars buried in the outer arms of this Seyfert spiral galaxy.'

Jim Bainbridge shuffled some papers into a neat pile on his desk and then got to his feet as well. 'Yes indeed. That is one of the clearest examples to date of multiple radztars associated with the Seyferts. I mean, one radztar close to a galaxy is perhaps questionable—but three? No, the odds of that are just too great for it to be a chance alignment.'

'I spoke to Monica about it, Lee, and she's prepared to have a go at reconfirming with a couple of people from her department. We should be able to fix that up soon.'

'That's great, Jim! Please tell Monica I'm very grateful.'

Jim Bainbridge walked to the door and took his jacket off the peg. 'Let's go over to the 'scope. I'll introduce you to our new night assistant.'

*   *   *

Two days later, the director, Lee, and Matt Mellencamp were in the photographic developing center, examining the result of their two nights' run on the 4-meter.

'How was it, Lee? Did you get any better resolution with the CCD cam? It takes awhile to get the best from it.'

Lee moved a small tubular magnifying instrument steadily over the photograph.

'Not sure, Jim. The atmospheric steadiness wasn't quite what we hoped it would be. The linear intensity response of the detector seems good though. Matt thinks he should be able to image-process the broader features of the bridge.'

Matt Mellencamp rested an arm on Lee's shoulder as he bent forward and traced the connecting bridge with his finger.

'It looks like there might be a counter-ejection in the opposite direction to 502. On the ultraviolet CCD frames, we detect a star-like object. From past experience with these kinds of objects near the end of a counter-jet, it usually turns out to be a radztar. We'll need to get a spectrum and measure the red-shift.'

Lee straightened. 'Jim, if it looks like there's something definitely worth following up, could you give us another run on the 4-meter? We'll probably need to use the spectrograph.'

'Sure, Lee. Let me know what you two come up with after you've done the image processing work back at the lab. In the meantime, I'll get Monica to check up on NGC 3701. Looks like we've got some very strong candidates that might finally convince the disbelievers. I'll continue urging my staff to search your other candidates.'

'Thanks, Jim. I'll be in touch as soon we've checked the results of our work here. Give my regards to Monica!'

They shook hands with the director and headed for the parking lot and the drive back to Pasadena.

10

The Net Closes In

Since first coming to Pasadena's Caltech Institute, Lee Drexler had maintained, as far as his observing schedule permitted, a regular Sunday tennis date with the 'discoverer' of radztars, Marty Schwitters. Today they would play their match at Marty's tennis club. Unfortunately for Marty, Lee was in particularly good form and enjoying the advantage of his newly-acquired carbon-compound racket.

'Thirty-Forty. Good shot, Lee. Hey, how did you get that back? I put everything into that forehand.'

'Doubles practice, Mart. You gotta be quick at the net in doubles. This new racket makes a difference, too—you gotta get one.'

Schwitters picked up the ball and returned to his serving spot. He served two double faults and ended up losing the second set.

'Heck, I feel a bit rusty, Lee. If you don't play every week, you soon lose your edge.' He sat down next to Lee and unscrewed the cap of a plastic water bottle.

'Yeah, sorry I wasn't able to play last week. Mind you, all *I* got to play up at Kit Peak was half an hour of table tennis with J. B. *Not* exactly a proper workout.'

Marty Schwitters took a swig from the bottle then raised it and let the contents rain over his head and shoulders in a refreshing splash. 'Jim's not the most athletic creature, that's for sure! Probably a leisurely round of golf would suit him better. So, what have you been up to since you got back? You said on the phone somebody was sending the director papers critical of your research—did you go see him about that?'

Lee rubbed a towel across the back of his neck and then folded it across his knees.

'Yeah, I sure did. I took along some more recent calculations, put them down on his desk, and said if he looked through them he would see the same result as before, even though they had been calculated differently.'

'And...what was the result?'

'Pretty negative. It seemed to annoy him that I was questioning him about it. Said it wasn't anything personal, but as the majority had concluded that my claims were misguided, it would better if I stopped trying to continue undermining the conventional position. He got pretty mad and muttered something about the observing committee taking a dim view of the value of my observations.'

'Well, I did warn you!'

'Yes, I know, Mart. But heck, I believe the observations are correct. What can I do? 'Well, as a member of that committee myself, I can tell you in confidence that some members are getting edgy, Lee. I have argued—even though I don't personally agree with your "local" radztar claims—that we should continue to allocate observation time even-handedly, both for and against the current position. I don't believe we have all the answers yet, and new discoveries will surely turn up as the instrumentation improves. But I do sense a hardening of attitudes, Lee.'

'So what's new?' Lee picked up his racquet and fiddled absent-mindedly with the strings.

'There were even some mutterings at the last meeting of sending some kind of written warning. It wasn't adopted—they decided to leave it for the moment.'

Marty Schwitters threw his towel aside and got to his feet.

'Hey, I shouldn't be telling you this...I'll be accused of leaking information to the other side!'

Lee pocketed some balls and moved to the service line in readiness for the third and final set. 'Oh, don't worry. I've probably got enough observational data now anyway, at least from the big optical 'scopes. The future will lie with the satellite observatories, X-ray, gamma, and infrared observations.'

By the time the final set drew to a close, the clock on the tennis club house indicated 3 P.M. and they had to make way for the next court reservation.

Lee walked to the net and shook hands with his opponent.

'Well played, Mart! I thought you were on the comeback trail there for a while. 1-3 down and nearly evened it. 7-5, 4-6, 6-4. Good match. Can you play next week?'

Marty Schwitters slid his racquet into its nylon cover and pulled at the zipper. 'Should be OK, Lee. I'll have to confirm later in the week. I'm attending a particle physics symposium in Austin on Thursday, but I plan to be back on Saturday.'

'Give me a call when you can confirm it.'

Marty closed the gate with a metal clang and patted his colleague on the shoulder with his racket. 'Will do.'

*   *   *

Dr. Ravindra Pondrabhann finally called it a day as editor-in-chief of the *Astrophysical News* and passed the responsibility on to his handpicked successor, Dr. Donald Trimble, a smooth-talking astrophysicist from the Smithsonian Institute in Washington. Lee had harbored the hope that a change of leadership at the *News* might ease the implacable opposition to his efforts to establish a connection between radztars and nearby galaxies, but he was soon disillusioned. In fact, the situation appeared to worsen. Donald Trimble was now becoming increasingly alarmed at the constant flow of submissions and had decided to do something about it.

Today, he picked up the telephone and dialed Dr. Dick Turtle, the new director at Mt. Palomar.

'Hello, Dr. Turtle. Trimble here, *Astrophysical News.*'

A voice crackled back down the line.

'Hello, Donald, what a nice surprise...no, no, no, of course you are not bothering me. We are always pleased to hear from the *News*. If it wasn't for your esteemed publication, we would all be groping about in the dark communicating with each other like ships passing in the night.'

Donald Trimble reached for the plastic Coca Cola mug—bequeathed by the late editor as a symbol of editorial continuity—and withdrew a pencil.

'Well, thank you, Dick. Congratulations on the appointment. What an honor to be entrusted with overseeing the achievements of your illustrious predecessor, Professor Hayman. He played such an important role in coordinating the task we have set ourselves. I know Ravi called to offer you his congratulations and to encourage you to continue the good work. He urged me to do the same, not that there was need for that, Dick!'

Dick Turtle surveyed the acreage of polished mahogany and green baize that lay before him. He spied an errant elastic band between his 'in' and 'out' trays, picked it up, and gently swung it to and fro between his fingers. 'And how is Ravi, Donald?'

'Ravi is very well. Largely retired now, of course, and basking in the glory of his Nobel Prize. Still keeps in close contact with us here at the *News*. Of course, we all still think of it as Ravi's Journal; after all, it was his visionary leadership that turned it into the renowned publication it is today.

'In fact, he urged me to get in touch with you on another matter that is of concern to us all, namely, the ongoing problem with your Dr. Drexler and his continuing efforts to undermine the orthodox position. I know Ravi raised this concern with your predecessor and that Professor Hayman spoke to Drexler about it, but it seems to have had little effect. We still receive a steady stream of contradictory submissions from Dr. Drexler. As soon as we counter with a quick response, back he comes, pulling another rabbit out of his celestial hat. He is a slippery customer, Dick, and some of us here think you may have to try a different line of *persuasion* if we are to get him to change course. Earlier attempts at appealing to the common good and the damage he is doing to the reputation of the institution appear to have fallen on deaf ears. Perhaps you will need to issue a firmer warning, to the effect that his radical views cannot be sanctioned by an official institution. If he wishes to continue arguing his bizarre claims, he should do it *independently*.'

Dr. Turtle maneuvered the elastic band to a small metal tray and dropped it on a pile of others of varying colors.

'Yes, Donald, I take your point and I am aware of the concerns you raise. Something needs to be done, and done soon. I had some words with Drexler in my office a few weeks ago and told him, in no uncertain terms, that he was wrong to pursue his efforts to undermine the established picture—and to do it from a renowned institution such as this. I can assure you, Donald, we are as concerned as you are, constantly on the receiving end of his improbable claims, and we are putting into place measures which we hope will deter further unnecessary waste of our valuable observing program. I will raise your concerns at the next TAC meeting and we will assess what further steps are to be taken. By the way, thank you for getting the report from *Cambridge Astrophysical Review* to my desk. I realize it would have been improper of you to send it to me directly.'

Donald Trimble snapped the pencil lead as he pressed it hard onto his note pad. 'Oh, you got that! I was wondering if Dr. Chandler had passed it on to you. I did recommend that he do so, to put you in the picture. I realize you don't have time to keep abreast of the many papers and reports that are published. I think Tester's statistics clarify the errors in Drexler's calculations and confirm the official position.'

'Perhaps it will have to come in the form of a written warning, as spoken admonitions seem to have had little effect in producing the desired result, Donald. We have already reduced quite considerably Dr. Drexler's allocation of observing time, but he is apparently now soliciting help from other observatories in his efforts to continue his research. He has a sympathizer there in the form of Professor Bainbridge. He is apparently making the telescopes available to Drexler.'

Donald Trimble put the pencil back in its holder and snapped his notepad shut.

'Well, we have every confidence that you will remedy the situation, Dick, one way or the other. I just wanted to convey the concerns here at the *News*. Once again, congratulations, and the best of luck with your speedy resolution of this troubling Drexler affair.'

'Thank you, Donald. Rest assured, your concerns are fully shared here, and steps will be taken to ensure our position is not undermined by a member of my staff. Thank you for relaying your concerns to me—good day to you, Donald.'

*   *   *

Dr. Drexler was rincing the dinner plates in the kitchen when the phone in the hall rang. 'Could you get that, Kay? I'm just washing up.'

'It's Jim Bainbridge, Lee!'

Dr. Drexler slid the plate into the wall-mounted wooden plate rack, dried his hands, and went to take the telephone from his wife.

'Thanks, honey.'

'Hi, Jim. How's things? I was going to call you. We need another short run on the 4-meter…yes, yes…it's almost impossible to get any useful time at Palomar now.'

Jim Bainbridge tapped ash from the bowl of his pipe into a glass ashtray and pushed it aside. He picked up a metal paperclip and turned it, end over end, between his fore and index finger as he spoke.

'Is it that bad, Lee?'

'Actually, it's worse than bad. The chairman of the telescope-allocation committee called me up to try and get me to change the object and purpose of my observations. Apparently, if I don't fall into line with the official view, they can't guarantee they will continue supporting my allocation for time on the 'scopes.'

Professor Bainbridge stopped playing with the paper clip and stood it vertically on end.

'What! That's unprecedented! I can't believe they would take such drastic action against one of their most senior observers. Heavens! I can't believe it. I thought we were on the road to convincing them that you had a good case. What did you say, Lee?'

Dr. Drexler saw his wife raise a pot of coffee in the kitchen and indicated silently that he would take a small one, by pinching his thumb and index finger.

'I said no, on principle. Apparently what got them real mad was that paper of mine in that *Cambridge Astrophysical Review* claiming a high statistical probability that radztars are more likely to be found around companion galaxies—you know, the result of the three-year study I did with Matt? Somebody sent a paper critical of my statistical method to Turtle.'

'Well, that's no reason to ban someone's research, Lee. Look, I might be able to help there. A member of our allocation committee has taken up a position overseas, and we'll need someone to step in to make the numbers up. If you're interested, I could put your name forward. I'm sure we could get someone with your experience onboard. It's not Mt. Palomar, but it might help redress the shortfall.'

Dr. Drexler laughed and winked at his wife as she set a small cup down next to the telephone. 'You mean I could vote for my own observing program, Jim?'

'Well, why not? Everyone else does!'

'Actually, Lee, I was calling about another matter, but having heard this, it will probably make things even worse! Monica has confirmed the three radztars in NGC 3701. She did the observations with the help of a couple of colleagues. They are all genuine high-redshift radztars, as you originally claimed. They're going to submit a report to the *Astrophysical News*.'

'Well, that is good news, Jim.' Lee picked up a small silver spoon and gave the coffee a stir. 'Maybe that'll force the board to climb down some. Please thank Monica for her help. They'll have to take the result seriously now, especially as they can't accuse me of doing the observation this time!'

Lee then added, 'You know, Jim? If we could prove the radztar candidate on the other side of NGC 502, that would be additional proof to support the claim that radztars really are ejected from the Seyferts.'

'Yes, Lee, we are rather more optimistic people will now see reason. I spoke to Ted Howell and he said the result shows that the standard theory is now in *big* trouble and clearly incapable of adequately explaining the observations. With regard to further time on the 4-meter, I'm sure we can weave an hour or two into the schedule—would July be OK, Lee? I think it's clear around the middle. I'm afraid we are rather committed until then.'

'That'll do fine, Jim. I have a meeting with some colleagues at the European Space Organization in Germany, so I'll be away for a week or so anyway. I'll get in touch when I get back and confirm. Thanks for the good news. Oh, by the way, what were the redshifts? Did they come out the same as my original measurements?'

Jim Bainbridge picked up his glasses and reached for a paper on his desk. 'Yes, 1.94, 0.59, and 1.41. We reckon the chances of finding *three* radztars this close to the center of a galaxy, compared to the average background number, is less than 1 in 50,000. I don't think anyone can argue that away, Lee. Looks like you were right all along.'

Lee twisted at the coiled cable with his free hand. 'Thanks, Jim. I'll be in touch just as soon as I get back from Europe. Thanks for calling.'

'Good news, Lee?' Kay looked up as her husband put down the phone and entered the kitchen.

'Sure was. Jim might be able to get me a seat on the allocation committee at Kit Peak *and* Monica confirmed the three radztars in NGC 3701. They can huff and puff as much as they like, but I didn't make the observations this time, Kay. They can't accuse me of malpractice this time!'

*   *   *

Lee Drexler looked at the calendar on his desk. It indicated July 16, 1980. 'Kit Peak with Matt' was circled in red ink. He picked up the phone and dialed Matt Mellencamp's number.

'Matt? It's Lee. I'm leaving now; be over in half an hour.'

'Ready when you are, Lee'

Lee replaced the receiver, gathered up some papers, grabbed his coat, and swept out of his office, locking the door behind him. He'd returned from the meeting in Europe four days earlier, had conferred with Jim Bainbridge as planned, and arranged to visit Kit Peak again today, with Dr. Mellencamp.

After picking up Matt at his office at JPL and negotiating a seemingly endless series of traffic lights and intersections, they joined the freeway that headed south to San Diego and then followed the road inland in the direction of Tucson and Kit Peak Mountain observatory. At a roundabout, exiting San Diego, they had been surprised to see Seth, the hitchhiker they had picked up the year before. He was heading in the opposite direction to Lee and Matt, but as Lee tooted his horn, Seth waved back in recognition and threw a battered Stetson wildly in the air.

Matt leaned out of the window and waved back as they passed.

'Would you believe it? Old Seth's still on the road. Remember when we gave him a ride to Tucson last year?'

Lee glanced in the rearview mirror and uttered sardonically, 'Bob Dylan must be in town.'

They hadn't seen any other interesting-looking travelers hitching a ride on their journey and stopped only once, for some lunch at a small 'wholefood' diner in Casa Grande, south of Phoenix. They arrived at the observatory around six thirty that evening and immediately made arrangements to begin the observations Professor Bainbridge had organized for that night.

Lee spent six hours in the cage. When he eventually climbed down he was tired but relieved to have had good, steady seeing conditions. It was almost six thirty by the time he eventually crawled into bed, and he fell immediately into a deep sleep.

He awoke around 2:00 P.M. to the jangle of an alarm clock that he had set to wake him for his meeting with Matt later in the afternoon. As arranged, Matt had already collected the plates from the night assistant, and taken them to the developing lab so they could view them when Lee got up.

After a shower and a quick coffee, he met up with Matt in the photographic lab and took a look at the night's photos. Having confirmed they did indeed look as good as he had hoped, they headed with the night's catch straight to the director's office for consultation. They found Jim Bainbridge at his desk, sifting through a pile of papers.

'Hey guys! How did the observations go? Any luck with that radztar candidate?'

Lee withdrew three large negatively printed photographs from a plastic folder and spread them on the director's desk. 'Not sure to be honest, Jim. We found a little emission spectra near the position of the star-like object; might be just an H-II region of hydrogen gas—the kind you normally see in the spiral arms—or it could be an indicator of recent ejection activity. We'll need to do a more thorough investigation when we get back to Pasadena. The photos look about as good as we hoped to get.'

Lee picked up one of the photos and studied it.

'It's puzzling, though. The hydrogen-alpha emission that normally characterizes spiral galaxies is almost completely absent. All we register over the entire galaxy is emission from ionized nitrogen, Jim. This is pretty unusual for a spiral, maybe an indication that recent violent activity has taken place.'

Matt picked up a photo and studied it closely. 'I guess the next step will be to have a look at the radio intensities across the entire region. We might be able to get someone at the Very Large Array of radio dishes in New Mexico to check for hot-spot emissions in the arms. Though most radztars are radio quiet, you never know, it might be worth a try.'

Professor Bainbridge shuffled the photos, scrutinizing the ghostly negative images carefully with a large, brass-handled magnifying glass.

'Yes, that would seem the logical next move, Matt, especially since we are finding compact double radio sources lying across the nuclei of these disrupted spiral galaxies. The VLA radio 'scopes might be able to resolve smaller and smaller compact sources within them. Perhaps radztar NGC 502 is just the most visible of a number of ejections from the nucleus.'

'Well, it's a long shot. But what isn't in this game! We sure appreciate your help, Jim. Now that the 200-inch is virtually off limits to us, it's vital we continue the observations at other observatories whenever possible.' Dr. Drexler pulled up a chair and straddled it, facing the back rest, his arms folded across the top. 'I hope this won't rub off negatively on your position here. You know, they could accuse you of aiding and abetting those they consider to be undermining the orthodox view.'

Jim Bainbridge's bloodhound-like jowls heaved as he laughed out loud. 'Oh, I think my views on this are pretty well known by now to most people! I have argued from the beginning of this radztar business that they simply cannot be at the distance indicated by their redshift. There is no way even nature can conjure up that much power from such a relatively small object, if it's at the distance implied by the redshift. No, it's their small size that really sets the limits on what's possible here. And then there's the observation of their seemingly preferred, or quantized, redshift. You simply couldn't have objects receding at certain velocities and not others. It doesn't make sense to have gaps like that.'

'No, if they were truly part of an expanding universe, we would expect to see them reflecting a continuous range of redshifts right across the board. That they are observed to reflect only certain steps suggests that redshift is not a result of velocity. It must be due to some intrinsic effect of the material out of which the radztars are formed.' The director put the photo down, picked up a pen, and spun it between his fingers. 'From that standpoint, Lee, in my opinion it is certainly valid to continue this research. We can't just sweep the issue under the carpet, as many would like to do, and pretend it will somehow go away. What's at stake here is much more than the personalities involved, much more.'

'Lee, this call you got from chairman of the allocation committee, threatening to cut your observing time unless you alter your research, this is unprecedented in the modern era. It smacks dangerously of the methods used against Galileo and his supporters in the seventeenth century.' He rapped the pen angrily on the desktop. 'It's outrageous, and a clear violation of the principles by which scientific research is supposed to be conducted. It will reflect badly on the board members and the institution in the long run.'

Matt Mellencamp turned from studying a shelf of neatly ordered astronomical journals. 'A clear case of censorship, Jim. Monica's confirmation of the three radztars in NGC 3701 will probably get them even madder. Heck, I wouldn't be surprised if they are piling the wood around the stake for us in Caltech's central plaza right now!'

Jim Bainbridge pushed his castored leather seat from the desk, stretched his legs before him, and gave a low whistle.

'These people at Caltech are really overstepping their bounds. It was bad enough when they unilaterally took over full control of the 200-inch last year. Now they want to kick the Carnegie Institution's senior observers off the voting committees because they don't like their research. Well, I'm going to take this matter up with some of my colleagues and see if we can't prevail upon them to consider the negative consequences of this before we start back down the road of censorship and persecution. Persecuting people because of their beliefs didn't work in the past, because it was wrong, and it won't work today, because it is wrong. What do you intend to do, Lee?'

'Well I'm not going to alter the research I've been doing for the past twenty years, that's for sure. The observations are too important for that. But if push comes to shove, we already have enough observations to prove the associations are valid. What's important now, Jim, is to consider the physics of the situation. How does new matter originate? How does it behave? What state is it in?

These are largely theoretical questions, and one doesn't really need to freeze one's butt in the cage all night seeking an answer to them. We need to find a physical explanation that will account satisfactorily for the discordant redshifts. Ted Howell and Jiri Rappannipan are exploring interesting variations of Dirac's variable particle mass solution.'

'Their so-called C-field equations?'

'Yes, the creation-event. The state elementary particles are in at time = zero. We have always assumed, based on Newton's Law of Gravity, that particle masses are constant. But it may be that in newly-created matter, this law is broken; we just don't know. It might be they are created with masses different to those which make up the matter around us today. Perhaps particles start out with zero mass and simply acquire it as they age?'

'It's an interesting possibility, Lee. So, in that scenario, the newly emerged radztars are composed of particles born with a large redshift and then, as they evolve and acquire mass, they become more like ordinary mass particles and the redshift decays to more normal levels.'

'Yes. That's the idea we are looking at. It is certainly true that low-mass particles *can* yield higher redshifts. One can think of atoms as small clocks, with their rates governed by the mass of their electrons. Lower mass equals slower frequency, and slower frequency equals higher redshift. It's a simple formula. It's amazing: Dirac considered this back in the 1920s, and only now, with the discovery of radztars, are we again seriously reconsidering it.'

Jim Bainbridge picked up a photo and studied it again. 'Some people are always way ahead of the pack—everything has a way of going full circle and coming out right in the end.'

Lee glanced at the electric clock over the door. 'I hope so, Jim. I hope so. Hey! It's getting late. We'd better head back, Matt.'

Matt gathered up the photographs, put them back into the plastic folder, and snapped the fastener down with a click.

'Jim, thanks again. I'll let you know how things progress with these observations—and the committee's attempts to stop them. You can be sure that whatever happens, the progress we are making won't be influenced or curtailed by threats to my personal standing at Palomar. The issue is too big now, too important to be deflected by that kind of thing.'

Professor Bainbridge followed them to the steps of the main entrance, stood there while they packed a couple of bags into the trunk of their car, and then gave them a friendly wave as they drove off.

11

The Trap Is Set

Had Dr. Drexler known his regular Sunday tennis partner had been called to give evidence at the previous day's secret meeting of the telescope-allocations committee, he would probably not have been reaching for the phone and dialing Marty Schwitters' number now. But he was unaware of the meeting and its result.

'Hi, Mart. Hey, howya doing? No, I'm just packing up for the day and heading back home. It's been a long one—statistics, statistics, statistics—they are the most tiresome and time-consuming aspect of the entire business. If people would just pay heed to the observations, it would make our job a whole lot easier. This numbers-crunching business just makes for so much extra work.'

'You can say that again, buddy. There are so many variables—and people can marshal only those that support their particular thesis if they want to. It can be a real melting pot depending on the parameters and methods used to quantify the significance.'

Lee wedged the phone between his right ear and shoulder; with his hands free he shuffled together some papers and slid them into a briefcase. 'Can you ever convince people with statistics, Mart? I guess one has to analyze the problem from every conceivable angle, but I wish things could be more clearcut. But enough of our astronomical problems, I was calling to see if you were OK for tennis Sunday? Kay's going up to Glendale to spend the weekend with her family. I'm free, if you can make it.'

Dr. Schwitters had hoped to avoid contact with his colleague, at least until after the committee's letter had reached its destination, which wouldn't be before Monday of next week at the earliest. He was now caught off guard and struggled to find an excuse to avoid the encounter.

'Oh…well…er…I'm not sure about this Sunday, Lee. Banged the old knee the other day on the edge of the bath—could hardly stand for a day. Don't want to make it worse. I've also got a pile of reports that must be in early next week. Listen, Lee, I think this weekend is going to be difficult.'

'Hey, sorry to hear about that, Mart. You sure it wouldn't stand up to a bit of light practice? We needn't run around too much.'

'No, Lee. This weekend is going to be difficult. Look, when the knee improves and I'm through with this mountain of darn paper work…can I call you on the tennis when I'm feeling 100% and I've got more time?'

Lee felt the reason for avoiding the game sounded a little contrived but conceded that he had little option but to accept it gracefully.

'Well, if you're sure, Mart, I suppose I can fix something with my doubles partner.'

'Maybe in a a week or two, Lee.'

'Don't worry, Mart. Take it easy. Call me when you're able to make it.'

Lee replaced the phone slowely; Had he detected a slight evasiveness in Marty Schwitters' response? He banished the thought. Marty was an old and trusted friend. He must simply be under pressure of work and in need of extra time in which to finish it.

Lee grabbed his coat, strode out locking the door behind him and went home.

*   *   *

On Tuesday, September 24, 1980, Dick Turtle, director of Mt. Palomar observatory, convened a special meeting of the telescope-allocation committee at the Mount Palomar offices to discuss the case of Dr. Drexler.

He had decided the time had come to put a stop to Drexler's wild and improbable claims, claims that had been repeatedly and roundly refuted by the majority of his colleagues yet which he persisted in advancing, using up valuable hours on the big telescope hunting for his imaginary 'local' radztars. The conflict of interest had grown so wide now between the opinion of majority and the heretic, as director, it was his duty to resolve the issue one way or the other. He had before him now the names of all six current TAC committee members: Marty Schwitters, Arni Strong, Scott Ferris, Barny Berisford, Dr. Bruce Cunningham, and Dr. Gerry Springer. He had just spoken to, and received confirmation that, the first five could attend the planned meeting, and he now dialed the last on his list.

'Hello, Gerry, Dick Turtle. I'm calling to confirm the allocations committee meeting in my office tomorrow. I'm afraid I've had to move it to a little later in the afternoon instead of midday, as previously planned. I've spoken to the other members, and they are all able to come at this new time. I wanted to check with you that this would not be an inconvenience…no, 4 P.M. if that's alright with you. I don't want any absentees on this one; we have to come to a consensus if we are to resolve this troubling Drexler affair, Gerry. Hopefully we can get this sorted out once and for all. I think we all understand the issues involved. There seems only one realistic option left to us now…yes, indeed. Thank you, Gerry. See you tomorrow.'

Dr. Turtle replaced the receiver with a sense of satisfaction. A line had now been drawn in the sand. He had taken a stand to end the strife within the astronomical community caused by Dr. Drexler's constant attacks on mainstream cosmology.

*   *   *

The following afternoon, Turtle and his committee members convened their meeting with a sense of urgency. Dr. Turtle sat at the head of a long polished table; three members sat on each side.

'Thank you all for coming to this special meeting. We are convened today, as you know, to review the research and the allocation of observing time of Dr. Lee Drexler. This meeting has special importance because of both the nature of Dr. Drexler's research and the lack of a positive response to our earlier appeals to him to modify his attacks on the goals we are all committed to and…' Dick Turtle paused a moment to emphasize the point and peered over the top of his glasses '…are so well advanced toward realizing.'

'This is not the first time this committee has had reason to discuss Dr. Drexler's research. We have, on two earlier occasions, warned him of the serious consequences of a misuse of observing time on these, the most valuable scientific instruments in our arsenal. But these warnings have fallen on deaf ears. Dr. Drexler, gentlemen, seems impervious to reason, to the opinions of his colleagues, and most recognized authorities in the field. Dr. Drexler is becoming an embarrassment to this institution and its aims with his constant attacks on the foundation of the expanding universe. He therefore forces us to take stronger measures to counter these attacks.

'In view of Dr. Drexler's attacks on the orthodox position and his refusal to support the institution's aim of endeavoring to refine the rate by which universal expansion is proceeding, I hereby move that the committee is left with no further option but to deny Dr. Drexler's requests for further time on the institute's telescopes, both here and in Chile, beginning next year—unless he redirects his research in accordance with the wishes and the aims of the institution. If Dr. Drexler wants to continue undermining the official position, he will have to make arrangements to do it elsewhere.'

'I formally move this proposal. Any questions or objections before we go to a vote? Yes, Dr. Schwitters?'

'This is a difficult decision for me personally, Dr. Turtle. Lee and I are old friends. Together with Scott Ferris here, we go back almost to the beginning of Palomar. Though these days we don't see eye to eye on the redshift issue, I don't believe it is right or necessary to start censoring people because of their professional views. My own personal position happen to coincide with the majority in the redshift debate, but I have to acknowledge the right of others to disagree. I believe we should keep an open mind to the possibility that new and unexpected discoveries may lie around the corner that may—and I repeat, *may*—alter the present position. For example, the very unexpected discovery I played a small part in some years ago.'

Chairman Turtle lowered his head and peered at Marty Schwitters over the rim of his glasses. 'You are referring to the puzzle over radztar redshifts, Dr. Schwitters?'

'Yes. But I am also concerned that some of Drexler's observations and claims have not been as fully and seriously investigated by researchers who are committed to the conventional picture as they might have been. Indeed, one must admit that Drexler has his supporters and sympathizers too, and some of these are very eminent in their field. I am concerned that attempting to prohibit research because it doesn't conform to the orthodox position is an unwise step and may set a dangerous precedent. It is a precedent that seems based more on emotion than reason. Telescope time is a valuable commodity, and of course it must be apportioned wisely if we are to get the most out of their use, but we must also respect the expert observational skills of our senior and experienced astronomers. We should also consider the possible negative fallout such a ban may engender should the general public get wind of the decision to ban a top astronomer because of his views. The credibility of the institution may be tarnished, not to mentioned the integrity of the scientific method. For these reasons, I believe a ban would do more harm than good. I feel obliged to abstain from this ballot.'

'Scott Ferris? What is your view on this proposal?'

'I have to agree with Dr. Schwitters. I think a ban would be a very unwise move. Look, I'm as opposed to Lee Drexler's claims as anyone. Heck, I didn't talk to him for five years because of our differences on the redshift issue. I really felt he was doing Hubble a great disservice, that he wasn't showing the great man his due respect! But hey, Lee *is* one hell of an observer, no question. And because he's been around here for so long, it seems unfair to summarily ban him from the tools of his trade because his views are unorthodox. I agree, a ban would probably do more harm than letting him continue his research, especially to Palomar's public image. I'm gonna have to go with Marty on this one.'

Dr. Turtle removed his glasses and looked about the table as he wiped them on a folded white handkerchief.

'Two abstentions—right, anybody else?'

Dr. Arni Strong raised his hand. 'I support the motion. I don't accept Scott's reservations that respect for experience or seniority should be the motivating consideration in this case. Both Dr. Drexler and Scott have over the years been assigned the lion's share of observing time at Palomar, and in Drexler's case, his research has failed to shift opinion in favor of his views. In my opinion, objective evidence of this failure can no longer be ignored, and Dr. Drexler's future applications must be judged on scientific merit. If we do not follow this principle, then we shall end up compromising the very goals we are all committed to. I second the proposal.'

'Two abstentions. One for. Dr. Berisford?'

'I support the motion, Dr. Turtle. Dr. Drexler simply hasn't convinced the majority of his colleagues in over twenty years of claim and counter-claim. There has been a steady decline in citations of his work in the annual reviews, and few young astronomers are coming forward to follow the lines of his inquiries. Drexler's research not only lacks focus and specific goals, it is now time to move on and give others a chance to help refine distance scales and the deceleration parameters of the expanding universe. I believe that it is now only right to give the younger generation a chance to use the facilities, and Dr. Drexler should not in the future expect privileged treatment based on his seniority.'

The director ticked at the names of his committee members on a piece of paper, then looked up. 'Two abstentions. Two for. Dr. Springer, can we have your decision on this.'

'I support the motion. We have to get on with the job of confirming the expansion of universe. The constant attacks on this, the most successful theory in the history of astronomy, are completely unwarranted and without foundation. We mustn't let one errant view hold us back or slow us down. We must move on to complete the job, even though our decision may be criticized in some quarters. If Dr. Drexler's claims were to be validated, they would have been by now.'

Dick Turtle looked around the table. 'Dr. Cunningham?'

'I'm afraid I can't support this motion, Dr. Turtle. Apart from the obvious ethical questions that have been raised by Dr. Schwitters and Scott Ferris, I have some sympathy for Drexler's position. I personally favor the views of those who argue for the continuous-creation theory. Yes, galaxies may be receding, but could this not be just part of the recycling process? As they recede, new matter may spring up in the space rendered vacant by their recession. It is conceivable that this new matter may appear in the form of radztars ejected from exploding galaxies. Yes, I am appealing for tolerance—and a little more time. Let us all think this through very carefully. One might not buy Drexler's claims, from the *single* big bang perspective, but they might conceivably be used to support a lot of little ones. Of course, no one wants to see a cosmological theory that has served us so well for so many years invalidated overnight. But what is of greater importance, gentlemen, the defense of a misplaced belief or the proof of a valid one? I must oppose the motion at the present time.'

'Thank you, Dr. Cunningham. I have taken note of your reservations. Any other objections? No? Right, we'll go to a show of hands. For the motion? Three. Against? One. Abstentions? Two. As chairman, it looks as though responsibility for casting the deciding vote falls to me. Thank you gentlemen. The "ayes" have it. The motion is carried, four votes to three.'

'The next item on the agenda is to agree on the text of the letter informing Dr. Drexler of the committee's decision and reason for the proposed denial of further observation time. I propose that we adopt a formal communiqué to the effect that the committee judges Dr. Drexler's research to be contrary to the aims and aspirations of the institute and that it is no longer reasonable to assign time to pursue research aimed at establishing the association of radztars with nearby galaxies. Starting next year, applications for observation time on the institute's facilities at Mt. Wilson, Palomar, and Chile are to be denied unless Dr. Drexler redirects his research. Any objections, amendments? No? Well, thank you all for attending. With due respect to the views of the abstainers, the motion is hereby duly adopted. Dr. Drexler will be informed of the committee's decision, in writing, forthwith.'

*   *   *

Lee rose late on Saturday morning, as was his custom on weekends when at home in Pasadena, and made it downstairs as Kay was clearing away the remains of her breakfast.

'Good morning! Good Lord, look at the time! I'd better call Marcus and see if he can play tomorrow.' Lee poured a coffee. 'You're off to your Mom and Dad's too!'

Kay dropped some crockery in the sink with a clatter. 'Yes, Connie and Alicia are coming over in the evening. What's up with Marty Schwitters? You normally play with him on Sundays.'

'Marty can't make it; banged his knee or something and says he's got a pile of paperwork. He sounded a little evasive on the phone, like he was embarrassed at having to refuse. It's not like him; he's as keen on playing tennis as I am. His excuse seemed a bit contrived to me.'

'Oh, don't worry, Lee. Marty's an old friend. I doubt there's anything up. He probably does have work to finish—that does happen.'

'Yeah, well, Marc can probably make it.'

'Hey, what time are you heading off to Glendale? I need to put some air in one of the rear tires before you go.'

'I should go soon, I told Mom I'd get there for lunch. You want some more coffee before I throw it out?'

'Thanks. Let me just call Marcus; he might be planning something.'

Lee received confirmation that Marcus Greenfield was available and happy to play then went to check the car. By eleven he was standing in the driveway, waving Kay off to Glendale, an hour's drive north of Pasadena.

'Have a good game tomorrow, honey. There's some pizza and stuff in the fridge—just put it under the broiler. See you tomorrow evening, I should be back around eight.'

'Maybe Marc and I'll go for some Mexican at the Ponderosa.' Lee stood a moment watching her back into the street then made his way over to the garage to check over his tennis gear.

*　　　*　　　*

Lee arrived at his office on Mt. Palomar Drive the following Monday morning. After parking his car he was greeted by Dr. Arni Strong, who had arrived at the same time.

'Hi, Lee. Have a good weekend? Do anything exciting?'

'No, Arni, nothing special. I was on my own. Kay went over to see her family for the weekend. I just relaxed at home, catching up on things one always puts off doing until times like that. Played some tennis with a friend of mine. Marty couldn't make it. He had a bad knee or something.'

'Oh, really? He was at the telescope-allocations committee meeting last week. Seemed OK then.'

Dr. Strong pulled a sheaf of papers and a briefcase from the back seat, locked his car, and headed with Lee toward the building's porticoed entrance. 'Hope they didn't vote to cut back on my observing allocation some more. If I lose any more time, I'll have to move to China and take up astrology or something!'

Dr. Strong tugged at one of the two heavy glass doors then stepped back to let Lee pass. 'Well, keep your passport up to date, Lee!'

Lee collected some mail from a row of personalized lockers in the hall, grabbed a coffee from the machine, and went to his office. Putting a couple of journals to one side, he opened a large white envelope with the official seal of the Palomar Observatory on it. After pulling the contents from the envelope, he started to read.

California Institute of Technology
Faculty of Astronomy and Astrophysics
Mt. Wilson and Palomar Observatories
318 Mt Palomar Drive
Pasadena, California

From: Telescope Allocations Committee
To: Dr. Lee DREXLER

The Telescope Allocations Committee is writing to advise you that, following their meeting today, further time using the institute's observa-

tional facilities cannot in the future be guaranteed due to the nature of your research.

In the judgment of the committee, because your persistent efforts to show a link between radztars and nearby galaxies has not been proved, next year may be the last for which allocation is granted unless a substantive redirection of your research is made. The following is the draft of the committee's principal concerns, communicated for your information.

'The TAC cannot continue allocating large amounts of valuable time to research that is incompatible with the aims of the institute and the opinion of the majority in the astronomical community. Despite receiving the lion's share of time on the institute's large telescopes over the past twenty years, you have failed to shift opinion to your point of view. On top of this, few students and undergraduates are coming forward to follow the lines of your inquiries, and fewer citations are appearing in the astronomical reviews.'

Though certain members of the committee voiced the concern this action might bring discredit to the institution, the majority agree priority in allocating time must in future be sanctioned by scientific merit.

The committee is unable to assign time to research that is deemed both unproductive and undermining to the aims of the institute. If, Dr. Drexler, you agree to use your expertise in assisting your colleagues in refining the rate of galactic recession, then we may review this decision. In view of the increasing demand from young astronomers who wish to use the telescopes, we cannot in future sanction time on research that runs contrary to the aims of the Mt. Palomar Observatory.

September 25, 1980

Lee put down his coffee and stared at the letter, face blank, drained of expression. After reading over the ultimatum again, he crossed to the window. A lone seagull was spiraling high above, first soaring and then diving in the wind. Lee suddenly felt wounded, vulnerable, and alone. Dazed and unsure what to do next, he had an overwhelming desire to escape the prison-like confines of his office and seek some open space where he could better breath. Picking up his coat, he stuffed the letter in his pocket and strode out. He crossed Mt. Palomar Drive, headed into the nearby park, and slumped onto a bench.

He pulled the letter from his pocket and read it again, slowly. Stunned by a mixture of confusion and disbelief, it was some time before he collected his thoughts sufficiently to be aware of his surroundings.

'So it's come to this? What are you protecting? The right to decree only your interpretation of nature's plan?' Lee kicked at the earth, muttering oaths born of indignation, rage, and despair. 'No! This can't happen again, not today.'

Slowly, he became aware of a young boy and girl lying on the grass a short distance away. He noticed the boy was holding a small brass telescope and was using it to follow a seagull floating high above.

'I spy with my little eye…hey, I could almost reach out and touch that seagull, Jeanie.' He looked at the telescope admiringly. 'Dad says we can go up on the roof tonight and look at the stars and planets if it stays clear!'

The boy rolled lazily on his side and turned the telescope on Lee. He waved his hand in the air as the figure in the long black overcoat slumped on the park bench, cupped both hands over one eye, and pretended to look back.

Dr. Drexler stuffed the letter back in his pocket, pulled himself upright, and walked slowly in the direction of the children.

'They say the rings of Saturn are a special sight!' Lee bent down as he reached the boy and looked admiringly at the small telescope. 'Hey, that's a mighty powerful 'scope you've got there!' Lee took the telescope and examined it. 'That'll show Saturn's rings real clear. You ask your dad where to look—that's a very special sight. Should show craters on the moon too!'

Lee smiled at the girl, handed the telescope back to the boy, and with a wave walked off into the distance. He was out of earshot when the boy rolled onto his back again and resumed his surveillance of the seagull and exclaimed disinterestedly, 'How would *he* know? I bet he's never even *seen* Saturn!'

Some three miles separated Mt. Palomar Drive from Lee's home, and he walked it now along the tow-path of the old canal that ran most of the way. Arriving unexpectedly, on foot and at midday, he surprised his wife, who was in the process of hanging out some laundry on a line in the backyard.

'Hi, honey. You're back early. I didn't hear the car.'

'Hi, Kay. The car? Oh yeah, I forgot about that. I walked back through the park and along the canal. I'm banned—they finally carried out their threat.'

Lee took the letter from his pocket and handed it to his wife.

'Oh, Lee, how can they do this? You were one of the first to observe with those great telescopes. You pushed them to the limits of observation, and now they repay your dedication by barring you from using them.'

'I opened the letter, and I just couldn't believe it. I just walked out. I wound up in the park and sat down to try and gather my thoughts. Palomar has been the center of my life for the past thirty years—I'm just trying to do my goddamned job, for Christ's sake!'

Lee took the letter from Kay's hand. 'They're making a big mistake. Marty was a part of that committee—no wonder he couldn't face me to play tennis. I felt something was up.'

He kicked at a green plastic watering can and sent it spinning along the side of the house. 'They didn't even have the courage to sign their names. Just "we" judge your work to be without value—without value! It's goddamned revolutionary—judge that!'

Kay picked up the laundry basket, slipped her arm into his, and coaxed her husband toward the house.

'What are you going to do, Lee. What can you do?'

'I'm going to call Turtle and demand an explanation. Find out what his little band of secret inquisitors is up to. There is no way they can say my research is valueless—it's absurd. This is gonna cause one mother of a barn dance. Some of my colleagues are going to get real mad when this gets out. This clique has overstepped the mark; this is outright censorship!'

'It doesn't speak well of the much-trumpeted "Age of Scientific Reason" we are supposed to be living in today.'

'You're damn right, Kay. These people are behaving like a bunch of medieval monks! I'm going to appeal; I want to challenge them to debate the facts openly. I don't accept these anti-democratic "behind closed doors" proclamations. What is this, the seventeenth century!'

Kay took her husband's coat and hung it on a peg in the hall. 'Well, I would wait awhile, until you've calmed down. Leave it awhile. I'll fix some lunch. Think over who you want to call first. Get some advice from Jim Bainbridge, or some other valued friend, before you go after these people.'

'Yeah, you're right, Kay. But I feel a sense of obligation here, a sense of responsibility. I, together with Scott Ferris and one or two others, have made an historic contribution to astronomical observations. Everybody acclaims our photographic atlases of galaxies—they just can't accept any opinion that contradicts the conventional belief, even when the observations demand it. Rather than consider modifications to their blessed beliefs, they are prepared to sacrifice their most experienced and dedicated astronomers. Hell, Kay, what's the point of looking through the goddamned telescope anymore if it is only to see what the director—what the committee—wants you to see? I can't do that.'

'Listen, you want me to call Jim and break the news to him, get some advice?'

He kissed his wife on the forehead. 'Yes, maybe I should call Jim first and talk with him about it. I just don't trust anyone at Palomar. How can I trust anyone there?'

Lee grabbed the phone, dialled Professor Bainbridges' number relayed the news.

'Yes, I know I had some warning shots, Jim, but I never really thought it would come to this. I didn't think they would go this far...yeah, you're damned right I'm going to appeal.'

The Kit Peak director pressed a lever on the side of his chair and snapped the backrest into a vertical position. He then leaned forward, rested his elbows on the desk, and spoke earnestly into the phone.

'Lee, I'm going to call some people. I'll see if we can't gather support to have Turtle revoke this decision. Good heavens! If we start condemning people for what amounts to a difference of professional opinion, we shall end up back in the middle ages before we know it. That won't do science any good at all.'

'Thanks Jim. I'll call you back later when I've contacted Turtle over this. I'll seek an appeal, I have a feeling that they won't listen, but it's worth a try.'

*　　　*　　　*

Dr. Drexler did indeed take his wife's advice and slept on the problem. The next morning, however, he knew the only immediate course of action was to call Dr. Turtle without delay to seek clarification of the letter and a possible appeal hearing. Upon reflection, he knew things had been moving in the direction that now transpired in the utlimatum thrown down by the establishment, but he never thought it would actually come to this. The sense of disbelief, betrayal and dispair left a sinking feeling in his stomach.

Lee went to the phone, dialed and then sat back and waited as the director's telephone rang for a moment.

'Hello? Turtle. Oh, Dr. Drexler, what can I do for you?'

'One thing you can do, Dr. Turtle, is arrange an appeals hearing. I want to ask your august committee what exactly their reasons are for finding my research without value and for refusing me observing time to pursue it.'

Turtle twisted in his chair. 'I'm afraid that it was a majority decision, Dr. Drexler. With a couple of abstentions, your continued research was deemed rather a waste of time. The general consensus amongst the committee members is that the redshift debate has been decided in favor of the cosmological interpretation and that the radztars have been assigned their correct redshift distance. That cannot be altered now.'

He droned on confidently, in a voice that sounded to Lee as though a carefully prepared script was being read aloud.

'...as that debate is now effectively closed, it seems rather pointless to allocate large amounts of observing time in a fruitless search to prove otherwise. If you would only agree to join our efforts to measure the expansion rate of the universe, our search for the mass that will allow us to decide whether it is open or closed, how it is decelerating, or any number of other mysteries pertaining to our goals, then we would welcome your expertise. But we cannot continue assigning time to those who undermine those goals, Dr. Drexler.'

Lee leaned forward and spoke into the mouthpiece with slow but polite deliberation.

'It is my contention, Dr. Turtle, that the conventional belief is mistaken. The observations clearly show that radztars violate Hubble's Redshift Law and therefore cannot be at their prescribed distance. I have produced not just one clear-cut example of a high-redshift radztar associated with a near low-redshift, galaxy—such as NGC 9134/502—but several others over the years. The real question, then, is why does the establishment persist in evading this evidence and prolonging the controversy? That is a question history will ultimately judge your committee's decision by—as it ultimately came to judge in the Galileo affair three centuries ago. In the meantime, I would have thought your committee might at least have the decency to put their signatures on the letter threatening to terminate my observing time, rather than hiding in anonymity like the referees who have so often frustrated and delayed the publication of my research papers. When news of this decision gets out, you may come to regret it. One thing that is for sure is that I won't be joining in your misguided efforts to measure the expansion rate of the universe. So, unless on appeal your committee rescinds its unjust and unwise decision, after some thirty years, Mt. Palomar and I will part company.'

Turtle brushed at his silver tie and let his gaze rest on the scene through the window.

'Well, that will ultimately be your decision, Dr. Drexler. With regard to leaks, someone has already informed the press about the committee's letter, and I've been asked to provide a copy to the *Los Angeles Times*. Indeed, they are sending a reporter to my office this very afternoon to seek clarification of the committee's decision. I am afraid this is not the way we wished for this to turn out, Dr. Drexler. We have tried in the past to persuade you to give up your heretical views and join us in mainstream research. We have even tried rather *stronger* methods, but you have consistently shown that appeals to common sense and the wishes of the majority in this matter are of little concern. Now, I'm afraid, you must shoulder the consequences. With regard to an appeal, yes, you will be entitled to one before the full committee. You will have the right to put forward your case for continued observational facilities, and you may seek the committee's reasons for their decision. Do you wish to lodge an official appeal, Dr. Drexler?'

'Yes, Dr. Turtle, I do.'

'Very well, I will notify the committee and get back to you when an appeal hearing has been arranged.'

Lee put down the phone and turned to his wife.

'What was his reaction?'

'He says I can continue observing so long as I concentrate on the things they are interested in—like helping to measure the speed of expansion of the universe! I really don't think they have ever listened to any of the evidence I've put forward. But I can appeal against their decision—not that it will do much good. Apparently the *L.A. Times* has gotten wind of the letter and wants to publish it. Should be interesting tomorrow! Turtle said he will call me back in the next few days after he has arranged an appeal hearing.'

12

The Appeal

The director of Mt. Palomar had indeed called back a few days after receiving Dr. Drexler's request for an appeals hearing, and Lee awoke today in the knowledge that he would mount his defense later that very morning—or, if defense was not possible, since he had declined the committee's offer to withdraw its threat if he changed the direction of his research, at least draw out from them a more explicit reason for his ban.

Kay was already up an hour before Lee, who, in the process of buttoning his shirt, eventually made it downstairs and entered the kitchen around 9:30.

'Well, decision day, Lee. I hope they listen to reason. Coffee?'

Dr. Lee Drexler fastened the topmost button of his shirt, pulled the plain red tie into place, and slipped on his jacket.

'Thanks, Kay. One can live in hope—no, one *must* live in hope—though I don't rate the chances too highly in this case. I don't think reason comes into it. If that were the issue, we'd probably be considering a different cosmology by now, following up on a different perspective. But at least it's a last-ditch opportunity to try and argue my case and draw them out on the real reason behind the allocation committee's decision.'

Lee checked his watch. 'Hey, I'd better move. Mustn't hold up the Inquisition. I'm supposed to be there by eleven o'clock.'

He sipped hurriedly at a cup of coffee then picked up some papers, put them in a briefcase, and headed for the door.

Kay followed her husband to the front porch and watched as he walked to the car and got in.

'Good luck, honey. Be sure to call me as soon as you know something, OK?'

Lee smiled as he turned the key and gunned the motor.

'Sure, I'll call soon as I know something.'

Kay lingered on the porch. 'Just remember, honey. If you are wrong, it doesn't make any difference. If you are right, it is enormously important—keep that in mind.'

Lee closed the door, wound down the window, and eased the car out of the driveway.

'I will. Maybe I'll offer that piece of wisdom to the committee to consider too. Thanks, see you later.'

Margaret Summers, the receptionist at Mt. Palomar Drive, was a light-hearted, cheerful soul who had been at the center for some twenty-two years, and Lee Drexler felt her good-natured personality even more strongly today as he entered the building and inquired sarcastically whether the members of the Inquisition had assembled yet.

'Good morning, Dr. Drexler, Yes, the committee is expecting you. Dr. Turtle and the other members have gone on up. Room 21A, second floor.' Margaret looked furtively up and down the corridor, then leaned forward, gave him a friendly wink, and whispered, 'Don't worry, this is the twentieth century; they won't put you under house arrest!'

Dr. Drexler checked his hair and straightened his tie in the reflection of the glass partition and thanked her for the good news and the directions.

'Better go up and face the music!'

Lee climbed the elegant curved marble stairway, the walls of which were lined with a series of black-and-white photographs of past Caltech members and portraits paying homage to astronomy's illustrious forefathers. He stopped a moment and stared at a photo of Hubble. 'This is your goddamn fault, Edwin. If you hadn't been so darned sure redshift equals distance, I wouldn't be in this mess fighting for my professional future.'

On reaching the second floor, he located room 21A by the large gold plaque that read: TELESCOPE ALLOCATIONS COMMITTEE.

Lee hesitated a moment then knocked at the door and pushed it open. Against a blindingly bright back-lit window, six figures—clothed in the scarlet robes of seventeenth-century Roman cardinals—sat behind a long table in throne-like high-backed gilded chairs. In front of them stood a chair and small table, upon which sat a glass and jug of water. To Lee's utter astonishment, the room appeared to be decorated in a style that would have befitted the trial of Galileo some three centuries earlier; with a polished marble-tiled floor, frescoed ceiling, and heavy draped curtains. A strong smell of incense pervaded the room, appearing to come from something smoldering in a tall copper vase standing in a corner.

As his eyes gradually adjusted to the bright light, a glimpse at the cardinals' faces revealed the grotesque and distorted features from a Hieronymus Bosch painting: distorted masks of clown-like characters, sick and ridiculous beyond redemption.

The middle figure, whose throne was raised slightly higher than those on either side, looked up as Lee took in the scene.

'Ah, Dr. Drexler! Come in.'

As he spoke, the scene reverted to normality, and Lee could make out the committee members, dressed in somber gray suits.

As he stepped into the room, the door, propelled by a sudden gust of wind, slammed shut behind him and he recognized the speaker in the high chair as Dr. Dick Turtle. Turtle gestured toward the small table.

'Please, sit down. The committee has convened this morning to hear your appeal following their meeting on September 25. At that meeting, the committee members, whose responsibility it is to allocate observing time on the institute's telescopes, voted not to renew your application unless a fundamental redirection of your research agenda is put into effect. Do you have a specific appeal or reason you wish to put forward as to why the committee should reconsider their decision, Dr. Drexler?'

Lee certainly did wish to sit down. The hallucinatory scene he had just witnessed induced a sudden weakness in his knees, and he willingly pulled out the chair and sat facing the long table. After a moment he collected his dazed thoughts, straightened his back and shoulders, and took a deep breath.

'I would certainly wish to ask exactly what reason and on what authority the committee bases its unprecedented decision to effectively obstruct my research. It is, in my view—and, I may add, in the opinion of several distinguished colleagues—unjust, unwarranted, and contrary to the principle of free and unfettered scientific inquiry.'

Dr. Turtle leaned forward in his throne-like chair, looked at Lee over the top of his glasses, and said gravely, 'As chairman of the committee and director of the institute's observing facilities, both I and my predecessor, Professor Hayman, have on more than one occasion urged you, Dr. Drexler, to give up your heretical notions and participate, along with your colleagues, in mainstream astronomical research. Sadly—and unfortunately, for yourself—my pleas and those of my fellow committee members appear to have fallen on deaf ears. No one is to blame for the current situation but yourself. Your constant efforts to undermine the orthodox view, the established cosmology, and replace it with your radical notions have left the committee with little choice, Dr. Drexler. Some of the greatest and most distinguished scientists of our era—and, indeed, long before it—have been involved in fashioning and refining the most convincing cosmological picture the human mind has ever conceived. For over seventy years, the observations have been tested and refined and then double-checked and further refined. No stone, no star, no galaxy has been left unturned in our efforts to reveal nature's true plan, culminating today, Dr. Drexler, in the most extraordinary knowledge that our universe is expanding in all directions following its primordial explosion fifteen billion years ago.

'A most marvelous and awe-inspiring achievement, most would agree. But you want to tear it all down, say it is not true! That all our efforts and those of our illustrious forbears—from Newton to Einstein, from Laplace to Hubble and Shapley—were all in vain! Do you mean to suggest that you, Dr. Drexler, have single-handedly succeeded where they have all failed to comprehend nature's grand plan?'

Lee had felt hunted for some time. Now he felt the members of the committee eyeing him with hawk-like scrutiny, waiting for the moment to swoop and devour their prey.

'I have the greatest respect for the pioneering work of our founding fathers, Dr. Turtle. Indeed, it is because of their heroic efforts that we stand here today. But the picture they derived was only as good, only as complete, as the observations of the day permitted. As technology has advanced and the observations improved, new data has constantly changed the evolving picture, to the point where, it is my thesis, the picture must be altered again to take into account the discordant nature of the radztars' high redshifts. Having due respect for the achievements of our forbears should not blind us to the inevitable shortcomings of theories and explanations that are derived from a technology less advanced and sophisticated than ours is today.'

Professor Turtle raised a hand as a barrier to Lee's verbal defense, leaned forward, and addressed the committee members with an ingratiating smirk.

'Dr. Drexler, are you suggesting *now* that the entire foundation of physics is wrong in order to justify your "local" radztar claims? I don't think that is going to help your case today.'

Suddenly Lee felt his vision blur, and for a brief moment he saw the figures arraigned before him dissolve back to characters from the Holy Roman Inquisition. The cardinals nodded and brayed in muffled agreement to the thrust of their leader's interrogation. Some hurriedly jotted down notes.

'Disagreeing with the established redshift doctrine is bad enough. *Now* he wants to sweep away the whole foundation of established physics in order to justify his heretical notions!' Turtle dismissed Lee Drexler's reply with a broad sweep of his outstretched arm. 'No, Dr. Drexler. This cannot be.'

Lee struggled to focus his mind on the charges being leveled against him and formulate a coherent line of defense.

'It is an explanation that may be proposed in order to account for the anomalous redshifts, Dr. Turtle. Indeed, it is *required*, in my view, in order to explain the observations that appear to show radztars and galaxies are physically associated. The way the majority apparently wish to proceed is by making observation fit a preconceived theory. I say theory must be made to fit the observations.'

A committee member from the chairman's left flank leaned forward.

'Dr. Drexler, you have been given a great deal of valuable observing time on the world's most powerful telescopes—over 100 hours prime time, in fact. If, in all that time, you have failed to convince the majority of your colleagues of your claims, what reasons can you offer now to convince this committee that more time will change the situation?'

Lee reached for the jug, half filled the glass, and took a sip.

'There are many galaxies that are yet to be searched for associated radztars, and I, along with my colleagues, have indicated around which particular galaxies we expect to find radztars. In my opinion, we have had a high success rate; therefore the prediction needs to be further investigated. If the prediction is vindicated, then it supports our thesis. We do not look for radztars around any galaxy; we can predict from past successes the more likely radztar-producing candidates, and this has been clearly and duly demonstrated in the many photographic observations and statistical tests that have been made. As prediction and verification are the twin pillars of the scientific method, it is incumbent upon the institution and this committee to allow this process to be carried forward. To arbitrarily deny this procedure, to withhold this right, is to conspire against the very principles science itself professes to aspire to, indeed, upon which its very foundation rests.'

'There are two issues on trial here, gentlemen. You charge that I deliberately set out to undermine the orthodox view, a charge I deny. The other is the charge that may be brought against the committee itself in that its action violates the very principles upon which the entire scientific enterprise has been founded. If the committee denies me the right to follow up a legitimate field of inquiry, then it is itself violating a fundamental principle of scientific research. Do we really know all there is to know about the universe at this particular point in time? It would indeed seem rather fortunate, and not a little arrogant of us, if we were to believe so considering the span of human recorded history and the great civilizations that have sought answers to the same questions we pursue today. In view of the long history of conceptual revolutions, it seems to me, gentlemen, a dangerous mistake to believe that at this particular moment in time we now know all there is to know, that the book of revelation is now closed. But that is what this jury's decision will look like if it denies the process of legitimate inquiry to continue.'

Turtle leaned back, crossed his arms, and looked up at the ceiling a moment before responding.

'Fine sentiments, Dr. Drexler. But we are not convened here today to listen to a philosophical treatise. What we are looking for is a firm commitment from you that you will stop your persistent attacks on mainstream cosmology. Your provocative claims are the cause of much frustration within the astronomical community and they bring discredit and ridicule to the institute. Can the committee conclude from your response that you remain unrepentant?'

The word 'unrepentant' so startled Lee he felt as though he was about to experience another bout of seventeenth-century deja vu, but he managed to rally his focus and concentrate on his defense.

'I have nothing to repent, as I have not sinned, Dr. Turtle. I have made a significant scientific discovery, one that should be evaluated and further examined by all responsible astronomers. I submit that the observations, as I have submitted them, are accurate, and that they call for an urgent review of our present understanding of the universe.'

Dr. Turtle removed his glasses and laid them carefully before him. He looked up and down the long table to confirm that other members had heard enough of Dr. Drexler's response, and said, 'Very well, Dr. Drexler, we have listened to your defense. I must now ask you to step outside while the committee considers its response to your appeal. Thank you. I will call you when we have reached a verdict in this matter.'

Lee got up, went out to the hall, and shut the door. He had time to smoke two cigarettes before the door was opened and he was called back to receive the judgment of the committee.

'Dr. Drexler. The committee, on reviewing your case and listening to your appeal, has judged that their original decision to revoke your observing status stands. As you are unwilling to abandon your heretical notions and conform to the direction and research priorities of the institution, the committee has no option but to terminate your observing status at the end of the present year, both here, at the Mt. Wilson and Mt. Palomar observatories, and at the institution's facilities in the Southern Hemisphere as well. The committee hearing is now terminated. Thank you, Dr. Drexler.'

*   *   *

Kay thought something must be up as she paced the front room nervously. The telephone had started ringing constantly with reporters wanting to get an exclusive interview with her husband—or, perhaps, if not with him, *Would she like to offer any information on the possible outcome of the appeals hearing and what their plans might be after it?* If it rang much more, Kay thought she would have to take it off the hook, but as she was waiting for Lee's call, she knew that wasn't really an option. She would have to endure the constant calls until he rang. She had drawn the curtains, though, and put the TV on in case of any breaking news.

Finally the call came from a callbox situated in the lobby of Mt. Palomar offices on Mt Palomar Drive. Dr. Drexler anticipated a lively meeting with the press assembled outside, but he wanted first to let his wife know of the committee's decision.

'Hi, honey. No, it's all over. They won't listen, they won't change their decision. No, just more of the same: "If you abandon your research and come and help us with ours you're welcome, etc." This is not going to look good…this is not going to look good.'

Kay sat on the arm of the settee and watched as reporters gathered outside the entrance of Mt. Palomar Drive on the television news.

'The phone just won't stop ringing here, Lee. You'll have to tell them something, make a statement. Both Jim Bainbridge and Ted Howell called. They want to know what happened. I told them to ring back later.'

'Kay, sit tight, I'll be back soon. I think the press is on Turtle's tail right now. The *L.A. Times* wants a statement from me too. I'll call you when I'm through with the interviews.'

Lee put the phone down and strode towards the throng of reporters waiting outside.

'Dr. Drexler, Bruce Morton, *L.A. Times.* Could you tell us the outcome of your appeals hearing. Did the committee agree to reinstate your observing allocation?'

Lee stood on the steps of the building's main entrance facing a multitude of reporters, each thrusting a microphone in his face, straining to record his first reaction to the committee's verdict.

'No. No, they did not. They presented me with an ultimatum: either I change my research or I'm barred from using the institute's facilities.'

'What did you say?'

'I said I wasn't prepared to accept their proposal, on principle.'

'So you are effectively barred from pursuing your research at Mt. Palomar, Dr. Drexler?'

'Yes, and at the institute's facilities in Chile, too.'

Bruce Morton continued, endeavoring to hold the microphone steady amidst the scrum of reporters, each trying to put their questions to the maverick astronomer.

'This kind of institutionalized decision to bar a scientist from the tools of his trade is unprecedented in the modern era, isn't it? What do you think about their decision?'

'I believe that it is an attempt by the establishment to stifle the voice of those who question current cosmological assumptions—the belief that our universe is expanding from some initial explosion. It is a blatant violation of the academic rules of tenure and freedom of research.'

'How will this affect your research, Dr. Drexler?'

'Luckily, I believe attempts to suppress the observations have come too late. Most of the important observations have already been made, at least in the visible part of the electromagnetic spectrum. The next stage will be to use satellites to study X-rays, infra-red, and microwaves—the part of the electromagnetic spectrum that is better observed from outside the Earth's atmosphere.'

'Do you plan to continue your research here, in the United States, or will you be seeking a position abroad, Dr. Drexler?'

'Well, I have been offered the use of some facilities at a privately-funded research center in Europe. So I will certainly consider that option, yes.'

'Do you feel personally victimized by the committee and your colleagues at the observatories?'

'Let me put it this way: I don't think it is necessarily a question of real science. It has more to do with sociology. By "real" science I mean taking accord of the facts; by sociology I mean taking accord of one's prejudices. But this is not something particularly new; the persecution of dissenting voices has a long history in human affairs.'

The *L.A. Times* reporter continued his barrage of questions in quick succession. He was aware this was an important event and he wanted to milk it for all it was worth. Not since the time of Galileo had a distinguished scientist been barred from the tools of his trade, and so publicly.

'Galileo, Bruno, Solzhenitsyn, the Senator McCarthy trials here in the United States in the 1950's...'

'Well, you draw the comparisons, Bruce. At least I suppose I haven't been burned at the stake or banished to a labor camp. But yes, I think the principle, the attempted coercion to try to get my research stopped or redirected, amounts to the same thing.'

Kay watched at home as her husband fielded several more questions, finally responding to one from a reporter from ABC television's *Nightly News*.

'And what are your plans now, Dr. Drexler?'

'Well, I'll be analyzing the satellite data closely and trying to develop an explanation for the intrinsic redshift of radztars. I believe redshift is a result of a variance in the mass of subatomic particles that make up the matter of the newly-emergent radztars. I also plan to write a book, setting out the observations so anyone who cares to acquaint themselves with the facts can judge for themselves the merits of the case.'

'Well, thank you, Dr. Drexler, and good luck.'

'This is Dan Arnold in Pasadena, handing you back to the studio in Washington.'

Kay suddenly felt devastated. She turned the sound of the television down, went to the window, and peeked through the curtain. Already, two mobile news teams were waiting in the road outside, one from a local radio station, Pasadena 3 FM, the other advertised as Red Mountain News, a television station covering the Bay area. She closed the curtain, returned to the kitchen, and filled a kettle. Though the sequence of events leading to today's dramatic outcome had been building for some time, the reality of the situation now left her saddened and concerned for the future. Lee had spent thirty years at Mt. Palomar, and now, even though he was approaching the age at which most men would be looking forward to retirement, he would have to uproot and seek facilities abroad to continue with his work.

They had talked before of the possibility of moving to another country as the opposition to her husband's research hardened at Palomar, but they had always agreed to let things ride. Lee always felt that 'just one more push' should convince the doubters and resolve the redshift debate in his favor. It had really been Kay's decision more than Lee's—he would get up and go anywhere, constantly traveling the world as he did. 'Sometimes I feel like I don't have a permanent place to hang my hat, Kay,' he once told her. But Kay had her family here, and although the girls had by now left home and were living independently, she still wasn't sure whether she could leave her elderly parents and all their friends at this stage in her life. It was one of those painful decisions, the kind which one postpones until circumstances conspire to make the choice for you.

Kay picked up a silver-framed photograph of Lee, taken on the day of his graduation from Caltech back in 1954. Starring at the black-and-white photo, she knew events had indeed now conspired to make the decision irrevocable.

She had not continued her job as assistant librarian at the faculty library after she met Lee and started a family. Lee's salary had been more than sufficient for them to live in modest comfort. But now the future was suddenly uncertain and they would have to consider their options carefully. She knew Lee had planned to write a book, but even when that was completed it wasn't certain he would find a publisher for it, or indeed that it would be promoted and read by many of his colleagues—not to mention the public in general.

Kay Drexler replaced the photograph and crossed to a window that looked out on the back garden, now crisscrossed with the lengthening shadows of an autumnal afternoon. She wished Lee were with her now. She worried desperately for him and what the future held.

13

A Conference of a Different Kind

Jack Astra, artist, sometime mystic, and longtime astronomy enthusiast, always made for the basement 'Astronomy' section of Barnham's Bookshop when he visited London from his home in the Canary Islands. There were other good bookshops to browse in, of course, but Barnham's, he thought, held the widest selection of astronomy titles, ranging all the way from introductory courses for beginners by the popular science writer Larry Longmann to specific and very technical texts for university graduates. Jack didn't look too closely at the thick academic volumes. This was partly due to the fact he was short and they were usually placed on the top shelves and therefore difficult to reach, but, more importantly, it was because he didn't understand the complex mathematical equations that filled them. He often mused to himself that he stood a better chance of unraveling the code embedded in the Rosetta stone than comprehending a page in the heavy volumes intended for the university students.

What Jack looked for were books by astronomers who tried to communicate the latest theories and discoveries in a way that could be understood by the general public. The less technical jargon and the more pictures the book had—especially pictures of exploding stars and galaxies—the better. But he was also particularly searching for anything on the mysterious radztars that had caused such dissent in the astronomical world, or books dealing with the subject written by their chief researcher Dr. Lee Drexler, his colleagues or collaborators. Jack already had several books on his shelf by Dr. Drexler's closest supporters, Professors Ted Howell, Jim Bainbridge, and Jiri Rappannipan.

Today, as he searched the tightly-packed shelves, he struck an astronomical goldmine. In the 'New Releases' section, he was surprised to come across a book entitled *The Redshift Mantra* by none other than Dr. Lee Drexler himself. Admittedly, it had been some time since he last had the opportunity to browse Barnham's shelves. There hadn't been a book by Drexler then, or at least he hadn't come across one, and he hadn't heard of one being published since his last visit to London some two years earlier. He had read some reports in the press that a Russian team under the direction of Boris Voronsky in the Ukraine was going to do some follow-up observations on some of Dr. Drexler's galaxy/radztar associations, but he hadn't heard any more on the subject.

Peering eagerly inside the front cover, he saw that it had been published only recently, in 1990, so it had been in print for only a few months. He took the book up to the check-out, made a purchase, and headed out the door for Baker Street Underground station, the Northern line, and the home of his computer-programmer friend, Martin Elliot in Belsize Park.

Flicking through the pages of Dr. Drexler's book while journeying to his friend's home in North London, he was delighted to find several black-and-white photographs of exploding galaxies. Furthermore, many showed the small star-like radztars apparently associated with the explosion. On some of the photos, radztars appeared to be buried in the actual spiraling arms of the disrupted galaxies; on others, they appeared to follow straight lines coming out of the nucleus, like peas from a peashooter. But something else also soon grabbed his attention, a small table listing the preferred values of radztar 'z.' Jack wasn't aware that radztars had 'preferred z' values. But now, as he glanced at the figures, his brain made a sudden and intuitive quantum jump to the mysterious harmonic scale of planetary distances from the Sun, which had so intrigued philosophers and physicists down the centuries, from Plato to Kepler, Bode, and Niels Bohr. He had made a point of memorizing the sequence of numbers in Bode's Law some time ago and now instantly recognized that the two sets of numbers closely matched, seemed to display a secret correspondence that was unlikely, he thought, to be mere coincidence. He would double-check as soon as he got to his friend's home.

'Hi, Jack, have a good day?' Martin spun on his computer stool as Jack entered the ground-floor flat, tossing his friend's set of spare keys on the side table as he did so.

'Sure did, Mart. Picked up a pile of oils and brushes. It's hard to get Rowneys in Spain sometimes. Found a book by the radztar astronomer, Lee Drexler, too. I didn't know he'd written one. Check this.' Jack pulled the book excitedly from a brown paper bag and handed it to his friend. '*The Redshift Mantra!*'

Martin Elliot took the book and leafed through it with interest.

'Hey! Great title! Where did you find it?'

'Barnham's. I found something quite curious when looking through it on the way back.' Jack Astra quickly turned to the page containing the table on the radztars' preferred 'z's. 'Look at this table here. Radztars apparently cluster around certain specific values. I didn't know that.'

'Don't think I've ever heard that they clustered either.'

'Yes, but do you know what? I think these preferred values match the harmonic spacing of the planetary orbits about the Sun—you know, Bode's Law? Do you have your astronomy encyclopedia handy? From memory, I'm sure these figures are pretty similar—I'd like to double-check.'

Martin pulled a thick encyclopedia from the bookshelf and opened it on an entry for Bode's Law. It didn't take them long to confirm Jack's suspicion as they ran their fingers excitedly down the list of numbers.

Jack bent close, as if willing the two sets of numbers closer together, but in his heart he knew they would find their own correspondence, as though somehow preordained. Like a key fitting a lock. 'Hey! Just as I thought, it is very close. That's remarkable! Look.'

They placed the two sets of tables next to each other for comparison. In five cases out of nine regarding planets' orbital distances, sure enough, preferred cases of radztar 'z' corresponded.

'Pretty amazing, eh? Radztars are supposed to be at the farthest edges of the universe. Well, they always did look like stars through the telescope, and now they seem to reflect the attributes of our Solar System. Could it mean the origin of the preferred 'z's *and* the formation of planetary orbits are somehow a result of the same processes—that they're linked in some way?'

'Well, I'm not an astronomer, Jack, but it sure looks like there could be a connection there.'

Jack stared at the two sets of numbers, absorbed by the implication that there might be some hidden connection between the origin of the planets and the radztars. 'Might be worth drawing Drexler's attention to this. I've got a friend living in Germany; maybe he can track down his mailing address. I'm sure he would find it interesting. It could be important. There must be some connection here.'

*   *   *

Dr. Drexler and his wife had finally decided on the move from the United States when it became clear his institution would no longer sanction further time for his research on the telescopes under their jurisdiction. Following the ultimatum, 'Change the direction of your research or find another place to do it,' Lee had decided on the latter and reluctantly, though gratefully, decided to take up a research position offered by the sympathetic director of AstroNet, a private space-research group operating satellites for various European universities and institutes, based in Landshut, Germany. Both of their daughters had left home by then, had secured good jobs, and were living in shared apartments with friends their own age. This arrangement also had the added advantage that Alicia, who worked as an assistant to the copy editor of the L.A. environmental protection publication *EarthScan*, could keep an eye on Kay's parents. Connie, too, though working in marine conservation up in San Francisco, managed to get home once a month to see them. Kay would split her time between Germany and California. It meant a lot of extra travel, of course, but if this was what circumstances required, she could see little alternative but to accept it gracefully.

AstroNet had gone out of their way to help locate a reasonably-priced apartment for them to rent close to the offices at Landshut, and although Lee wasn't given a salary as such, a car and generous 'living' expenses were provided. If it was a step back from the glamorous, almost movie-star-like lifestyle he had enjoyed in California for most of the past thirty years, at least he was able to continue his research, making use of the latest data coming down from the new orbiting satellites the agency were operating. He also remained in close contact with a few sympathetic colleagues around the world who would make observations for him, clandestinely if need be.

Lee had finished writing his book and had managed to find a publisher for it in the form of an acquaintance who had started a small publishing company in Pasadena. It was not a massive print run; the reviews that appeared in the press were skeptical of his claims, to say the least, but the book had been extensively promoted and ordered by several university libraries and commercial bookstores in the U.S. and Europe. Life and research went on, and Lee felt a measure of comfort in the knowledge that now the general public had access to the facts if they wanted to study them.

Dr. Drexler was comparing two sets of tables in his office at Landshut when one of the two telephones on his desk rang. Without looking up, Lee stretched out a hand and inadvertently picked up the wrong telephone, then replaced the receiver and quickly grabbed the second.

'Drexler…'

'Lee, Jim Bainbridge. Great news, listen to this! Boris Voronsky's team in the Ukraine have confirmed the material bridge between NGC 4319/502 by observing the gas and dust lanes between the two in the far infrared. Looks like you were right all along! This is going to stir things up.'

'Are you sure, Jim?'

'They apparently got a very high definition picture, Lee. When they processed the plates and removed residual background glare, the bridge was there for all to see. This proves what you've been claiming all these years. This is sure going to cause some red faces back at Palomar.'

Lee laughed. 'Maybe they'll give me my telescope back! At least it should make it easier to publish the new book. It was tough getting the first one out.'

'Galileo had to wait awhile longer to get his dues, Lee.' Jim Bainbridge laughed. 'You'll soon be on your way to Stockholm. Congratulations!'

'Thanks, buddy. Maybe the tide is finally turning in our favor. Didn't think I'd live to see it, though, after all the fuss my observations created. Where did you see it?'

Astrophysical News. There's even a positive review in the editorial: "Do New Observations Support Radztar Astronomer?" Who knows where this will lead, Lee.'

'Hey, I was just looking at something I got in the mail. Apparently someone living down in Spain has noticed some kind of correspondence that appears to link Bode's Law and the preferred redshifts.'

'Is he an astronomer?'

'No, an artist. Says he's a cosmic surrealist—whatever that is.' He saw the figures in my book. I haven't had time to check yet, but the correspondence does seem to be there all right; check it out for yourself. You and Monica still going to the Madrid conference on 'High Energy Extragalactic Gamma Ray Sources' in December?'

'Yes, Lee. We're confirmed for that one'

'OK, Look forward to seeing you both—and hey, thanks for the news.'

Dr. Drexler hung up and stared thoughtfully at the tables.

*　　　*　　　*

The Russian confirmation of Lee's claims spread like wildfire. Soon teams in both China and Jodrell Bank in the UK confirmed their photo of bridging material, thus proving beyond doubt the nearby galaxy and the high-redshift radztar must be physically connected. Several leading cosmologists came forward and supported Lee, suggesting his observations would force astronomers to view galaxies and their evolution very differently in future. Physicists, too, were forced to reconsider the fundamentals of their own laws, for if redshift was not the result of velocity, then perhaps gravity and the mass of particles varied in the cosmic scheme of things, as some had predicted.

This belated acknowledgement of Lee's claims had a beneficial impact on Lee's publishing career. His first book was translated into six languages and was reprinted five times in the ensuing six years. His second, an autobiographical affair focusing on the sociological aspect of the radztar controversy, topped the best-seller lists and stayed there for several weeks. For the first time since leaving the United States some ten years earlier, Lee now had a measure of material security and, more importantly, a measure of recognition from the scientific community that his claims were valid after all. An official acknowledgement even appeared in the *Mt. Palomar Bulletin*, conceding that a grave professional injustice had been afforded Dr. Drexler (though, they claimed, it had been due to both the pressure to satisfy telescope demand and the enormity of the implications deriving from Dr. Drexler's claims).

Lee had also kept in touch with his artist aquaintence in the Canary Islands and promised, whenever time and circumstance permitted, to visit—if not in his professional capacity then perhaps for a short holiday. Lee had become convinced the correspondence between Bode's Law and the radztars' preferred redshifts was of fundamental importance and wanted to discuss the connection with him. A visit would also provide an opportunity to see the artist's paintings. The opportunity finally came when the Astronomy Institute, on the Island of Tenerife, invited Lee to give a talk on the implications of his radical proposals. Lee had sent a message enquiring whether Jack would be home around mid-January, when he was due to arrive.

*   *   *

This was certainly exciting news to Jack Astra, and as he scanned the short note now he hailed the news aloud to his long-time partner, Sutra Diamond, in the adjoining room. Jack had already learned from their correspondence that Lee's father had been a member of an avant-garde group of New York artists in the early part of the century. It seemed Lee rather admired his own form of 'Space Art,' though he wasn't too sure what Lee thought of his rather bizarre views on the cosmos.

'Hey, Su, Lee Drexler's coming to Tenerife!'

Jack and Sutra met in London in '87 when she was on a three-month working holiday from Australia, teaching English to foreigners at a small private school in Fulham. At the time, Jack was squatting a particularly leaky old house in Kilburn and gratefully accepted Sutra's offer of a room in her flat for a share of the rent. Eventually Sutra applied for and got a post at a language school in the Canary Islands, and they decided to move to Tenerife. Jack had imagined the Canary Islands would be quite tropical: Golden sandy beaches, swaying coconut palms, and grass-skirted girls dancing topless to the hypnotic rhythm of steel guitars, à la Gauguin's Tahiti.

Jack got the palm tree part right—the island was covered with them—but was somewhat dismayed to find it was actually very mountainous (at 12,000 ft, the volcano that straddles the island of Tenerife is the highest peak in all of Spain.) Furthermore, he soon learned that the sand was black—and, in Jack's view, sand wasn't sand if it wasn't white. Still, it did have it's compensations; the girls were certainly very beautiful, and he soon found the easy, relaxed pace of life and year-round temperate climate more than compensated for the topographical shortcomings. He would have to learn Spanish, of course, but that shouldn't be an insurmountable problem.

'Be great to meet up and talk over my ideas with him. Probably thinks them pretty whacky, but at least he can see the paintings. His father was an artist.'

Sutra stepped into Jack's studio and studied the letter carefully. 'Oh, I'm sure he finds your ideas interesting, Jack, or he wouldn't have kept up the correspondence all this time.'

'Yeah, maybe. I think my microcosmos idea is too far out, even for him.'

Sutra examined the postage stamp, which depicted a dark, romantic landscape of forested mountains partly shrouded in deep mist. 'Hey, you said he plays tennis. You could probably interest him in a game if he has time. When did he say he was coming again?'

'January 22, for four days.'

*   *   *

Jack Astra had confirmed that he would be at home when Dr. Drexler visited and told him if he wanted to bring his tennis racket, he would be delighted to reserve an hour or two at his local court. Jack played most weekends with his friend Juan García and looked forward to having a hit with his astronomical hero, if time permitted.

Jack had received a telephone call on the evening of his arrival and they arranged to meet at Dr. Drexler's hotel in La Laguna, the small university town situated some eight kilometers inland from the capital, Santa Cruz, at eleven o'clock the following day. As Dr. Drexler wasn't due to give his talk until late that evening, they agreed to play a little tennis in the morning and then visit Jack's home and view his paintings.

Jack pushed through the doors of the hotel lobby at the appointed time, asked the receptionist to call room 41, and waited for Dr. Drexler to appear. After a few minutes, a tall, mustached, aristocratic-looking gentleman wearing a sober long black coat and carrying a tennis racket under one arm pushed through a side door and entered the hotel lobby. Jack's immediate impression of the figure, who extended his hand in greeting, was that of a scholar from a bygone era, the Edwardian era perhaps. A time when the great questions of the age, concerning the measure and the fate of the universe, were debated politely by a handful of eminent gentlemen philosophers in paneled, book-lined drawing rooms. It was a time far removed from the myriad white-coated technocrats who toil today in a kaleidoscope of specialization in clinical laboratories filled with computers crunching numbers at the speed of light.

But the sober impression didn't last long. As Jack clasped his visitor's hand in a warm shake, Dr. Drexler's nasal East Coast twang sounded full of friendly, down-to-earth humor.

'Lee, welcome to Tenerife. Great to meet you.'

'Hi, Jack, you too! I've been to most mountain-top observatories in the world, but not this one! Since they moved the big UK 'scopes down here, I've always been meaning to visit but somehow never got the opportunity. It's fortunate my Mexican friend, Pedro Delgado, joined the team down here and invited me to give the talk. I probably wouldn't have made it otherwise—at least not for a while, anyway.'

If Jack Astra had been misled by Lee's outwardly serious appearance, Lee Drexler was surprised to be met by someone whose age he found difficult to ascertain. Jack was dressed casually in a pair of worn Levis, sneakers, a white tee shirt, and a blue windbreaker that had 'outsider' stitched in small red letters on the front. But it was Jack's thatch of long, tousled blond hair that gave him an appearance of youthfulness and helped mask his true age. Though actually in his early fifties, Jack still looked like he would be quite at home at Big Sur or Bondi Beach, riding the crest of a wave. He had the look of someone who had spent a good deal of his life on the beach.

Dr. Drexler took the tennis racket from under his arm. 'Brought my trusty old Wilson, Jack. Should I change here or at the courts?'

Jack Astra ushered Lee toward the lobby door. 'Leave it 'til we get to the courts, Lee, they have changing rooms there.' Jack checked his watch. 'I've booked for twelve o'clock, so we should get going.'

As it turned out, Lee soon proved to be a much fitter and more skilful tennis player than his sixty-nine years would suggest, and to Jack's embarrassment he easily out-played an opponent nearly twenty years his junior.

'Hey, Lee, you're too darn good for me! How long have you been playing this game?'

Dr. Drexler stooped to pick up some balls by giving them a sharp pat with his racket, a simple trick of controlled recoil Jack had never been able to master. 'Oh, I've been playing since college. I usually manage to play on weekends in Landshut with our doubles partners. It's a faster kind of game, Jack. I think that's why I had the advantage over you at the net.'

Jack tossed his racket on the bench, wiped his brow with a towel, and responded with a laugh.

'Did you ever think of turning pro. You could probably give McEnroe a game! Hey, let's take a break. I can show you some of the newer paintings I've been working on.'

'Lead the way, Jack!'

Jack picked up his car keys, swung his tennis gear over his shoulder, and they headed for the exit.

'You've been down here awhile now. You must like the Canary Islands.'

'Yeah. Fifteen years now. Sutra and I felt we had to leave the UK—couldn't stand what the Iron Lady was doing to the place. We lived in London for several years, but when she closed down the GLC, that was the last straw!

Sutra—actually, she used to be called Sally but she became a Buddhist and changed her name—got a teaching job in the linguistics department of the university here after she finished her MA. Can't say I regret it, Lee. You can't beat the climate, and if you want know what the surface of the moon or Mars looks like, just drive up to Mt. Teide, our volcano! It's the closest view you're going to get without going there.'

They drove the short distance to Jack's flat and then climbed—as the building hadn't been equipped with an elevator—the six flights of stairs to the top floor, the *atico*.

'Keeps you fit, Lee,' the artist quipped as they reached the top floor.

Jack usually offered this heartening good news to visitors—especially those of more advanced years—who would arrive at his door breathless and seemingly on the point of expiration.

'You're an exile too, Lee.' Jack laughed. 'How are you handling Germany? Must be a big change from sunny California?' Jack pushed at the door and ushered Lee through.

'Well, actually it's a return to my family roots. My grandfather emigrated from Germany to the U.S. at the turn of the century, so it's brought us full circle in a roundabout kind of way. I sure appreciate the folks at AstroNet for giving me an office and the facilities to continue my research. Without their support, it would have been tough.'

Jack took Dr. Drexler's heavy overcoat and hung it on the back of the door. 'I doubt you'll be needing this here, Lee—unless you go up to the volcano. We've just got the first winter snowfall around the high ground up there already.'

Jack picked up a note from the table and scanned it. 'Sutra's had to go up to the uni; says she'll be back in the afternoon. You must be angry over what happened in the States, the way they barred you from using the big 'scopes. I thought that kind of thing got straightened out following the Galileo affair.'

'Yeah, so did I!' Lee seemed uncomfortable, as though he wished to put the experience of the past thirty years behind him, but he continued with an air of resignation.

'Sure I was angry, but above all I felt betrayed and saddened by the realization that the real loser in all this was science itself and that the opportunity had been missed to move toward a truer understanding of the cosmos. The coercion, the intrigue, the jealously, the foot-dragging over publishing—it just gets in the way of the research, makes it that much harder. But I don't hold a personal grudge. Look, it's natural to attempt to defend a belief that for many years seemed to be supported by the observations. It only became a real problem when the defense of that position somehow elevated it to the point of dogma and resulted in the outright persecution of those who questioned it. The *principle* of defending the status quo became more important than the observations. *That* is indefensible, and it made me very angry.'

Lee scanned the paintings, which seemed to occupy every inch of wall space in the small flat. 'Hey, I really like your paintings. The photos you sent don't do them justice, Jack. They're inspiring! You know, I once considered taking up art, but I went into science because I considered it more rigorous, you know, less open to subjective judgment. Your work seems to avoid that trap. It encapsulates the most inspiring aspects of both worlds.'

Jack went to a stack of canvases leaning up against one wall and carefully pulled a couple out.

'Well, I've always been interested in both worlds, Lee. Since childhood I've drawn and painted, and I guess I've been interested in astronomy for as long. As a kid I would spend time at night lying on the beach, looking up at the stars, and wondering how far away they were, how far it all stretched. I just try to combine the two interests. Perhaps there are some aspects, some concepts, in science that may better be expressed or visualized through art. I mean, mathematical equations don't really cut it with most people. If you don't understand that language, the concepts can be very difficult to convey. The best scientists, in my view, seem able to express their ideas simply—you know, by using a picture, a metaphor from nature that we can all relate to. You said you come from an artistic background?'

'Yes, my father was a painter, a member of a group called the Trashcan School in Greenwich Village in the 20s. There were always artistic folk around when I was a kid. People from the movement would often drop by; it was a very intellectually charged atmosphere, quite revolutionary, with the painters and the poets wanting to record the reality of life, warts and all, in the great urban metropolis. I guess it was somewhat equivalent to what was happening around the same time in Europe with the Expressionist movement.'

Lee stood back and admired an oil painting that depicted a large yellow buttercup in place of the metal dish on a radio telescope. 'That's great,' he said admiringly. He then laughed at the thought. 'Hey, perhaps if I had been a painter, I would have struck out on my own path in that field also and upset the art establishment!'

'Well, at least *they* wouldn't ban you from buying paint and canvases,' Jack joked. He then continued, 'But seriously, I wouldn't want to experience the kind of battle you've had to endure, Lee. To get your ideas accepted, you have to convince your peers and colleagues that your results, your proposals, are to be taken seriously—that they are important. Artists don't have to present their work to a peer review committee—well, unless they are entering it for a prize in a major competition, perhaps. The work is created and—hopefully, if it is successful—it is applauded.'

Lee laughed. 'Beauty is in the eye of the beholder!'

Jack replaced the 'sunflower telescope' and carefully withdrew another canvas, which depicted what looked like a small brass telescope fitted in place of the focusing tube on a microscope.

'It can go the other way too, I guess. I wrote a book setting out my cosmological ideas, but then I couldn't find a publisher for it.' Jack laughed at his own misgivings and added hurriedly, 'Well, that might have been because it wasn't any good, of course. But it might also have been a result of academia's disciplinary apartheid and the general nervousness today of overstepping the arbitrary boundaries that separate art and science. People are nervous about commenting on subjects that are considered the domain of specialists and professionals.'

Jack led the astrophysicist into his small studio, where several more canvases were stacked up against the walls. A half-finished canvas stood on a large wooden easel that appeared to be a variation on the artist's micro/macro theme. This time the picture depicted a giant microscope standing sentinel-like on the floor of a domed building that normally housed a telescope.

'That's far out! You sure know how to turn the perspective upside down, Jack. Do you have a title that one?'

'*Mirrorscope.*' It's a play on concepts really.'

Lee stood admiring the surreal image.

'Yes, science wants to describe the universe solely on its own mathematically-provable terms. But I'm not sure that is entirely possible. It is a very ambitious quest, this search for the science's Holy Grail, but it has little or no "fall-back" strategy if it should fail.'

Lee was surprised at the number of canvases stored in the small apartment and wondered to himself if Jack was successful in selling them.

'Do you sell, Jack?'

'Oh, not much. People seem to find the pictures interesting but would probably rather buy a new fridge or something of practical value—something useful! But it's all right, I inherited some shares from my late grandmother's estate in Australia—I live on that. It's not a million bucks a year,' Jack said with a laugh, 'but I guess I'm luckier than a lot of artists!'

He stopped, absorbed in thought, and turned to Lee.

'You mean because so much has been invested in the big bang, expanding universe theory?'

'Yes. We have invested everything over the years in Newton's belief that the mass of elementary particles never varies. That is the physical foundation of the present belief, and the result is always the same: redshift equals expansion.'

Jack Astra looked up with interest when he heard this. 'Are you saying Isaac was wrong, Lee?'

Lee paused a moment to consider his answer. 'Oh, not entirely. The problem is, he only had the local experience of space/time to work with and *assumed* the entire universe was always governed by the laws and forces he had measured here. It's like he caught a minnow one day while out fishing and assumed the ocean contained only minnows. If he had cast his net wider—as we do today, cosmically speaking—he would have found it contained many other species of marine life of varying sizes, and his original assumption would have been incorrect. Trouble is, today, we have become more concerned with defending his legacy than making an objective assessment of the facts. For this reason, we are unable to consider any observations that question Newton's laws. It is simply inconceivable that Newton may be wrong.'

Jack picked up on Lee's argument. 'So you really see it as a question of starting from scratch—let's accept the reality of Dr. Drexler's claims and start over from there?'

'Yes, I think so, Jack. Allowing mass to vary may scuttle the big bang, but it would allow us to consider that radztars are ejected from the exploding galaxies, like seeds from a pod. This, to me at least, seems quite natural when you consider the same process takes place throughout the natural world. Maybe the planets too, formed this way.'

Lee noticed that Jack's studio, which had a slightly sloping red-tiled floor, indicating that it had perhaps once been an outside terrace, was a decent size. The outer wall now consisted of a series of broad windows from which hung white roller blinds, affording bright but muted light. Several Buddhist images and artifacts occupied the shelves, and in one corner of the studio a small shrine had been made around a carved wooden Buddha statue that was decorated with brightly-colored dried flowers.

Jack removed an assortment of magazines from a folded futon and gestured for Dr. Drexler to sit down. He pulled up a stool for himself and continued.

'Yes, I think so too, Lee. I wanted to draw you on this, because if redshift doesn't offer a means of measuring space and time, then our perception—our sense of cosmic scale—is open to alternative speculations, it seems to me. This is what fascinates me about the implications of your research.'

'Well this is why I found your correspondence between Bode's Law and the preferred redshifts of radztars important, Jack. It appears to support the initial observation that radztars simply *look* very star-like. Now they also appear to follow some kind of quantized pattern in their very creation, which corresponds to the planetary orbits of the solar system. It may be that this is something that goes even deeper than Bodes' Law and is somehow a reflection of the quantized nature of the microscopic world, perhaps something to do with the electron orbits of atoms themselves.'

'You mean where electrons may only occupy certain discrete, quantized orbits, or shells, within the atom?'

'Yes, that's the idea I'm exploring right now. It's really rather simple. If particle masses are variable and are a function of time, the younger, more recently created electrons have smaller masses. When a less massive electron makes a jump or a transition between atomic orbits, the energy packet involved—the photon—has lower energy, and the resulting spectral line is redshifted toward the red end of the electromagnetic spectrum.'

Dr. Drexler cupped his hands as though clasping a tennis ball and slowly expanded them outward as he spoke.

'Consider a single electron at the moment of creation. It has no mass, because it cannot be compared to anything else. When it communicates with another electron, it acquires the property of mass; as it ages, the light signal sphere within which it communicates enlarges, and it therefore communicates with more and more particles and acquires more and more mass, and the initially high redshift decays to more normal levels.'

Lee hesitated, wondering if his artist friend would grasp the concept he was outlining. He didn't want to get too deep into the technical detail; most ordinary folk, even most 'experts,' seemed happy enough to learn the universe was expanding in all directions and didn't have much sympathy for those who might question it. But his concern was quickly allayed as Jack Astra simply picked up a paint brush, turned it thoughtfully between his fingers, and asked, 'So, if two differentially redshifted objects were close enough together in space so that their spatial coordinates didn't matter, the only real difference between them would be their relative location in time?'

'Yes, that's it, Jack! The high-redshift object, the radztar, and all the matter in it *could* have been created, or could have appeared in our universe, at a relatively later time. In this way, we may follow a single object which starts out small with a very high redshift: it evolves gradually into a high-redshift companion galaxy and then, finally, into an only slightly redshifted companion galaxy.'

Jack went to a bookshelf, which appeared to contain equal numbers of books on astronomy and art, and pulled out Dr. Drexler's *The Redshift Mantra*.

'In your book, Lee, you say, "Quantization as a physical phenomenon is a property only of matter with at least one very small dimension. Matter on the large scale does not show quantization effects." But the spacing of planetary orbits seems to reflect the property of quantization, as does the preferred 'z' of radztars. These are objects of matter on the large scale—well, certainly the solar system is.'

Dr. Drexler shifted a little awkwardly and cleared his throat.

'Well, yes that's true, but remember, that was written before you noticed the correspondence between Bode's Law and the preferred redshifts, Jack. I now believe that we are seeing the effects of quantization right across the board and on every level, from atoms to stars and galaxies. It is almost as though the universe were built on the principle of...of a fractal, where each different scale reflects the one below and above it.'

Jack stared at the cover of Lee's book and added quickly, 'Then, if all things and scales are fundamentally equal, perhaps we are simply making an incorrect assumption in attributing to objects a hierarchical scale based on the only system we are familiar with, the solar system. If our system is unique, and we still have no direct proof that it isn't, then we could not use it as a method to scale cosmic phenomena. For all we know, the 'stars' out there might be simply atomic phenomena—a sort of mirror image, or reflection, of the microcosm. The dimension that underpins this one.'

Jack balanced the long, finely-pointed paintbrush horizontally between the palms of his hands. He felt privileged to be discussing such grand questions with one of the world's leading cosmologists—and he wasn't even an astronomer. Most, he felt, wouldn't have the time or the inclination to discuss such topics with non-scientists. He continued, choosing his words carefully.

'It seems to me, Lee, in freeing us from the notion that redshift may be used to scale the universe, you have opened the cosmological debate up to these kinds of speculations. In the past, we have developed our cosmologies on the assumption of a duality between the atom, on the one hand, and the planets, stars, and great spiraling galaxies, on the other. Could that perception be a delusion? Could we have got our sense of cosmic scale so completely and fundamentally wrong? I don't mean the scale of things in the solar system, but *beyond* that. The solar system *might* be the only truly large-scale structure in the universe—a sort of physical summation of all the atoms it is composed of and created by the same physical processes that operate on the subatomic level.'

Dr. Drexler leaned forward in a show of interested encouragement. He had a hard time on most occasions debating such issues with his fellow scientists, himself, and here he was discussing such notions with an artist, who appeared to have little difficulty embracing the ideas he was discussing.

'I think we are poised on the threshold of something big, something very big.'

Jack thought so too and had for some time now. He also thought, as it was now half past four and Lee was scheduled to give his presentation at the *Instituto de Astrofísica* at six, perhaps they should continue their discussion after the meeting, an arrangement to which Dr. Drexler happily agreed.

Lee's talk was attended mostly by post-grad students, and the auditorium was full to capacity. Many professionals were in attendance, including the director, who made an impassioned speech in favor of dialogue over detention. The response to Lee's talk during the Q&A session was mixture of die-hard skepticism and admissions of recent conversion to Lee's research. Jack thought the talk interesting and well presented, with 'state of the art' visuals and many previously unseen photographs. The seminar was also punctuated throughout with many interesting personal anecdotes from Lee's side of the debate. The only time Jack noted a measure of remorse was when Lee related the story of Virginia Warner, a retired astronomer who, in her 70s, had spent four hours in the freezing cold at Mt. Palomar one January confirming the existence of one of Lee's radztars because none of the younger staff was willing to do it for him. Apart from that, he seemed buoyed, good humored, and confident throughout.

They met up in the bar after with a few others sympathetic to Lee's research and arranged to continue their discussion the next morning with a stroll along the nearby beach.

'Sounds like a great idea, Jack; always like to see as much of the places I visit as possible! Meet you in the hotel foyer.'

'Bring a jacket, Lee. It's never exactly cold here, but it can be windy.'

Jack picked Lee up at the appointed hour and they drove the short distance to the beach in some twenty minutes. After pulling into the parking lot at the back of the beach, they walked up a concrete ramp that housed a toilet, changing room, and shiny chrome shower. Lee stood and surveyed the stretch of long sandy beach, which was decorated at the back with a scattering of palm trees. It was soon apparent he had done some homework on the island's geology, for he immediately exclaimed, 'Hey, I thought the sand here was supposed to be black!'

'Most of it is, Lee. This beach was created by bringing ship loads of sand from the Sahara, just seventy miles to the east, over there. Before that, it was a two kilometer scarp of rock and black sand, backed by these mountains behind us. It still needs to be topped up every few years'

Jack thought they must have made a rather odd impression as they strolled along the beach together: Lee, tall, aristocratic looking, wrapped in his Edwardian greatcoat and still sporting the pop-art tie he wore at the talk, sharply contrasted the artist's compact stature and informality of dress: worn jeans, a tee shirt with a colorful Tibetan *mandala* printed on the front, lightweight windbreaker, and sneakers. *Simon & Garfunkel*, he mused wryly to himself at the thought, the picture from the cover of *Bridge over Troubled Water* springing to mind—or was it *Sound of Silence*? He wasn't sure.

Lee pulled at the lapels of his greatcoat. 'I see what you mean about the wind, Jack. Is it always like this?'

'Windy' was something of an understatement at Las Teresitas; 'gale force' was often a more accurate description, and to Jack's dismay it looked as if the latter might be the better one today. It was already blowing the sand in fierce gusts along the beach. More than once they had occasion to abruptly turn their backs against particularly nasty gusts that stung at their faces with driving sand. Soon Jack began to think this wasn't such a good venue after all in which to discuss the mysteries of the universe. But they were here now, and he would have to make the most of it. Perhaps the small bar, El Ultimo, at the end of the beach might be open. That, at least, might provide a temporary refuge from the wind.

'The summer months can be pretty impossible. I think it's the mountains at the back here that create the temperature inversion and turbulence. I was hoping it wouldn't be too bad—just our luck.' Actually, Jack had wondered at one time if the wind came with the sand, like it did in the Sahara. Maybe you couldn't have one without the other. The Australian aboriginals or native

American Indians, those who felt the bond between nature's physical and spiritual forces, he thought, would probably agree with the sentiment.

Jack braced himself against the elements and continued walking and talking alongside his guest.

'Getting back to the discussion we had yesterday, Lee. If everything seems pretty much equal from the mass-quantization point of view, wouldn't it allow us to consider a completely different sense of cosmic scale? I mean, we *could* let our imagination run wild and consider the universe to be simply a reflection of the microcosm—all things being fundamentally equal!'

'You mean...like...thinking of the telescope as just a giant microscope, something like that—a *mirrorscope*, like in the picture you have on your easel?'

Jack picked up a small, flat stone and sent it skipping across the water, the small splashes it generated being instantly whipped into fine spay by the gusting wind. 'Exactly! Why not?'

'Well, I'm not sure I'm prepared to go *quite* that far, Jack, but it's a daring thought. I haven't pushed it to that extreme, but...'

'Think of a galaxy as a cosmic cell, Lee. Then the galaxy's stars—or what we *believe* are objects like our sun—automatically become the *atoms* that make up the 'cosmic' cell. Do you see how it neatly snaps into place, or at least could when you look at the problem from this perspective? I love to do that.'

Lee brushed at his hair then smoothed his graying moustache thoughtfully by slowly spreading the thumb and forefinger of one hand over it. 'I never thought of altering the perspective so radically, Jack. That is a pretty amazing concept. If it were true, it would cause a rethink regarding our place in the universe, that's for sure. Let me get this straight: are you suggesting that the stars in all those galaxies out there are really...some kind of cosmic cell's atoms?'

'Well, I'm suggesting they *could* be considered that way.'

Lee stopped a moment and turned to the artist. 'If it were true, then the planets, if any existed, would be kind of like the atom's *electrons*—is that the picture you are painting, Jack?'

'You've got it! It's the logical next step, isn't it?' Jack gave a happy kick at a crushed 7-Up can. 'Look, not so long ago, people believed the Earth was the center of the universe, with the sun and planets revolving about it. People accepted that until Copernicus came along and revealed the true picture. I'm just taking that position a step further.'

Jack paused again, searching for words to better illustrate the point he was trying to convey.

'In practical terms, it wouldn't make any difference. If the universe really is on the scale we assume it is today, space travel between the stars—let alone galaxies—is still only for science-fiction enthusiasts. Indeed, returning to the notion that the Earth is the center of all creation would confer upon us a much greater sense of responsibility to preserve life rather than destroy it.'

Dr. Lee Drexler listened intently as he walked, head and shoulders above the artist friend at his side.

'But even that perception, as improbable and crazy as it might sound, is nothing to what follows, Lee, because *then* we might ask, "Well, if all that is up there is really the microcosm, then how do we *relate* to it?"'

Lee stopped and looked at the artist. 'Jack, you are jumping way ahead of me here, but keep going; it's a fascinating picture you're painting. Now I begin to see where you get the inspiration for your marvelous images.'

Jack continued, 'Well, looking at it from this inverted perspective, the cosmos simply becomes the *microcosmic crucible* for life that blossoms here.'

'You mean like some kind of cosmic egg? But then how does life pass from that dimension, the microcosm, to this one?'

'Quantum tunneling!' Jack shouted excitedly above the wind. 'The ability to jump from one state to another that transcends, or suspends, the limitations imposed by the space/time continuum we are used to here, today, in our macro world. You know, I have an intuitive feeling that this transition begins at the point of conception. That is the departure point that results, eventually, in our appearence here.'

Jack reflected a moment, then added. 'Kind of like waking from a dream, Lee.'

Lee laughed out loud, wiping a tear from his eye with the back of his hand. For a second Jack wasn't sure if this was a result of the elements or Lee's amusement at what he was suggesting. But his uncertainty was quickly dispelled when Lee added, 'And then spend the rest of our days wondering how far away the stars and galaxies are and what in heaven's name it all means, when all the time we had the answer within us: that it wasn't to be found outside, by looking through the magnifying lens of a giant telescope!'

Jack felt elated—like he had successfully passed some crucial test in a particularly difficult school exam—but managed to conceal his relief and carried on as though his companion now fully followed his line of reasoning. 'In my view, Lee, we are backing up huge numbers when we should really be downsizing. When we look back in time, everything gets *smaller* rather than bigger.

When we retrace our steps, everything dissolves back to the dimension of cells, atoms, and their constituent particles—'

Lee cut him short. 'The dimension *we* were a part of, on the microcellular level, when we started out on this miraculous journey.'

'Yes. But it's not only on the physical level. Birth doesn't mean being transformed from a *non*-physical level—we are already a part of that material state. Birth means passing from an *unconscious* state to a conscious one.' Jack gave a wry smile, 'and consciousness is a slippery customer. Looking at the physical cosmos from this perspective, one can see the fabric of the universe doesn't change or evolve by expansion. It is simply *our* creation as living beings endowed, ultimately, with consciousness that makes the temporal move from that dimension, the one we look upon today as the starry cosmos. It is surely this that gives the *illusion* of the infinitely large universe.'

Jack turned his back momentarily against a blast of stinging sand then continued.

'Conventional wisdom has the universe starting out from the expansion of some infinitesimally small particle, but it may be nearer the truth to propose that it is *we* that start out from this small state, Lee.'

'Well, your explanation certainly gives the cosmos a new meaning, Jack! I've never thought of it like this. I've been in the business some forty years, and I've never heard a scientist offer such an amazing description. As extraordinary as it sounds, I have to admit, it puts the universe into some kind of perspective whereby we could get a handle on it...something we can get our heads around...rather than continuing with the puzzle of infinity that has always plagued purely physical, geometrical, or mathematical descriptions. You should write another book, Jack. I'm sure people would find these ideas of interest—make a novel out of it.'

Jack laughed. 'Well, it's certainly a novel idea! Maybe it would make a good science-fiction story. You know, I couldn't believe it myself at first, because it goes against everything we have been brought up to believe. But, interestingly, it seems to be supported by the very embryonic-like images of nebula captured by the Hubble Space Telescope. It might also offer an explanation of what comets are. One could imagine that they are the primordial harbingers that bridged the dimension between the universal microcosm—the cosmos—and the planet's original 'fertilization.' It also naturally assumes the entire universe to be the origin, the crucible, where Earth's teeming sphere of life got started and the incredible diversity of it.'

Jack added as an afterthought, 'Perhaps if the universe always existed there would be infinite time for life to evolve and diversify.'

'So the Earth is the center of it all in your view?'

'Well, not only in my view, Lee. Eastern religions and mystics of all persuasions have maintained this link between both sides of our existence: an eternal, cyclical dance between life, death, and rebirth. The impermanent and illusory nature of material existence. In astrology too, the belief is that our origins and our destiny are closely governed by cosmic events and forces, so I'm not completely alone on this. Hey! El Ultimo is open. Do you fancy a beer—we could get out of this hurricane?'

They battled against the wind and crossed to a beach bar that looked like Rambo had taken a can opener to a shipping container. Painted red and adorned with Pepsi Cola signs, two wide hatches appeared to have been hewn in the side facing the beach and one of those was now propped partially open by metal struts. A flat steel ledge served as a counter. Although there were a number of similar bars spaced equally along the beach, all painted different colors and adorned with the logo of their multinational patrons, Coca Cola, 7-Up, Pepsi Cola, and Fanta, El Ultimo appeared to be the only one open today. At least the tin shack offered a temporary respite from the elements, so they entered, claimed a small round metal table in the back, and ordered a couple of beers. Even inside the bar they needed on occasion to cover their glasses against the flying sand, but this was certainly preferable to conditions outside. Jack took a sip of his beer and reflected upon the cosmological theme he was outlining to his astrophysicist friend.

'An interesting aspect of this picture of the cosmos being simply the crucible, the dimension from which we all spring, is that it implies a self-sustaining cosmos, Lee, where matter and energy are continually transformed in a constant symbiotic dance between life, death, and rebirth.'

Dr. Drexler put his glass down and stared for a moment at the sand rippling across the beach, then turned back to study his companion.

'Well, I have no quarrel with that, Jack. I think it sits very well with the picture that is emerging of what we call a 'steady-state' universe. One that is constantly recycling its basic elements, from the largest structures—the galaxies—right down to cells, atoms, and subatomic particles. I believe that we are now witnessing galaxies dividing, throwing out new seeds in the form of radztars, which then grow into second generation galaxies, and so on, ad infinitum. In this sense, the latest scientific picture bears comparison to the one you are describing.'

'Yes, Lee, but the trick is to think of it, *the cosmos*, as the *micro*-cosmos, the *microcrosm!* When you do that, your dividing galaxies *automatically* become 'cells', dividing as living cells do, creating the genetic code for life that blosooms here. However, only when consciousness appears may we reveal it.'

Jack Astra took a crumpled packet of Drum from his jacket, opened it, and withdrew a packet of cigarette papers.

'But there's another side to this which has always intrigued me, Lee. If the cosmos is really better considered to be the *micro*-cosmic dimension, the dimension we are conceived in, then we may have a direct connection to it—or we may at least be responsible, in some way, for the condition, both psychologically and physically, we find ourselves in today.'

'You mean like the Eastern notion of karma, where one's actions always incur an equal and opposite reaction?'

Jack placed a little tobacco on the paper, rolled it tight, drew his tongue quickly across the gummed strip, then gave the end a brief flame with a flick of his Clipper and stuck the Drum back in his pocket. It occurred to Lee that this whole process had been achieved automatically, while Jack's mind was grappling with another dimension. Perhaps it was force of habit, something done so often it could serve as a prop to help deflect the distractions of the physical world for a moment and help keep his mind focused on the metaphysical concepts he was struggling to convey.

After blowing a column of smoke toward the ceiling and watching a moment as it tangled with the vortex of turbulence created by the conditions outside, Jack returned to the train of thought he was following.

'Well, I guess I am thinking as much on the spiritual plane as the purely material, Lee. Whatever ripples, waves, or changes we make are absorbed and then reflected back by the universe—which then affects the present, and so on, in an eternal symbiotic, interactive dance. When we eventually revert back to the microcosmic universe, presumably, we will inherit the changes that are taking place right now—just as *we* are the product of changes that took place in the past, before we were conceived.'

Lee looked suddenly serious. 'And many of the changes taking place today—over-population, climate change, GMOs—*are* very negative. So you're suggesting unless we alter these negative aspects of our behavior *now*, things are only going to get worse in the future?'

'I'm afraid if we don't attend to it now, Lee, we might reach a point where we find we have pushed too far, have become so estranged from nature that sustains us we cannot get back to the point of salvation. We, like the dinosaurs, may actually die out as a species. Hey, let's get some *tapas*.'

Jack went to the bar and came back with a couple more beers, a plate of diced tortilla, bread, and olives and set them down carefully on the table.

'Well, I think I see what you're trying to get at, Jack, but getting back to this idea that we start out in the microcosm—or what historically we have looked upon as the vast universe stretching all about us—how do we get from that state, that dimension, to the dimension we experience today? What's the mechanism?'

'Very simple. As I said before, Lee, quantum tunneling. Our connection must be via some form of a quantum jump that involves a metaphysical transition that operates beyond the laws of time and space—at least, as understood from measurements conducted in the present dimension.'

Jack took a coin from his pocket and laid it on the table. 'Look, think of the physical universe as simply consisting of two sides of a coin—let's give them a positive side and a negative side. Consider the solar system as representing one side, say the positive side, the cosmos of stars and galaxies the negative.'

Lee listened intently to what Jack Astra was suggesting as he broke a piece of bread in two and herded a piece of tortilla onto one half with the other.

'Now, consider that life, also, comes in two halves, Lee—life and death—and apply each to our "universal" coin. Apply "death" to the stars and galaxies side and "life" to the solar system side.' Jack picked up the coin and stood it on end. 'In this way, we may begin to glimpse the possibility that we are conceived in the death, or negative, side of the coin and, through the miracle of conception and birth, pass between the two halves to suddenly wake up here, in the solar system, our present center of reality.'

Dr. Drexler pulled a small notepad and pencil from a shirt pocket and scribbled something in what appeared to be some kind of mathematical formula. 'So, you believe it is some kind of quantum tunneling that enables us to make the transition between the two...dimensions, or sides of existence?'

'Yes. But, of course, we have no *awareness* of this miraculous transition from one side of the coin to the other in its duration, simply because we have not yet attained consciousness. The journey takes place before consciousness evolves. Our parents know the journey takes nine months, according to their clock. But for us? Well, we have no knowledge of when our clock started ticking, of our own conception, or of the dimension we sprang from. All we are eventually aware of is opening our eyes in *this* dimension, on our birthday.

Similarly, and perhaps for the same reason, we can have no knowledge of the beginning of the universe itself—if indeed it has one.

Jack stubbed his roll-up in a tin-foil ashtray then picked up the coin and spun it like a top on the metal table. 'Another way of looking at it, Lee, is to think of the act of being born, the instant we become conscious, as like the click of a shutter on a camera. But in this case, instead of using film to record both positive and negative sides of our existence, it is *consciousness* that records the event. *It* snaps an imprint of the negative side we have tunneled out of—the cosmos—and of course we get the lovely "Kodachrome color image" of the positive side we experience right now. This, I believe, is why the universe seems so perplexing today. We haven't followed our own origin, our own evolution, right back to the microcosmic realm of cells, "stars," "galaxies."

'This is really a relativistic view, Lee. Only by considering consciousness as an integral part of our actual transition, in a *relativistic* context, can we make sense of the stuff you guys study—the cosmos of stars and galaxies.'

Dr. Drexler spiked an olive with a small wooden tooth pick, raised it vertically, and studied it a moment. 'So, you're suggesting that modern science has created a most sophisticated camera, in the form of a telescope, but that it doesn't yet have the film—the convincing *conceptual* explanation—that allows the camera to develop the full picture. Is that it, Jack?'

Jack picked at the last piece of tortilla and pushed away the plate. 'Yes. Only by putting a film labeled "consciousnesses" in the camera are we able to develop the whole picture—both aspects of reality, positive and negative, life and death. You know, Lee, I'm always reminded of a letter Vincent Van Gogh wrote to his brother, Theo, when I attempt to discuss these ideas. If I quote correctly—and he was talking about his painting *Starry Night*—he said:

> This picture raises the eternal question whether we can see the whole of life or only a hemisphere of it before death. I have no idea of the answer myself, but the sight of stars always sets me dreaming just as naively as those black dots on a map set me dreaming of towns and villages. Why should those points of light in the firmament, I wonder, be less accessible than the dark ones on the map of France? We take a train to go to Tarascon or Rouen and we take death to go to a star. What is certainly true about this argument is that as long as we are alive we can't visit a star any more than when we are dead we can take a train.

'From Vincent's perspective then, one could argue that we are connected to the starry heavens not by the physics of material existence but through consciousness, which is rather similar to the picture I'm trying to describe.'

'That's a marvelous insight, Jack. I've always admired Van Gogh's painting, but I hadn't realized he entertained such profoundly cosmic thoughts.'

Jack Astra looked at his watch. He had lost all track of time relating his views to the astronomer and now suddenly became aware that it was getting late. Lee was being shown around the institute's Las Cañadas facilities the next day and would have an early start planned.

'Hey Lee! I should get you back to the hotel; you'll want to rest up before your tour of the facilities tomorrow.' Jack called for the bill, with a '*La cuenta, por favor!*' paid, and then joined Lee outside. Together, they headed back along the beach.

'Lee, you know, I sometimes wonder whether we have overstepped a fundamental metaphysical boundary in our reliance on a telescopic view of the cosmos. A boundary that separates reality from illusion and, like Alice stepping through the looking glass, unwittingly entered a world filled with fantasy, illusion, and paradox. Maybe it's time to call a rain-check on the big questions and try a different approach—try a different conceptual perspective.'

'So this is the center of the universe, in your view, Jack?' Lee repeated his earlier question in order to draw the artist's definitive opinion before they parted.

'Well, I wouldn't go back to a completely pre-Copernican perspective.' Jack wiped a wind-induced tear with the back of his sleeve, leaned into the wind, and shouted across to his companion. 'No, I would simply suggest that the solar system encompasses the largest single entity in the universe today, with the sun lying at the center of it all.'

'Then, after some three centuries of telescopic observation of the heavens, we've gone full circle and arrived back where we started.'

'I think we will, Lee. I think we will.'

They had almost reached the end of the beach and were within sight of their own starting point when Dr. Drexler pulled up, put his hand on his friend's arm to stay him a moment, and asked unexpectedly, 'Is there an art supplies store on the way back, Jack? I have a mind to see if I can paint something.'

Jack Astra laughed at the thought that Lee Drexler, one of the great astronomers of the day, felt that art was as important a tool in our efforts to describe the mystery of existence as science.

'Now, that would be going full circle, Lee. That would be going full circle!'

THE END

0-595-32217-4

Printed in the United Kingdom
by Lightning Source UK Ltd.
103576UKS00003B/127